ANZIA YEZIERSKA was born in a shtetl, probably Plotsk, in Russian Poland and emigrated to the United States in 1890 when she was about eight years old. One of nine children in a very poor family headed by her father, a Talmudic scholar, she grew up in the Jewish ghetto on New York's Lower East Side. At the age of seventeen, against her father's will, Anzia Yezierska left home and worked in sweatshops and laundries while going to school and then university. In 1915, she began to publish short stories about "her people," the Jews of the Lower East Side. Her first book, a collection of stories entitled *Hungry Hearts* (1920), was made into a Hollywood film. Its success brought Yezierska wealth and fame. She went on to publish another collection of stories, *Children of Loneliness* (1923), and a succession of novels, including *Salome of the Tenements* (1922), *Bread Givers* (1925), *Arrogant Beggar* (1927), and *All I Could Never Be* (1932). Then, in the 1940s and 1950s, her writing went out of vogue, and Yezierska fell into poverty again. In 1950 she published her final book, *Red Ribbon on a White Horse*, a semi-fictional autobiography. Anzia Yezierska died in 1970.

Since Persea's republication of *Bread Givers* in 1975, Anzia Yezierska has been recognized as an important American author, and her work is now widely read. Persea also publishes all of Yezierska's short stories in one volume, *How I Found America: Collected Stories;* her autobiography, *Red Ribbon on a White Horse;* and a biographically arranged selection of her fiction, *The Open Cage.*

ALICE KESSLER-HARRIS, who initiated the rediscovery of Yezierska, is Professor of History at Columbia University and the author of *Out to Work: A History of Wage-Earning Women in the United States* and *A Woman's Wage: Historical Meanings and Social Consequences,* among other books.

BREAD GIVERS

Anzia Yezierska

BREAD GIVERS

A Novel

ANZIA YEZIERSKA

Foreword and Introduction
by Alice Kessler-Harris

with photographs

A Karen and Michael Braziller Book
PERSEA BOOKS / NEW YORK

I should like to thank Louise Levitas Henriksen for her generous help in reconstructing the details of her mother's life, and Joy and Marchette Chute and Rose Goldberg for sharing their memories of Anzia Yezierska with me. Karen Braziller and Jane Ross were instrumental in rescuing this novel from the world of out-of-print books.

A. K. H.

The publisher would like to thank the Samuel Goldwyn Company for helping to make possible the use of stills from the 1922 film "Hungry Hearts" for this edition of *Bread Givers*.

Persea Books, Inc.
853 Broadway
New York, New York 10003

Library of Congress Cataloging-in-Publication Data

Yezierska, Anzia, 1880?–1970
Bread givers : a novel / Anzia Yezierska ; foreword and introduction by Alice Kessler-Harris with photographs.— 3rd ed.
p. cm.
"A Karen and Michael Braziller book."
ISBN 0-89255-290-5 (pbk. : alk. paper)
1. Lower East Side (New York, N.Y.)—Fiction. 2. Assimilation (Sociology)—Fiction. 3. Children of immigrants—Fiction. 4. Fathers and daughters—Fiction. 5. Women immigrants—Fiction. 6. Jewish families—Fiction. 7. Young women—Fiction. I. Title.
PS3547.E95 B74 2003
813'.52—dc21
2003007187
Printed and bound by the Maple-Vail Book Manufacturing Group
Designed by Rita Lascaro

Third edition
Fifth printing

FOREWORD

Finding *Bread Givers*

Like every book, *Bread Givers* has had a life of its own since its original publication nearly three quarters of a century ago. And like most of those that survive to become "classics," this one speaks to each generation of readers with a voice that is both timeless and quite particular. It was like that for me. When I discovered Anzia Yezierska, I thought I had found my own voice.

It was the 1960s. I was spending most of my days in the New York Public Library researching a doctoral dissertation on New York Jews in the 1890s. I'd stumbled across Anzia Yezierska by accident and was fascinated. After I sampled one short story, then another, I was hooked. At half past four every day, I abandoned the microfilm machines and the reels of Yiddish newspapers, and made my way up to the third-floor reading room. There I sat, day after day, until I had worked my way through all of Anzia's books.

I was dismayed when I reached the end. Dismayed and at a loss. Until it occurred to me that there might be a way to acquire a copy for myself. I leafed back through the disintegrating volumes and chose the one I liked best: *Bread Givers*. My own biography explains the choice. Like Yezierska, I was an immigrant: a young woman in a world where ambition was the path to Americanization and ambition seemed designed for men. My father, like hers though for vastly different reasons, could not bear to see his daughter tread a path he thought foolhardy. In his eyes, universities were for males; girls might aspire to teachers' colleges. Nothing more. So like Sara Smolinsky, I broke away. And like Sara, I would spend years trying to reconcile what appeared even to me to be my own selfish desires with the profound need to find a place in the culture I had adopted. When Sara Smolinsky declared her independence by selling herring at two cents a piece, the act penetrated my flesh. I read this book as an immigrant, a woman, a Jew, and a "person."

I did not want to let it go. Looking back on what happened next, I am sure that there must have been easier ways to get what I wanted. I might have canvassed used bookstores or called the old publisher. Instead I gingerly approached the desk. Could the library photocopy the book? What would it cost? The librarian took one look at the old pages and the tight spine and immediately refused. Then he asked, what about photo-offset? More expensive, of course, but safer for the book. Two weeks later and $57.20 poorer, I walked out of the NYPL with my own squeaky-clean copy of *Bread Givers*.

For several years, I used the novel as my private source of solace and inspiration. Then, in the light of a new women's movement, and thinking that it might speak to others as well, I began to look for a publisher. In the interim Anzia Yezierska died in California. I did not know: I had never thought of her as a real person and imagined her long dead. No one was much interested in her work. The editors to whom I showed *Bread Givers* found a very different book from the one that had so affected me. From their perspective, the book's vernacular style and emotional appeal posed a barrier rather than a vehicle to understanding. To them, *Bread Givers* seemed of little significance, limited to a particular ethnic experience. At the time, ethnic literature had little resonance. Nor could social historians drum up any enthusiasm for a woman's version of the immigrant experience. Women's history remained in its infancy, concerned with celebrating successful achievement rather than with exploring the anguish of the daily struggle to live against the grain.

By 1972, the idea of republishing *Bread Givers* had become something of an obsession. Whenever I sensed an opportunity, I carried the offprint with me, cajoling and pleading with publishers' representatives to take a look at it. Then, bingo. A friend read it and wept, passed it on to her editor friend, whose company was not right for it, and who persuaded her husband, also an editor, to look at it. The deal was cut. And so began Persea Books' commitment to Anzia Yezierska, a commitment that continues to this day.

Now my education began. Successful publication would require an introduction, which I was eager to write. I went to work. It didn't take long to discover the small collection of Yezierska's letters and unpublished work at Boston University and the rest of her published stories and reviews. But the woman herself remained elusive. If the big attraction of *Bread Givers* was its capacity to render the immigrant woman's life as a piece of the fabric of social history, I had to discover whose myth and memory I was reading: to locate the autobiographical core within the fiction. Then a friend who knew my obsession well sent me a magazine column written by Shana Alexander. I've long ago lost the column, but the words remain etched in memory. "A once-famous great aunt of mine named Anzia Yezierska ... " she wrote. It was all I needed. Shivering, I dashed off a note: could I interview her about this aunt, I asked. Just as quickly she replied: she'd be happy to talk, but there was a better source: Anzia's daughter Louise lived in California. The phone number was enclosed.

When I found Louise Levitas Henriksen in 1973, just a few years after her mother's death in 1970, and requested permission to reprint *Bread Givers*, the attention could not have been entirely welcome. Louise, past sixty, was eager to resurrect her own suspended writing career and to leave her mother's life behind. Under these circumstances, renewed attention to her mother, so soon after her death, must have seemed a mixed blessing: yet another incursion on Louise's own desires. In the last several years of her mother's life, Louise had urged Anzia to move from New York to California, where she could be near her. Though her mother had lived in a nursing home, Louise had been her primary caregiver.

She greeted our first contact with great ambivalence. Louise had watched a spurt of renewed attention that accompanied her mother's last years impatiently, correcting what she saw as the tendency of a new generation of scholars to take Yezierska's fictional characterizations of self as the literal truth. She was not sure, she said, that any of the early fiction merited republication: it was not of very high quality; it lacked subtlety; at best, the novels were period pieces lacking in universal appeal. She would give her permission but could not imagine that she had much to contribute. Her mother had been interviewed before her death to no great effect. Louise didn't think she had very much more to say about her; there were other relatives and a couple of friends who might.

I retrieved the flavor of Yezierska's extraordinary personality from these sources, and as I began to think about her in the given name everyone used to speak of her, Anzia came alive. From her friends and family I learned about her willful and solipsistic nature, about the hunger to write that overwhelmed any capacity to think about others and that permitted her literally to take the food from the mouths of her sisters' children when she needed it to fuel her own energy. From them I began to understand the fiery spirit that drove Anzia's longing to become somebody in the world; that confusion that possessed her when she tried to reconcile herself to the life of a traditional wife and mother; the strength of her desire to articulate the unspoken feeling. She would be the voice of the voiceless, the interpreter who could simultaneously validate cultural difference and bridge it. Hers was a mission, a "holy calling," her daughter would later call it. She enlisted every willing soul to accomplish it, and fearlessly, outrageously she demanded their participation, briefly incorporating into her tornadolike vortex the talents of such well-known writers as Dorothy Canfield Fisher and Zona Gale as well as casual friends, the neighbor downstairs, and all of her daughter's acquaintances. Everyone admired her and no one could bear to be with her for very long.

Persea's edition of *Bread Givers* appeared in 1975 not to wild acclaim but to steady success. Its first audiences may well have come from an older generation of women, themselves children of immigrants eager for the nostalgia of a lost world. They recalled the pleasure and pain of Yezierska's conflicted immigrant family lives; remembered the Lower East Side she so brilliantly painted; and resonated to a language that had filled their childhood imaginations. Then Persea reprinted a selection of some of her best short stories in *The Open Cage* (1979), a collection that included an afterword by Louise Levitas Henriksen. The success of these two volumes led Persea to republish Yezierska's first book of short stories, *Hungry Hearts* (1985), and finally to produce a complete edition of all of Yezierska's short stories, including those in *Children of Loneliness* and *The Open Cage*. These are contained in *How I Found America* (1991).

Scholarly and literary interest grew. Slowly the grandchildren of immigrants found the book. Schools adopted it; classes read it. Yezierska became the bridge she had always wanted to be, the "voice of the voiceless" speaking to the generations to come after. To them, *Bread Givers* served a more complicated function. In a generation eager to find the meaning of ethnicity and to uncover the roots of individual identity, Sara Smolinsky's search took on a new life. Because she so effectively captured the tension between an America that longed to maintain the community of a traditional old world and yet sought the material goods and individual satisfactions of the new, Smolinsky reached beyond the specifically Jewish situation into the heart of the shared immigrant experience. Her woman's voice found a universal audience in a generation that sought to locate its own identities more firmly, and mined memoir and biography for the larger meaning of a materially laden world. The threads of family, autonomy, and self, so apparent in *Bread Givers* and so astonishingly modern, snake through Yezierska's work, providing one explanation for why all her work is now back in print.

From the distance of New York to California, interspersed with intermittent visits, Louise slowly came to terms with her mother's heritage. In 1978, when she agreed to write an afterword to the short stories collected in *The Open Cage,* there were things she wanted to say. The piece stands as a testament to a daughter's struggles to abandon her own position at the center of her mother's life and to read her mother's work through the eyes of a larger public. "Often as a child," she begins, "I had reason to regret that she was first of all a writer." Now she could appreciate the force of the talent, but her reading remained autobiographical. As Louise described it, Anzia wrote out of her emotions, to still the loneliness engendered when the endless demands produced an inevitable withdrawal of friendship. She needed, the daughter averred, "to explain her experiences to herself."

Louise wanted to correct the record, to refute what she called the "Hollywood myths" that had grown up around her mother. Most of these were Anzia's own doing: she had, according to Louise, "a talent for dramatizing and enlarging her own life for an appreciative listener." More bluntly put, her mother was "incapable of telling the plain truth." At different times, in interviews as well as for the documentary record, she made up everything, from her date of birth to her family relationships, her work experience, and her education. To make her point, Louise provided her account of Anzia's biography. Anzia, she insisted, was not the ignorant immigrant of her fiction but an educated woman with a passion for politics and philosophy. Her sisters were not the unhappy creatures of their father's will; they led fulfilled and satisfying lives. Their father was less tyrannical than traditional.

Louise herself was part of the myth that had become Anzia's reality. She was the child for whom Anzia had refused to sacrifice, the four-year-old who had been sent clear across the country to live with her father. Louise was the daughter whose mother earned fame by insisting on the force of individual ambition. Yet the daughter had not abandoned the mother in her turn. Louise had admired and cared for Anzia even as she became increasingly difficult. Louise was living testimony to Anzia's willful insistence that devotion to a life-calling need not eliminate human love. Anzia's penchant for fabricating the circumstances within which she lived did not, as Louise acknowledged, detract from the brutal honesty with which Anzia recorded the intensity of her desire. Where the mother had held the facts in far less esteem than the larger truths they asserted, fearlessly intertwining them, the daughter insisted on separating the life from the text, in finding her mother at last amid the mists within which she had hidden herself. So while the daughter read to locate her mother in familiar terrain, she listened to the mother's voice echoing in a larger canyon. It is no accident, then, that in her seventies Louise turned to writing a biography of her mother.

In the biography, *Anzia Yezierska: A Writer's Life* (Rutgers, 1988), published more than a decade after her first printed efforts to fathom her mother, Louise acknowledged that her mother's books were now often read from the perspective of a newly revived feminist movement. Yezierska's search for independence, she thought, resonated with the efforts of a new generation of women to find satisfying work lives, even at the expense of family. In that spirit, Anzia had "sharpened the drama of real events by eliminating muddy contradictions." To Louise, *Bread Givers* was a case in point. A family saga loosely based on Anzia's own childhood, it explores the devastating effects of patriarchal traditions on women. But Anzia had chosen not to include characters who represented any of the six brothers who had formed her own family. And she had altered the lives of her sisters—who had not been forced into marriages, and whose lives were for the most part happy—in order to enhance the significance of her own rebellion. Still, Louise recognized the power of the fictionalized account as an expression of the difficult search for autonomy faced by women, a search of which she had been both victim and beneficiary as a child.

Before she died, in September 1997, Louise had not only learned to live with her mother's success, she had transcended it. Engaged in writing her own autobiography, an account that acknowledged and demonstrated her own quite considerable talents as a writer, she had learned, perhaps better than her mother had ever taught, how to meld her own ambitions with the demands of family life.

Anzia, college-educated, and in a position to earn a perfectly decent living even if she chose not to live with her husband, had willingly given up rearing her only child to pursue a writing career. Louise understood the decision, sometimes admired it, and seemed relieved to have been able to retreat to the calm and orderly framework her father and grandmother provided. Yet she had never come to terms with her mother's choice. As a small child, she had received letters from Anzia that professed her great love and asked forgiveness for the long absences demanded by her need for time to write. Later, when her mother returned to New York, Louise basked in her celebrity, enjoying the glamour of seeing her books in shop windows and thrilled at attending an occasional gala with her. At the same time, she resented the restrictions imposed by Yezierska's insistent efforts to organize life around her writing. She could not bear the frequent demands to read the latest bit of manuscript, to correct its grammar, or to find exactly the right word or phrase to evoke the depth of Anzia's powerful feelings. Still, when she went off to college as a sixteen-year-old, Louise chose the University of Wisconsin, where her mother was spending a fellowship year. Unaccountably, the two remained close: the mother's loneliness and dependence fueling the daughter's sense that she alone could lift the despair and earn her mother's caring presence after all.

All this, of course, is to be found in *Bread Givers*. At one level, the novel reflects Anzia's condemnation of the most traditional form of family life, her doubt that it can ever accommodate a woman's thirst for individual satisfaction and fulfillment. But at another level, the novel persistently seeks reconciliation, first for Sara Smolinsky with her dying mother, and then with her unrepentant father. Anzia's voice reflects a historical moment in the 1920s when many educated women questioned the rigid boundaries of family and insisted as fiercely as Anzia on pursuing their own ends. At the same time, because she is an immigrant, coming from a working-class culture that attempted to channel women's aspirations into narrow frames, the voice anticipates the frustrations of our period and our tormented debates as to the human costs exacted when women combine family and career. No wonder *Bread Givers* has had such staying power.

Yet the modern reader finds much more. In the eyes of some contemporary critics, Sara Smolinsky emerges as a witness to subjective self-creation. Our modern eyes read her less as a creature of rebellion—a young woman who defies her father's bullying denigration—than as a person who remakes herself in his image. In the American tradition of self-reliance, she takes her life in her hands and shapes herself after the models provided by her family. If her traditional father searches for God through the Talmud and religious study, Sara Smolinsky finds her own commitment to the American values of individual self-realization through secular education. She will reach out to the children of America. His spiritual search finds its articulation in a religiously enjoined rigidity and intolerance that wipes out the individuality of his wife and daughters. Hers takes on an American vein: exalting her quest to marry cultural tradition to new world values into the salvation of her adopted country. Sara's self-sacrificing mother, who appears a diminutive character at first glance, becomes a more powerful figure. If her mother believed she might earn her place in heaven by serving her husband well, Sara expands the object of devotion from a single male to all the poor and the lonely. If Sara cannot adore her father as her mother does, she can and does imagine the fathers she might adore. Invariably they are well-bred, American-born older men, cultured and schooled in American traditions. As she educates herself, she searches for a companion who will encourage her to be all she can be, to whom she will devote her life and with whom she will work in partnership.

For the modern reader, the book speaks most powerfully to issues of diversity. Yezierska constructs herself as the quintessential "other"—the outsider perpetually seeking to belong. She wants desperately to be an American but first has to figure out what that means. More than any other piece of Yezierska's fiction, *Bread Givers* seems to offer answers, regretting the loss of community and the disintegration of family as it spurns the transient satisfactions of material success. When Sara Smolinsky dons her simple blue suit, moves into the starkly decorated white room in which her visitors speak in quiet voices, and begins the process of reconciling with her tradition-laden father, Yezierska seems to be telling us how we too can become Americans, that we too might give something back in order to earn our insider places.

To the extent that she never escaped these themes, all of Anzia's work is autobiographical. Each of her novels and each of her short stories can be read as part of a larger "cry of the heart." But like all of Anzia's life and work, including the fictionalized autobiographical account of her life she rendered in *Red Ribbon on a White Horse* (Persea, 1981), *Bread Givers* blurs the boundaries of self and the world, fiction and truth, myth and self-creation. She never did reconcile the dichotomies in her life. Until she died she remained torn between the possibilities offered by fame and fortune and the poverty of her childhood; between success and continual fear of failure; between individualism and loneliness; between her earned status as insider and her self-perception as outsider. All of us who are "outsiders" at some point in our lives recognize the struggle to put some meaning into the idea of becoming American, and in the end, Anzia Yezierska's struggle is accessible to all of us. Her elusiveness captures what is most American about her.

She willed it so, frustrating forever her daughter's efforts to sort out what was the life and what was the fiction, and ensuring that each reader would find a book of her own creation. In this respect she may have anticipated the postmodern. I still find myself in *Bread Givers* as the judgmental teenager ashamed of her family's poverty, language, and manners; as the young woman yearning to find a place in the world; as the aspiring intellectual trying to figure out what to give back; as the isolated adult searching for community. But my reading of *Bread Givers* is as idiosyncratic as that of every other outsider. And like Sara Smolinsky and Anzia Yezierska, I expect never to give up searching for my own definitions of the meaning of "American."

Alice Kessler-Harris
New York, 1999

A NOTE ON THE PHOTOGRAPHS

The photographs that illustrate this edition of *Bread Givers* are drawn from the 1922 film of Anzia Yezierska's first published book, *Hungry Hearts*. The film, contracted by Samuel Goldwyn and for which Yezierska was brought to Hollywood as a consultant and script-writer, helped to spread her fame as an immigrant writer. Like her fiction, the film chronicles the dreams of a young, newly arrived, girl on American shores. But Anzia never liked the film. She left Hollywood shortly before its completion, furious because the heroine's salvation through marriage contradicted her own blazing desire to become a person in her own right.

We have used the stills here because many of the film's scenes beautifully evoke the universal themes in Yezierska's stories: the pressure of poverty, the role of tradition, the ambivalent relationship to family, the desire for education. I learned about the existence of the film from Joyce Antler, a leading historian of Jewish women, who told me of its careful restoration by the National Center for Jewish Film at Brandeis University and arranged for me to view it. The stills are reproduced here with the kind cooperation of Sharon Pucker Rivo and Mimi Krant of the Jewish Film Archive.

Alice Kessler-Harris
2003

For those who want to read more:

BOOKS IN PRINT BY ANZIA YEZIERSKA

Arrogant Beggar (Duke University Press, 1996)

How I Found America: Collected Stories of Anzia Yezierska (includes all the stories in *Hungry Hearts, Children of Loneliness,* and *The Open Cage)* (Persea Books, 1991)

The Open Cage: An Anzia Yezierska Collection (includes short stories and excerpts from *Red Ribbon on a White Horse)* (Persea Books, 1979)

Red Ribbon on a White Horse: My Story (Persea Books, 1981)

Salome of the Tenements (Illinois University Press, 1995)

OTHERS BOOKS OF INTEREST

Boydston, Jo Ann, ed., *The Poems of John Dewey* (Southern Illinois University Press, 1977)

Cahan, Abraham, *Yekl: A Tale of the New York Ghetto* (Dover Publications, 1970)

Cohen, Rose, *Out of the Shadow: A Russian Jewish Girlhood on the Lower East Side* (Cornell University Press, 1995)

Dearborn, Mary, *Love in the Promised Land: The Story of Anzia Yezierska and John Dewey* (The Free Press, 1988)

Gold, Michael, *Jews Without Money* (Carroll & Graf, 1996)

Henriksen, Louise Levitas, *Anzia Yezierska: A Writer's Life* (Rutgers University Press, 1988)

Lang, Lucy Robins, *Tomorrow Is Beautiful* (Macmillan, 1948)

Samuel Ornitz, *Haunch, Paunch and Jowl: The Making of a Professional Jew* (Markus Wiener, 1986)

Rosen, Norma, *John and Anzia: An American Romance* (E. P. Dutton, 1989)

Roth, Henry, *Call It Sleep* (Noonday Press/Farrar, Straus and Giroux, 1991)

Schoen, Carol, *Anzia Yezierska* (Twayne, 1982)

Spewack, Bella, *Streets: A Memoir of the Lower East Side* (Feminist Press, 1995)

Zipser, Arthur, and Pearl Zipser, *Fire and Grace: The Life of Rose Pastor Stokes* (University of Georgia Press, 1989)

INTRODUCTION

All of the six books Anzia Yezierska published between 1920 and 1932 are in some sense autobiographical, but none more so than *Bread Givers*. An immigrant, desperately poor and often hungry, Yezierska wrote realistic stories of Jewish immigrant life on New York's Lower East Side. Her constant themes are the dirt and congestion of the tenement, the struggle against poverty, family, and tradition to break out of the ghetto, and then the searing recognition that her roots would always lie in the old world. If in her other work Yezierska offers glimpses of the language and culture of immigrant Jews at the turn of the century, in *Bread Givers* she opens the door wide and leads us through the days of her childhood to the impetuous decision to reject her parents' home. Along the way, she lays open the woman's experience of immigration, revealing the ways in which Jewish women encountered the new world and tried to reconcile it with the old.

Yezierska's old world was like that of many turn-of-the-century immigrants. She was born in a small town—probably a shtetl called Plotsk—in Russian Poland about 1882. The exact date of her birth went unrecorded, for her family was large—there were nine children—and her parents poor. Her father, a Talmudic scholar, had chosen, Yezierska later wrote, "to have his portion in the next world." The family lived off the neighbors' contributions of food and clothing and the mother's occasional earnings from selling small items in the local market. But her father was a learned man who spent his days in Talmudic study and religious discussion. Since the community honored a wife and children who supported such a man, poverty was a source of pride as well as of hunger and cold.

For the shtetl wife, poverty meant constant work and continuous sacrifice for husband and children. Although women complained often and bitterly, Jewish faith provided both solace and rationalization for their hard life. Only men could study the Torah. Their wives and daughters were destined to smooth the path. A woman's virtue was measured by how well she helped her husband to live a pious existence, free from daily worry and encouraged by her orthodox observance of ritual in the home. To serve her husband and father should be a woman's highest wish, and it was, in any event, her only hope of heaven. In the name of religious duty, husbands who were otherwise entirely dependent on their wives and children tyrannized them. "It says in the Torah," says Sara Smolinsky's father in *Bread Givers,* horrified that his daughter might live alone, "only through a man has a woman an existence. Only through a man can a woman enter Heaven." Most shtetl women were therefore married in their teens to men chosen by their families. If love came at all, it came afterwards.

Religious injunction encouraged sexual intercourse, and women began to bear children soon after marriage. Mothers coddled each baby until the next appeared. Their daughters were quickly put to work caring for younger children and doing household chores. Unlike their brothers who spent their days in religious instruction, most girls went to school only long enough to learn the rudiments of Hebrew letters and to become literate in Yiddish. After that they learned by following their mothers' examples. Too much learning, even for the well-off, was frowned upon, for a girl who developed a "man's head" would not make a good wife.

If she had been well provided with a dowry or her husband was wealthy a woman might have a servant to help with household tasks. But most women not only cared for house and children alone, they also helped to sustain the family economically. Wives and husbands worked together in small shops; women peddled produce or goods in the marketplace. Their husbands spent long hours in the synagogue and, contemptuous of non-Jews, dealt with them as little as possible. Women, unrestricted by the fetters that bound their husbands, frequently developed greater familiarity with the worldly ways of the marketplace than did their husbands. Paradoxically, though intended to produce submissive and retreating women in the domestic sphere, exclusion from most religious activity placed major economic burdens on many women and encouraged them to develop aggressive and articulate roles in the larger world.

Not accidentally, many young women broke out of their confined spheres even in Russia. A long tradition of exciting and alive Jewish women—a bit eccentric and marvelously self-willed—testifies to the emerging contradiction between the reality of women's economic contribution and their low status. Emma Goldman, the famous anarchist, insisted on joining her sister in America. Rose Pesotta, later to become a labor union leader, said she had left her Russian village at the age of seventeen because she "could see no future for herself except to marry some young man and be a housewife." In contrast with the restricted options of the shtetl, America seemed to offer boundless opportunities even for girls. Some of Yezierska's best-known stories are about young girls who dream of America as a place where they can freely meet the ideal lovers who surely await them.

If women in the old country were beginning to chafe at restrictions and to become aware of new possibilities, their conflicts multiplied enormously in America. When Yezierska came in the 1890s, she was one of a hundred thousand Jews who each year sought security and prosperity in the new world. Like most other Jews, Yezierska disembarked at Ellis Island and went to live with relatives in Manhattan's crowded Lower East Side. There Jews tried to reconstruct the old world in the landscape of the new. But in America pious poverty earned no approbation. Most Jews quickly shed their traditional garb and, drawing on shtetl-nurtured talents for business and learning, began their rapid march to upward mobility. A few, Yezierska's father among them, clung resolutely to old paths, spending their days in holy study and remaining untempted by money.

For many women, the transition to America aggravated the tension between their religiously enjoined subservience and their actual economic importance. In the old country strong community sanctions and religious edict kept women in their place despite their economic activity. But now, without the protective cloak of persistent religious observance, women's secondary position in the new world seemed anachronistic: a matter of outmoded custom and tradition. A new world demanded a new rationale for keeping women down. It found it in the strong family structure sustained by women's developing economic dependence.

Most immigrant women, of course, never considered these questions. The ghetto that seemed so full of life and color to casual observers meant for them a constant battle against bugs, dirt, and poverty. Their economic contribution was as necessary on the Lower East Side as it had been in the shtetl, and they quickly wore themselves out caring for boarders, sewing at home, or husbanding the family's little income. As levels of prosperity rose, however, women who believed their lives derived meaning from family service found themselves with time on their hands and diminished economic importance. In *Bread Givers,* Zalmon the fish peddler gleefully reports that he can make his new wife "a lady with nothing to do but stay home and cook for me and clean the house and look after the children." Women who wanted to break out of these old patterns violated not only the expectations of their own immigrant community, but also American social prescription that confirmed dependent roles for women at the turn of the century. Some women, nevertheless, found new outlets for their aggressive energies. Most continued to live their lives through husbands and to sacrifice for children. In the absence of a vital economic need, this became a narrowing pursuit whose results can sometimes be seen in the overly concerned and child-centered woman we have come to know as the American version of the Jewish mother.

Daughters of immigrants, nursed on family tradition, often fell into these patterns. A few objected from the very beginning. Socialist or trade unionist activity stimulated many young women to rebel. Yezierska lived at the socialist Rand School for a while. Other immigrants, like Sara Smolinsky in this novel, took America at its word and tried to live by its ideals. At least in theory the ideology of success offered opportunities for women to make the most of their capacities. Here women could choose their husbands, could marry for love. And if, in Yezierska's words, "they don't get a husband, they don't think the world is over, they turn their mind to something else." The ability to earn one's own living was in one sense only an extension of what Jewish women had been doing all along. Jobs and education that contributed to family life were applauded. After their sons had been educated, families sacrificed to keep their daughters in school and even to send them to college. But at its extreme, when a woman's autonomy involved the search for personal fulfillment, it became nothing short of revolutionary. It violated a basic tenet of Jewish family structure: that women were merely the servants of men, the extensions of their husbands.

Anzia Yezierska was, in that sense, a revolutionary. Passionately convinced that her life was her own, she deliberately rejected traditional home and family roles. There is no evidence that she developed friendships with any of the "New Women" who populated New York's Greenwich Village in the decade surrounding World War I, but she seems to have shared many of their ideals. She was fiercely independent: an individualist who did whatever she wanted to do. Sympathy with the oppressed and outrage at tyranny of any kind came naturally to this child of a tyrannical father. Traditional notions of marriage discomfited her, yet she sought out male companions and lovers. Contemptuous of the ordinary and impatient with the unimaginative, she could not conform to social convention for its own sake. She was never bored—never did anything by halves. Aggressive, dynamic, demanding and forceful, she sought and created a satisfying, self-directed career. It was not so much that she was a feminist, her daughter said of her later: she was just herself.

When Yezierska left home at the age of seventeen, rejecting her parents' attempt to mold her into acceptable roles, she wanted most of all to become a "person." Education seemed the plausible route, so she worked in sweatshops and laundries, living in dark and smelly hall rooms until she had learned enough English to begin writing. At first, she paid a janitor's little daughter to teach her the lessons from her school books. Then she went to night school, and finally attended college lectures. Around 1910 she married an attorney: the union lasted only a few months before it was annulled. Almost immediately, she married again. This time, wary of legal complications, Yezierska chose to have only a religious ceremony, and Louise, the child born of this match, had to be adopted by her father for the sake of formal legitimacy. Yezierska did not take well to cooking and housekeeping. Marriage proved too restrictive for her explosive personality and after three years she left, taking her daughter with her. It was not long before the pressures of earning a living became too great. Reluctantly she surrendered four-year-old Louise to her father and thereafter lived the independent life she wanted.

All the while she describes herself as having a "burning eagerness" to become an American: to look and dress with the assurance of the native-born. She felt something different, she recalled later, so different that it had to come out. During this period she had a close and apparently unconsummated relationship with John Dewey. They exchanged poetry and sought each to delve into the other's sensibilities. In 1922 Yezierska described her efforts to write as her contribution to making an America that was not yet finished. She wanted, she wrote, "to build a bridge of understanding between the American-born and myself... to open up my life and the lives of my people to them." Miraculously, she says, in writing about the ghetto she found America.

The miracle had only begun. *The Forum* printed her first story, "The Free Vacation House," in 1915 and other publications followed. In 1919, "The Fat of the Land" won the coveted Edward J. O'Brien award for Best Short Story of the Year. In 1920 her tales were collected in a volume called *Hungry Hearts.* Then came a Hollywood contract. The book was purchased by Sam Goldwyn and the studio wanted her to help write the script: a $10,000 purchase price, a $200 a week salary. Fame. Praise. Success. Riches beyond her wildest dreams. What more could a poor immigrant want? All the Sunday magazines featured articles on the "Rags to Riches" girl. The literati competed for the honor of discovering her: she was a realist, her book was full of color and action, out of her simple words burst tremendous emotional energy. But Yezierska's soul was not appeased. Her heart was still empty.

It was not that fame did not appeal to her but that her muse lay in the ghetto and without it she could not write. In her semi-fictional autobiography, *Red Ribbon on a White Horse,* written when she was 65 and long after her fame had passed, Yezierska described her longing for her own people. Money removed her from Lower East Side life and from old friends who now came to see her only to beg. She was, she wrote, "without a country, without a people. . . . I could not write any more. I had gone too far away from life, and I did not know how to get back." Caught between two worlds, the muse faltered and she could not write. Within a year, she gave up the wealth of Hollywood to return to the East.

Yezierska continued to publish steadily through the 1920s. First came *Salome of the Tenements* in 1922, then *Children of Loneliness* in 1923. *Bread Givers* followed in 1925 and *Arrogant Beggar* in 1927. In 1932, she published *All I Could Never Be* in which, presciently, her major character explained, "I don't believe that I shall ever write again unless I can get back to the real life I once lived when I worked in the factory." After that her voice was curiously quiet. Magazines occasionally published her stories and book reviews appeared regularly. But she published only one more book-length manuscript: *Red Ribbon on a White Horse,* which appeared in 1950.

Perhaps Yezierska had said her piece, spoken her mind—or the muse had simply deserted. She wrote, and destroyed, two unfinished novels in these years, and when she died many short stories remained unpublished. Possibly her tales of people living in poverty and struggling to rise above it ran counter to the anxious pessimism so prevalent in the depression years. In the thirties she found work on the WPA Writers Project. In the forties and fifties she was out of vogue. *Red Ribbon on a White Horse,* the final volume of this once famous writer, found a publisher only with difficulty. Poor again, she lived most of the time in a single room, stretching a meager income from royalties and the earnings of her pen. Still fiercely independent and still writing, she began in the last years of her life to publish stories about old age. The burning eagerness had not diminished. A friend who knew her in 1961 describes her then as "literally strangling" to get out the story that was inside her. She must have been about eighty years old when people began to discover her work again. Students invited her to lecture. She accepted delightedly. Less than three years before she died she wrote, "What makes writing so difficult? Isn't it the blind craze to say too much?"

Perhaps the nostalgia of an old woman distorted her perspective. In any event, Yezierska ended her life convinced that her obsession to lift herself out of material poverty had resulted in poverty of the soul. Perennially lonely, she spoke of the barren road of her success. She saw rebellion against her father as an attempt to be like him: to search for a vocation as strong as his. Because she was a woman, that was sinful. She had rejected family life and violated cherished Jewish tradition. In what may be a tribute to the power of cultural heritage, as well as to the folly of chasing after the American dream, she acknowledged finally the truth of her father's conviction that fire and water would not mix. "Hell," she wrote, "is trying to do what you can't do, trying to be what you're not." But she never wavered from the conviction that had guided her life: "The glimpses of truth I reached for everywhere, all that I could ever be was in myself." She died in 1970, an old woman with failing eyesight, still a marvelous teller of stories and, by her daughter's account, "an explosion to everyone."

If Anzia Yezierska was not typical of immigrant women, neither was she unique. Her struggle, in lesser proportions, went on everywhere. A stubborn and unrelenting father, more firmly rooted in old world traditions than most, and a willful daughter, convinced of her own right to make choices, merely highlighted tensions implicit in the transition to the new world. Yezierska's great gift was her ability to capture the ambiguity created by America's consistent temptations. She could write about the warmth and closeness of the immigrant community as she rejected the dirt and poverty that accompanied them. She could describe the pull of prosperity and the urge for adequate food as she warily watched for the trap that the marketplace surely laid. She condemned the endless toil and incessant anxiety that bound America's workers, but she remained eternally optimistic that its promise would be redeemed. She offered no answers, but she was sure that America somehow had them. Her reviewers used to say that she wrote about "life." And she did. Deceptively simple in plot and structure, her work is suffused with the unending trauma of adjustment, with the psychic stress of adaptation, with alternating currents of exhilaration, weariness, fear, self-doubt, self-loathing, and quiet acceptance that were all part of every individual's entry into America.

In his introduction to Yezierska's fictionalized autobiography, *Red Ribbon on a White Horse,* W. H. Auden wrote that the book was "an account of her efforts to discard fantastic desires and find real ones." I prefer to see her work as an attempt to reconcile American ideals with Jewish culture. For what seemed to Auden fantastic desires were for Yezierska only the wish to take the promise of America literally. America offered two things, both equally unattainable for the shtetl woman and, Yezierska was convinced, simultaneously available in America. America held out the possibility of love and of satisfying work. Yezierska's task was to find out if they could be achieved without giving up the best of the old culture and without the dreadful pangs of rootlessness that would follow.

Life in America did not begin and end with marriage. It offered the opportunity to reject old roles—to be unlike the women she knew. Thus, her heroine responded in *Arrogant Beggar* to the pride of a neighbor woman who had spent her life serving her husband and son, "I loved her because she gave up so much of herself. But I knew I could never, never be like that." Work could be a satisfying alternative. "Don't take pity on my years," shouted the heroine of one of her short stories to an uncle who wanted to marry her off. "I'm living in America not in Russia. I'm not hanging on anybody's neck to support me. In America if a girl earns her living she can be fifty years old and without a man, and nobody pities her." And so she set out, like many of Yezierska's heroines, to "make herself for a person" to rise out of poverty and find a satisfying life by her own efforts.

The road to becoming a person lay through the dangerous territory of Americanization. Yezierska is at her best when she describes the anguished journey. Americans were clean, so immigrants had to get out from under the dirt. But tenement apartments were crowded and dark. Few had running water. Soap cost money and washing took precious time away from sleep or studies. Americans were neat and stylish. But what immigrant girl had the money for clothes? Or the time to remake hats and learn new manners? Americans were soft-spoken and educated so the struggle to learn English, to finish high school, even to attend college became a single-minded obsession for those who wanted to shed the greenhorn image. A jumble of emotions assaulted the poor immigrant who tried to absorb these rules all at once. In her short story, "When Lovers Dream," Yezierska reflected on the cost of the process for a girl trying to live up to the image of her medical student boyfriend of what she should be.

David was always trying to learn me how to make myself over for an American. Sometimes he would spend out fifteen cents to buy me the 'Ladies Home Journal' to read about American life and my whole head was put away on how to look neat and be up-to-date like the American Girls. Till long hours in the night I used to stay up brushing and pressing my plain blue suit with the white collar what David liked, and washing my waists, and fixing up my hat like the pattern magazines show you. On holidays he took me out for a dinner by a restaurant, to learn me how the Americans eat, with napkins, and use up so many plates— the butter by itself and the bread by itself, and the meat by itself, and the potatoes by itself.

She didn't make it. David, afraid she would burden him, took the advice of a rich uncle and left her.

Americanization brought self-assurance and a change in personality that would transform the crude immigrant into a suave native. The tall Anglo-Saxon male appears repeatedly in Yezierska's work. To the immigrant girl he is an inspiring figure. Older and infinitely more sophisticated than she, he appears as the measured and calm epitome of her aspirations. To her, he represents reason and civilization. To become like him, she strives to get away from the Yiddish language and to suppress her displays of feeling. Yet it is precisely these qualities that he admires. To his Anglo-Saxon imagination, she seems, in her roughness, the essence of life. Her emotional energy and excitement draw him. He is captivated by the color and vitality of the immigrant community. His romantic vision of the ghetto leads her to see beyond its poverty and to recognize that her roots lie in the community she is trying to escape. In *All I Could Never Be,* Yezierska explores the conflict between reason and emotion in a love affair apparently modeled after her sad experience with Dewey. For a while the lovers complement each other. In the end, however, their differences irreconcilably divide them. The passionate immigrant and the cool son of privilege part.

On the way to successful Americanization lay another kind of anguish. Becoming an American cut women off from their culture and their past. It brought the fearful recognition that they were adrift in the world. "I had gone too far away from life and I did not know how to get back," lamented Yezierska. One of her characters, an immigrant's college-educated daughter, echoed the cry: "I can't live in the old world and I'm yet too green for the new. I don't belong to those who gave me birth or to those with whom I was educated." Yezierska offers some possibilities of solace. The educated daughter of immigrants could return to the ghetto in a spirit of love for her people. Together they might forge a new world out of her book knowledge and their knowledge of life.

The best part of America was freedom. As she was obsessed with her own need to be free, she gloried in the country that made it possible. This was a place in which all could aspire to the "democracy of beauty," she wrote in 1922. Yet she saw clearly America's failure to live up to its potential. In the midst of the depression she wrote sadly of her fellow immigrants, "We foreigners are the orphans, the stepchildren of America. The old world is dead behind us, and the new world—about which we dreamed . . . —is not yet born." And again, "How many get the chance to give to America the hope in their hearts, the dreams of their minds?" Greedy landlords and bosses shared the blame for poverty's distortion of the dream. Still her faith remained intact. Friends described her late in her long life as a woman instinctively opposed to "oppression of the spirit."

Many of these themes, of course, are present in the work of other first generation Jewish immigrants and their children. Poverty, Americanization, family tensions, the ambiguity of success are the painful realities of which immigrant drama was made. The pain surfaces in great novels like Henry Roth's *Call it Sleep,* in forgotten entertainments like Samuel Ornitz's *Haunch, Paunch and Jowl,* and in rediscovered sagas like Abraham Cahan's *The Rise of David Levinsky* and Michael Gold's *Jews Without Money.* In Fannie Hurst's thinly disguised didactic stories, the process of adaptation finds a picturesque frame. Everywhere there is the degradation of poverty mediated by a caring community and redeemed by a vibrant hope for the future.

Yezierska shares with her fellow immigrants the ability to evoke vividly the religion and tradition of the shtetl which she rejects. The intensity of her rejection contributes to the liveliness of her memories. Her heroes and heroines are in constant motion. They do not meander through the streets of the Lower East Side like Ornitz's street gangs. They rush headlong, hunting for a way out and pausing, like Michael Gold, to dwell on the distortions that poverty creates in the personalities of the people they pass along the way. Gold, like Cahan in *Yekl,* comments on the disjuncture between husbands who have found the way to the new world and wives who hang back, comfortable in their old patterns. Yezierska offers another and no less real syndrome: the wife who pleads, threatens, and nags her husband into American ways. Samuel Ornitz's Meyer Hirsch, who became a corrupt lawyer, and Abraham Cahan's David Levinsky, a wealthy cloak manufacturer, take their place alongside Yezierska's Sara Smolinsky as vivid warnings of the abject emptiness of lives lived to someone else's tune. David and Meyer, rich and dissatisfied, fall into the yawning chasm between two worlds. Sara, for whom success was not measured by money alone, is saved by making her peace with her immigrant childhood and her father.

If Yezierska has none of Ornitz's sense of humor or Gold's sense of the absurd, she may more accurately represent the way Jewish immigrants managed to struggle out of the Lower East Side. Relatively few became socialists, like Gold, or petty gangsters. Many nourished themselves on hope while they slaved to educate themselves and their children. And if Yezierska has neither the symbolic depth of Henry Roth nor the epochal power of Abraham Cahan, she offers unrivaled ability to bring life to a neglected aspect of Yiddish culture, plunging us directly into the woman's experience of immigration.

When women appeared at all in the novels of her fellow-writers, they were likely to be creatures of male sexual imagination, manipulative and overly protective mothers, or dependent wives made fearful by their helplessness. Mary Antin's romanticized and sentimental *The Promised Land* provides no antidote to this view. Fannie Hurst occasionally offers glimpses of autonomous women, but their freedom is bounded by severe moral constraints.

Yezierska, in contrast, offers independent and self-willed women, and she does not hide the psychic pain of their sacrifice. The struggle out of poverty, never easy, posed for women a unique problem. Those who shared the mobility aspirations of a larger society had to violate family and community tradition in order to achieve them. Many women brave enough to risk transgressing drifted towards radical activity where they could more readily find support. Even so, their lives were filled with conflict.

We find bits and snatches of rebellious womanhood scattered in the literature of Jewish labor and socialist leaders. Pauline Newman and Fannia Cohn, who worked for the Jewish International Ladies Garment Workers Union in the period when Yezierska was writing, complained bitterly of their lonely and rootless existences. Autobiographies like Rose Cohen's *Out of the Shadow,* Lucy Robins Lang's *Tomorrow Is Beautiful,* Emma Goldman's *Living My Life,* Rose Pesotta's *Bread Upon the Waters,* and Rose Schneiderman's *All for One* offer poignant testimony to the pain of women who rejected the injunction to marry and rear families as their major responsibility. They indicate that the current of discontent ran deep. Yezierska speaks for all of them and nowhere more fully than in *Bread Givers.*

She later commented of this novel, "I felt I had justified myself in the book for having hardened my heart to go through life alone." Perhaps, in the end, it is the need for self-justification that invests *Bread Givers* with its powerful emotional force. Anzia Yezierska and Sara Smolinsky, the novel's narrator, are emotionally interchangeable. Sara, as a small child, watches her self-righteous father successively drive off the suitors of each of her three sisters and marry off his daughters to men of his own choosing. The horror and injustice of her sisters' broken lives lead her to vow that she will not become a fourth sacrifice to his rigid conception of Jewish womanhood. So she escapes. But her father's curses ring in her ears and memories of her mother's boundless and forgiving love mock her own self-centered life. Sara, repeating Yezierska's own experience, struggles upward. She drives herself through night school and college, thrusting out of her mind questions about what she was doing and why. Successful at last, she visits her parents, teacher's diploma in hand, to hear her unrelenting father proclaim: "She's only good to the world, not to her father. Will she hand me her wages from school as a dutiful daughter should?" Is there then any reconciliation between the legitimate search for self-fulfillment and duty to family? Yezierska, like Sara, opted for self and built her life around her own authentic needs. She freed herself from a tradition few of her countrywomen could ignore in that first generation, and she did it against the heaviest odds. But she paid an enormous price. This book was part of her attempt to seek absolution.

In the light of the continuing women's movement, *Bread Givers* has become more meaningful than ever. When it was first published in 1925, reviewers praised its blistering intensity and translucent prose. They talked about its crisp quality, its vitality. "One does not seem to read," commented critic William Lyons Phelps. "One is too completely inside." Today these qualities are enhanced by Yezierska's scrutiny of issues that are the subject of wide concern. In her life and in this book, Yezierska questioned the limited roles offered to women by traditional families. She rejected the constraints that community pressure imposed on her freedom. She presented the possibility of men and women who could acknowledge each other's legitimate needs. *Bread Givers* makes no judgments of people who choose other paths. For freedom is at the pivot of this book as it was the driving force of Yezierska's life. Three quarters of a century after she wrote, the power and intensity of her message remain intact.

Alice Kessler-Harris
New York, 1975, 1999

BREAD GIVERS

CONTENTS

Book I: *Hester Street*

Book II: *Between Two Worlds*

Book III: *The New World*

BOOK I

Hester Street

Chapter I

HESTER STREET

I had just begun to peel the potatoes for dinner when my oldest sister Bessie came in, her eyes far away and very tired. She dropped on the bench by the sink and turned her head to the wall.

One look at her, and I knew she had not yet found work. I went on peeling the potatoes, but I no more knew what my hands were doing. I felt only the dark hurt of her weary eyes.

I was about ten years old then. But from always it was heavy on my heart the worries for the house as if I was mother. I knew that the landlord came that morning hollering for the rent. And the whole family were hanging on Bessie's neck for her wages. Unless she got work soon, we'd be thrown in the street to shame and to laughter for the whole world.

I already saw all our things kicked out on the sidewalk like a pile of junk. A plate of pennies like a beggar's hand reaching out of our bunch of rags. Each sign of pity from the passers-by, each penny thrown into the plate was another stab into our burning shame.

Laughter and light footsteps broke in upon my dark thoughts. I heard the door open.

"Give a look only on these roses for my hat," cried Mashah, running over to the looking glass over the sink. With excited fingers she pinned pink paper roses under the brim. Then, putting on her hat again, she stood herself before the cracked, fly-stained mirror and turned her head first on this side and then on the other side, laughing to herself with the pleasure of how grand her hat was. "Like a lady from Fifth Avenue I look, and for only ten cents, from a pushcart on Hester Street."

Again the door opened, and with dragging feet my third sister Fania came in. Bessie roused herself from the bench and asked, "*Nu?* Any luck with you?"

"Half the shops are closed," replied Fania. "They say the work can't start till they got a new president. And in one place, in a shirt factory, where they had a sign, 'Girls Wanted,' there was such a crowd of us tearing the clothes from our bodies and scratching out each other's eyes in the mad pushings to get in first, that they had to call two fat policemen with thick clubs to make them stand still on a line for their turn. And after we waited for hours and hours, only two girls were taken."

Mashah looked up from the mirror.

"Didn't I tell you not to be such a *yok* and kill yourself pushing on a line a mile long, when the shop itself couldn't hold those that were already on the doorstep? All the time that you were wasting yourself waiting to get in, I walked myself through the stores, to look for a trimming for my hat."

"You heartless thing!" cried Bessie. "No wonder Father named you 'Empty-head.' Here you go to look for work, and you come back with pink roses for your doll face."

Undisturbed by the bitter words, Mashah finished the last stitch and then hung up her hat carefully over the door.

"I'm going to hear the free music in the park tonight," she laughed to herself, with the pleasure before her, "and these pink roses on my hat to match out my pink calico will make me look just like the picture on the magazine cover."

Bessie rushed over to Mashah's fancy pink hat as if to tear it to pieces, but instead, she tore her own old hat from her head, flung it on the floor, and kicked it under the stove.

Mashah pushed up her shoulders and turned back to the mirror, taking the hairpins carefully from her long golden hair and fixing it in different ways. "It ain't my fault if the shops are closed. If I take my lunch money for something pretty that I got to have, it don't hurt you none."

Worry or care of any kind could never get itself

into Mashah's empty head. Although she lived in the same dirt and trouble with us, nothing ever bothered her.

Everywhere Mashah went men followed her with melting looks. And these melting looks in men's eyes were like something to eat and something to drink to her. So that she could go without her lunch money to buy pretty things for herself, and not starve like the rest of us.

She was no more one of us than the painted lady looking down from the calendar on the wall. Father's preaching and Mother's cursing no more bothered her than the far-away noise from the outside street.

When Mashah walked in the street in her every-day work dress that was cut from the same goods and bought from the same pushcart like the rest of us, it looked different on her. Her clothes were always so new and fresh, without the least little wrinkle, like the dressed-up doll lady from the show window of the grandest department store. Like from a born queen it shined from her. The pride in her beautiful face, in her golden hair, lifted her head like a diamond crown.

Mashah worked when she had work; but the minute she got home, she was always busy with her beauty, either retrimming her hat, or pressing her white collar, or washing and brushing her golden hair. She lived in the pleasure she got from her beautiful face, as Father lived in his Holy Torah.

Mashah kept part of her clothes in a soapbox under

nke Meg'.

4

the bed. Everything in it was wrapped around with newspapers to keep the dirt out. She was so smart in keeping her things in perfect order that she could push out her box from under the bed in the middle of the dark night and know exactly where to put her hand to find her thin lace collar, or her handkerchief, or even her little beauty pin for the neck of her shirtwaist.

High up with a hanger, on a nail nearly to the ceiling, so that nobody's dirty hands should touch it, hung Mashah's white starched petticoat, and over it her pink calico; and all around them, an old sheet was tacked about with safety pins so she could tell if anybody touched it.

It was like a law in the house that nobody dared touch Mashah's things, no more than they dared touch Father's Hebrew books, or Mother's precious jar of jelly which she always kept ready for company, even in the blackest times, when we ourselves had nothing to eat.

Mashah came home with stories that in rich people's homes they had silver knives and forks, separate, for each person. And new-ironed tablecloths and napkins every time they ate on them. And rich people had marble bathtubs in their own houses, with running hot and cold water all day and night long so they could take a bath any time they felt like it, instead of having to stand on a line before the public bath-house, as we had to do when we wanted a bath for the holidays. But these millionaire things were so far over our heads that they were like fairy tales.

That time when Mashah had work hemming towels in an uptown house, she came home with another new-rich idea, another money-spending thing, which she said she had to have. She told us that by those Americans, everybody in the family had a toothbrush and a separate towel for himself, "not like by us, where we use one torn piece of a shirt for the whole family, wiping the dirt from one face on to another."

"Empty-head!" cried Mother. "You don't own the dirt under their doorstep and you want to play the lady."

But when the day for the wages came, Mashah quietly went to the Five- and Ten-Cent Store and bought, not only a toothbrush and a separate towel for herself, but even a separate piece of soap.

Mother tore her hair when she found that Mashah made a leak of thirty cents in wages where every cent had been counted out. But Mashah went on brushing her teeth with her new brush and wiping her face with her new towel. And from that day, the sight of her toothbrush on the shelf and her white, fancy towel by itself on the wall was like a sign to us all, that Mashah had no heart, no feelings, that millionaire things willed themselves in her empty head, while the rest of us were wearing out our brains for only a bite in the mouth.

As Mother opened the door and saw all my sisters home, the market basket fell from her limp arm.

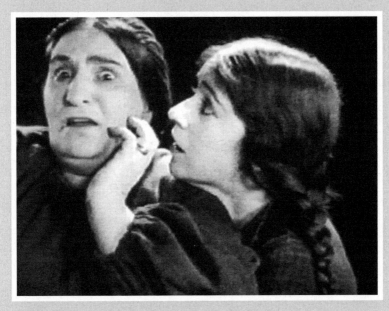

"Six hungry mouths to feed..."

"Still yet no work?" She wrung her hands. "Six hungry mouths to feed and no wages coming in." She pointed to her empty basket. "They don't want to trust me any more. Not the grocer, not the butcher. And the landlady is tearing from me my flesh, hollering for the rent."

Hopelessly, she threw down her shawl and turned to me. "Did you put the potatoes on to boil?" Then her eyes caught sight of the peelings I had left in the sink.

"Gazlin! Bandit!" her cry broke through the house. She picked up the peelings and shook them before my eyes. "You'd think potatoes grow free in the street. I eat out my heart, running from pushcart to pushcart, only to bargain down a penny on five pounds, and you cut away my flesh like a murderer."

I felt so guilty for wasting away so much good eating, I had to do something to show Mother how sorry I was. It used to be my work to go out early, every morning, while it was yet dark, and hunt through ash cans for unburned pieces of coal, and search through empty lots for pieces of wood. But that morning, I had refused to do it any more. It made me feel like a beggar and thief when anybody saw me.

"I'd sooner go to work in a shop," I cried.

"Who'll give you work when you're so thin and small, like a dried-out herring!"

"But I'm not going to let them look down on me

like dirt, picking people's ashes." And I cried and cried so, that Mother couldn't make me do it.

But now, I quietly took the pail in my hand and slipped out. I didn't care if the whole world looked on me. I was going to bring that coal to Mother even if it killed me.

"You've got to do it! You've got to!" I kept talking to myself as I dug my hand into the ashes. "I'm not a thief. I'm not a thief. It's only dirt to them. And it's fire to us. Let them laugh at me." And I did not return home till my pail was full of coal.

It was now time for dinner. I was throwing the rags and things from the table to the window, on the bed, over the chairs, or any place where there was room for them. So much junk we had in our house that everybody put everything on the table. It was either to eat on the floor, or for me the job of cleaning off the junk pile three times a day. The school teacher's rule, "A place for everything, and everything in its place," was no good for us, because there weren't enough places.

As the kitchen was packed with furniture, so the front room was packed with Father's books. They were on the shelf, on the table, on the window sill, and in soapboxes lined up against the wall.

When we came to America, instead of taking along feather beds, and the samovar, and the brass pots and pans, like other people, Father made us carry his books. When Mother begged only to take along her pot for *gefülte* fish, and the two feather beds that were handed down to her from her grandmother for her wedding presents, Father wouldn't let her.

"Woman!" Father said, laughing into her eyes. "What for will you need old feather beds? Don't you know it's always summer in America? And in the new golden country, where milk and honey flow free in the streets, you'll have new golden dishes to cook in, and not weigh yourself down with your old pots and pans. But my books, my holy books always were, and always will be, the light of the world. You'll see yet how all America will come to my feet to learn."

No one was allowed to put their things in Father's room, any more than they were allowed to use Mashah's hanger.

Of course, we all knew that if God had given Mother a son, Father would have permitted a man child to share with him his best room in the house. A boy could say prayers after his father's death—that kept the father's soul alive for ever. Always Father was throwing up to Mother that she had borne him no son to be an honour to his days and to say prayers for him when he died.

The prayers of his daughters didn't count because God didn't listen to women. Heaven and the next world were only for men. Women could get into Heaven because they were wives and daughters of men. Women had no brains for the study of God's Torah, but they could be the servants of men who

9

studied the Torah. Only if they cooked for the men, and washed for the men, and didn't nag or curse the men out of their homes; only if they let the men study the Torah in peace, then, maybe, they could push themselves into Heaven with the men, to wait on them there.

And so, since men were the only people who counted with God, Father not only had the best room for himself, for his study and prayers, but also the best eating of the house. The fat from the soup and the top from the milk went always to him.

Mother had just put the soup pot and plates for dinner on the table, when Father came in.

At the first the look on Mother's face he saw how she was boiling, ready to burst, so instead of waiting for her to begin her hollering, he started:

"Woman! when will you stop darkening the house with your worries?"

"When I'll have a man who does the worrying. Does it ever enter your head that the rent was not paid the second month? That to-day we're eating the last loaf of bread that the grocer trusted me? Mother tried to squeeze the hard, stale loaf that nobody would buy for cash. "You're so busy working for Heaven that I have to suffer here such bitter hell."

We sat down to the table. With watering mouths and glistening eyes we watched Mother skimming off every bit of fat from the top soup into Father's big plate, leaving for us only the thin, watery part.

If they let the men study the Torah in peace ...

We watched Father bite into the sour pickle which was special for him only; and waited, trembling with hunger, for our portion.

Father made his prayer, thanking God for the food. Then he said to Mother:

"What is there to worry about, as long as we have enough to keep the breath in our bodies? But the real food is God's Holy Torah." He shook her gently by the shoulder, and smiled down at her.

At Father's touch Mother's sad face turned into smiles. His kind look was like the sun shining on her.

"Shenah!" he called her by her first name, to show her he was feeling good. "I'll tell you a story that will cure you of all your worldly cares."

All faces turned to Father. Eyes widened, necks stretched, ears strained not to miss a word. The meal was forgotten as he began:

"Rabbi Chanina Ben Dosa was a starving, poor man who had to live on next to nothing. Once, his wife complained: 'We're so good, so pious, you give up nights and days in the study of the Holy Torah. Then why don't God provide for you at least enough to eat?'... 'Riches you want?' said Rabbi Chanina Ben Dosa. 'All right, woman. You shall have your wish.'... That very evening he went out into the fields to pray. Soon the heavens opened, and a Hand reached down to him and gave him a big chunk of gold. He brought it to his wife, and said: 'Go buy with this all the luxuries of the earth.'. . . She was so happy, as she began planning all she would buy next day. Then she fell asleep. And in her dream, she saw herself and her husband sitting with all the saints in Heaven. Each couple had a golden table between themselves. When the Good Angel put down for them their wine, their table shook so that half of it was spilled. Then she noticed that their table had a leg missing, and that is why it was so shaky. And the Good Angel explained to her that the chunk of gold that her husband had given her the night before was the missing leg of their table. As soon as she woke up, she begged her husband to pray to God to take back the gold he had given them. . . . 'I'll be happy and thankful to live in poverty, as long as I know that our reward will be complete in Heaven.'"

Mother licked up Father's every little word, like honey. Her eyes followed his shining eyes as he talked.

"*Nu, Shenah?*" He wagged his head. "Do you want gold on earth, or wine of Heaven?"

"I'm only a sinful woman," Mother breathed, gazing up at him. Her fingers stole a touch of his hand, as if he were the king of the world. "God be praised for the little we have. I'm willing to give up all my earthly needs for the wine of Heaven with you. But, *Moisheh*"—she nudged him by the sleeve— "God gave us children. They have a life to live yet, here, on earth. Girls have to get married. People point their fingers on me—a daughter, twenty-five years already, and not married yet. And no dowry to help her get married."

"Woman! Stay in your place!" His strong hand pushed her away from him. "You're smart enough to bargain with the fish-peddler. But I'm the head of this family. I give my daughters brains enough to marry when their time comes, without the worry of a dowry."

"*Nu,* you're the head of the family." Mother's voice rose in anger. "But what will you do if your books are thrown in the street?"

At the mention of his books, Father looked up quickly.

"What do you want me to do?"

"Take your things out from the front room to the kitchen, so I could rent your room to boarders. If we don't pay up the rent very soon, we'll all be in the street."

"I have to have a room for my books. Where will I put them?"

"I'll push my things out from under the bed. And you can pile up your books in the window to the top, because nothing but darkness comes through that window, anyway. I'll do anything, work the nails off my fingers, only to be free from the worry for rent."

"But where will I have quiet for my studies in this crowded kitchen? I have to be alone in a room to think with God."

"Only millionaires can be alone in America. By

Zalmon the fish-peddler, they're squeezed together, twelve people, in one kitchen. The bedroom and the front room his wife rents out to boarders. If I could cook their suppers for them, I could even earn yet a few cents from their eating."

"Woman! Have your way. Take in your boarders, only to have peace in the house."

The next day, Mother and I moved Father's table and his chair with a back, and a cushion to sit on, into the kitchen.

We scrubbed the front room as for a holiday. Even the windows were washed. We pasted down the floppy wall paper, and on the worst part of the wall, where the plaster was cracked and full of holes, we hung up calendars and pictures from the Sunday newspapers.

Mother sent me to Muhmenkeh, the herring woman on the corner, for the loan of a feather bed. She came along to help me carry it.

"Long years on you!" cried Mother, as she took the feather bed from Muhmenkeh's arm.

"Long years and good luck on us all!" Muhmenkeh answered.

Muhmenkeh worked as hard for the pennies as anybody on the block. But her heart was big with giving all the time from the little she had. She didn't have the scared, worried look that pinched and squeezed the blood out of the faces of the poor. It breathed from her the feeling of plenty, as if she had Rockefeller's millions to give away.

"You could charge your boarders twice as much for the sleeping, if you give them a bed with springs, instead of putting the feather bed on the floor," said Muhmenkeh.

"Don't I know that a bed with a spring is a good thing? But you have to have money for it."

"I got an old spring in the basement. I'll give it to you."

"But the spring needs a bed with feet."

"Do as I done. Put the spring over four empty herring pails and you'll have a bed fit for the president. Now put a board over the potato barrel, and a clean newspaper over that, and you'll have a table. All you need yet is a soapbox for a chair, and you'll have a furnished room complete."

Muhmenkeh's bent old body tottered around on her lame foot, as she helped us. Even Mother forgot for a while her worries, so like a healing medicine was Muhmenkeh's sunshine.

"*Ach!*" sighed Mother, looking about the furnished room complete, "God should only send a man for Bessie, to marry herself in good luck."

"Here's your chance to get a man for her without the worry of a dowry. If God is good, he might yet send you a rich boarder——"

From the kitchen came Father's voice chanting:

"*When the poor seek water, and there is none, and their tongue faileth for thirst, I, the Lord, will hear them. I, the God of Israel, will not forsake them.*"

Mother put her hand over Muhmenkeh's mouth to

stop her talking. Silent, breathless, we peeked in through the open crack in the door. The black satin skullcap tipped on the side of his head set off his red hair and his long red beard. And his ragged satin coat from Europe made him look as if he just stepped out of the Bible. His eyes were raised to God. His two white hands on either side of the book, his whole body swaying with his song:

"And I will bring the blind by a way that they know not; I will lead them in paths that they have not known; I will make darkness light before them, and crooked things straight. These things will I do unto them and not forsake them."

Mother's face lost all earthly worries. Forgotten were beds, mattresses, boarders, and dowries. Father's holiness filled her eyes with light.

"Is there any music on earth like this?" Mother whispered to Muhmenkeh.

"Who would ever dream that in America, where everything is only business and business, in such a lost corner as Hester Street lives such a fine, such a pure, silken soul as Reb Smolinsky?"

"If he was only so fit for this world, like he is fit for Heaven, then I wouldn't have to dry out the marrow from my head worrying for rent."

His voice flowed into us deeper and deeper. We couldn't help ourselves. We were singing with him:

"Sing, O heavens; and be joyful, O earth; and break forth into singing, O mountains; for the Lord hath comforted his people."

[handwritten marginalia: idolizes him]

Suddenly, it grew dark before our eyes. The collector lady from the landlord! We did not hear her till she banged open the door. Her hard eyes glared at Father.

"My rent!" she cried, waving her thick diamond fingers before Father's face. But he didn't see her or hear her. He went on chanting:

"Awake! Awake! Put on strength, O arm of the Lord: Awake, as in ancient days, in the generations of old. Art thou not he that hath cut Rahab and wounded the dragon?"

"Schnorrer!" shrieked the landlady, her fat face red with rage. "My rent!"

Father blinked his eyes and stared at the woman with a far-off look. "What is it? What do you want?"

"Don't you know me? Haven't I come often enough? My rent! My rent! My rent I want!"

"Oh-h, your rent?" Father met her angry glare with an innocent smile of surprise. "Your rent? As soon as the girls get work, we'll pay you out, little by little."

"Pay me out, little by little! The cheek of those dirty immigrants! A fool I was, giving them a chance another month."

"But we haven't the money." His voice was kind and gentle, as hers was rough and loud.

"Why haven't you the money for rent?" she shouted.

"The girls have been out of work." Father's innocent look was not of this earth.

"Hear him only! The dirty do-nothing! Go to work yourself! Stop singing prayers. Then you'll have money for rent!" She took one step towards him and shut his book with such anger that it fell at her feet.

Little red threads burned out of Father's eyes. He rose slowly, but quicker than lightning flashed his hands.

A scream broke through the air. Before we had breath enough to stop him, Father slapped the landlady on one cheek, then on the other, till the blood rushed from her nose.

"You painted piece of flesh!" cried Father. "I'll teach you respect for the Holy Torah!"

Screaming, the landlady rushed out, her face dripping blood as she ran. Before we knew what or where, she came back with two policemen. In front of our dumb eyes we saw Father handcuffed, like a thief, and taken away to the station house.

Bessie and Fania came home still without work. When they heard that Father was arrested it was as though their heads were knocked off.

Into this thick sadness, Mashah came, beautiful and smiling, like a doll from a show window. She hung up her hat with its pink roses on her nail on the wall, and before she had time to give a look at her things in the box, to see that nobody had touched them, she rushed over to the mirror, and with her smile of pleasure in herself, she said:

"A man in the place where I was looking for work

asked to take me home. And when I wouldn't let him, still he followed me. The freshness of these men! I can't walk the street without a million eyes after me."

Silence and gloom were her only answer.

Mashah stopped talking; turning from the mirror, for the first time gave a look at us.

"What happened? It's like a funeral in the house."

"The landlord's collector lady was here—and——"

"Well? What of it?"

"She was hollering for the rent."

"Then why didn't they pay her the rent? asked the innocent doll face. "Don't everybody pay rent?"

Mother began to scream and knock her head with her fists. "A stone! An empty-headed, brainless stone I had for a child. My own daughter, living in the same house with us, asking, 'Why did the landlady come? Why don't they pay her the rent?'"

Not listening to Mother's cursing and screaming, Mashah looked about for something to eat. The stove was cold. No food was on the table.

"Why ain't there something to eat? I'm starved."

Then Mashah caught sight of two quarters on the table that Muhmenkeh had left when she came to comfort us.

"What should I buy for supper?" Mashah asked, reaching for the money.

Before she could get to the quarters, I leaped to the table and seized one of them.

"Mammeh!" I begged. "Let me only go out to peddle with something. I got to bring in money if nobody is working."

"Woe is me!" Mother cried. "How can I stand it? An empty-head on one side and a craziness on the other side."

"Nobody is working and we got to eat," I kept begging. "If I could only peddle with something I could bring in money."

"Let me alone. Crazy-head. No wonder your father named you *'Blut-und-Eisen.'* When she begins to want a thing, there is no rest, no let-up till she gets it. It wills itself in you to play peddler and waste away the last few cents we got."

"As long as we're not working," said Bessie, "whatever Sara will earn will be something. Even only a few cents will buy a loaf of bread."

Without waiting for Mother to say yes, I ran out with the quarter in my hand. I saw Mashah go to a pushcart of frankfurters. But I, with my quarter, ran straight to Muhmenkeh.

"I got to do something," I yelled like a fire engine. "Nobody is working by us. Nobody! Nobody! What should I buy to sell quick to earn money?"

Muhmenkeh thought for a minute, then said. "I got some old herring left in the bottom of this barrel. They're a little bit squashed, but they ain't spoiled

"Let me only go out to peddle with something."

yet, and you'll be able to sell them cheap because I'll give them to you for nothing."

"No—no! I'm no beggar!" I cried. "I want to go into business like a person. I must buy what I got to sell." And I held up the same quarter that Muhmenkeh had given Mother.

"Good luck on you, little heart!" Muhmenkeh's old eyes smiled into mine. "Go, make yourself for a person. Pick yourself out twenty-five herring at a penny apiece. You can easy sell them at two cents, and maybe the ones that ain't squeezed for three cents."

On the corner of the most crowded part of Hester Street I stood myself with my pail of herring.

"Herring! Herring! A bargain in the world! Pick them out yourself. Two cents apiece."

My voice was like dynamite. Louder than all the pushcart peddlers, louder than all the hollering noises of bargaining and selling, I cried out my herring with all the burning fire of my ten old years.

So loud was my yelling, for my little size, that people stopped to look at me. And more came to see what the others were looking at.

"Give only a look on the saleslady," laughed a big fat woman with a full basket.

"Also a person," laughed another, "also fighting already for the bite in the mouth."

"How old are you, little skinny bones? Ain't your father working?"

I didn't hear. I couldn't listen to their smartness. I was burning up inside me with my herring to sell. Nothing was before me but the hunger in our house, and no bread for the next meal if I didn't sell the herring. No longer like a fire engine, but like a houseful of hungry mouths my heart cried, "Herring—herring! Two cents apiece!"

First one woman bought. And then another and another. Some women didn't even stop to pick out the herring, but let me wrap it up for them in the newspaper, without even a look if it was squashed or not. And before the day was over my last herring was sold.

I counted my greasy fifty pennies. Twenty-five cents profit. Richer than Rockefeller, I felt.

I was always saying to myself, if I ever had a quarter or a half dollar in my hand, I'd run away from home and never look on our dirty house again. But now I was so happy with my money, I didn't think of running away, I only wanted to show them what I could do and give it away to them.

It began singing in my heart, the music of the whole Hester Street. The pushcart peddlers yelling their goods, the noisy playing of children in the gutter, the women pushing and shoving each other with their market baskets—all that was only hollering noise before melted over me like a new beautiful song.

It began dancing before my eyes, the twenty-five herring that earned me my twenty-five cents. It lifted me in the air, my happiness. I couldn't help it. It began dancing under my feet. And I couldn't stop myself. I danced into our kitchen. And throwing the fifty pennies, like a shower of gold, into my mother's lap, I cried, "Now, will you yet call me crazy-head? Give only a look what 'Blood-and-iron' has done."

Chapter II

THE SPEAKING MOUTH
OF THE BLOCK

"**E**ven butchers and bakers and common money-makers have sometimes their use in the world," said Father.

He had just come home free from the court. And Mother was telling him how the butcher and baker and Zalmon the fish-peddler left their work to bail him out. And how they raised the money together for the best American-born lawyer to take his part.

Community

"*Nu?* Why shouldn't they take my part?" said Father. "Am I not their light? The whole world would be in thick darkness if not for men like me who give their lives to spread the light of the Holy Torah."

It was like a holiday all over the block when they had Father's trial. The men stopped their work. The women left their cooking and washing and marketing, and with babies on their arms, and babies hanging on to their skirts, they crowded themselves into the court to hear the trial.

In high American language the lawyer made a speech to the judge and showed with his hands all those people who looked up to Father as the light of their lives. And then he told the Court to look on

Father's face, how it shined from him, like from a child, the goodness from the holy life of prayer.

"He couldn't hurt a fly," the lawyer said. "Reb Smolinsky would turn aside not to step on the littlest worm under the feet." And he called on the neighbours to give witness how Father loved only stillness and peace and his learning from his books. And if he hit the landlady, it was only because she burst into the house in the midst of his prayers, and knocked his Bible out of his hands and stepped on it with her feet.

"It's a lie!" cried the collector lady.

Then our smart lawyer asked the judge to have made a print of her foot on a white piece of paper. And when he showed up together the page in the Bible where her wet, muddy foot stepped, and the print on the white paper, everybody could see it was the same shoe.

For a minute it was so still in that court, as if somebody had just died and everybody was scared to draw his breath.

"Prisoner discharged!" said the judge.

The crowd got so excited, yelling and shouting with gladness, they almost carried Father home over their heads.

For weeks after, everybody was talking about Father. By the butcher, by the baker, by the fish market, everybody was telling everybody over and over again, as you tell fairy tales, how Father hit the landlady when she stepped on the Holy Torah.

In the evening, when everybody sat out on the stoop, the women nursing their babies, the men smoking their pipes, and the girls standing around with their young men, their only talk was how Father was the speaking mouth of the block. Not only did he work for the next world, but he was even fighting for the people their fight in this world.

Everybody was scared to death when the landlord came around. And Father hitting the landlord's collector lady was like David killing Goliath, the giant.

Shprintzeh Gittel put the baby down in the gutter, stuck a nipple into its mouth to keep it quiet, and right before everybody on the stoop, acted out, like on the stage, the way Father hit the landlady first on one cheek and then on the other.

All the people stamped their feet and clapped their hands, with pleasure of getting even, once in their lives, with someone over them that was always stepping on them.

"She deserves it yet worse—the fresh thing!" said the rag-picker. "She insults enough the people."

"But a man shouldn't hit a lady," said Shprintzeh Gittel's Americanized daughter who was standing around with her American-born young man.

"A collector for the landlord ain't a lady," cried Shprintzeh Gittel. "For insulting her own religion they should tear her flesh in pieces. They should boil her in oil and freeze her in ice. . . . "

"I hate the landlord worse as a pawnbroker," Hannah Hayyeh, the washwoman. "Every month of your life, whether you're working or not working, whether you're sick or dying, you got to squeeze out so much blood to give the leech for black walls that walk away, alive with bedbugs and roaches and mice."

"He lives himself on Riverside Drive, and his windows open out into sunshine from the park, so why should he worry if it's to get choked with smoke in my dark kitchen every time I got to light the fire to cook something," said the shoemaker's wife from the basement.

"If the landlord wills himself another diamond on his necktie, or if his wife wants a thicker fur coat, all he got to do is to raise our rent."

"But you people are unreasonable," said the bookkeeper, who was always wearing a white, starched collar on his neck.

"Poor people are yet too much reasonable, because they can't help themselves," interrupted Hannah Hayyeh. "It's the landlords who don't want to fix or paint the houses and yet keep on raising the rent what are unreasonable."

"But the landlord has to pay taxes. And when they raise his taxes, he must raise the rent. . . . "

"Taxes? Rich people got enough money for taxes and other pleasures. I should only have the worry for paying taxes on a million dollars."

And so it kept on. And the arguments always ended with, "Long years on Reb Smolinsky to fight the landlords for the people!"

Soon everybody from all around knew us so well, it got easy for us to rent the front room. First one came, then another, and then a third. And when Mother wanted to squeeze in another boarder, they said they'd better each pay yet another quarter a week more and not have another boarder in the same room.

Things began to get better with us. Bessie, Fania, and Mashah got work. But still I kept on peddling herring. Earning twenty-five and sometimes thirty to fifty cents a day made me feel independent, like a real person. It was already back of me to pick coal from ash cans. I felt better to earn the money and pay out my own earned money for bought coal.

Mother began to fix up the house like other people. The installment man trusted us now. We got a new table with four feet that were so solid it didn't spill the soup all over the place. Mashah got a new looking glass from the second-hand man. It had a crack in the middle but it was so big she could see herself from the head to the feet. Mother even bought regular towels. Every time we wiped our faces on them it seemed so much behind us the time we had only old rags for towels.

We bought a new soup pot and enough plates and spoons and forks and knives so we could all sit down

Things began to get better with us.

by the table at the same time and eat like people. It soon became natural, as if we were used from always to eat with separate knives and forks instead of from the pot to the hand as we once did.

Once in a while we even had butter on our bread. And when eggs were cheap and Mother got a bargain at a pushcart, a lot of cracked eggs, then we had eggs for breakfast just like the boarders. Now all of us had meat for the Sabbath—not only Father. And sometimes Mother had a half chicken for Father.

But the more people get, the more they want. We no sooner got used to regular towels than we began to want toothbrushes, each for himself like Mashah. We got the toothbrushes and we began wanting toothpowder to brush our teeth with, instead of ashes. And more and more we wanted more things, and really needed more things the more we got them.

With the regular wages coming in each week, Mother became a new person. There was a new look in her eyes, and a new sound in her voice when she went to the grocery store, with the dollar in her hand, and bought what she wanted for cash, instead of having to beg them to trust her.

Sometimes almost a whole day would pass without a curse or a scream from Mother. She even began to laugh, once in a while, and make jokes about soon buying a house and a fur coat for winter.

When we sat down to our dinner she'd begin to tell us of the years back when she was a young girl.

"Who'd believe me, here in America, where I have to bargain by pushcarts over a penny that I once had it so plenty in my father's house? Pots full of fat, barrels full of meat, and boilers full of jelly we had packed away in our cellar. I used to make cake for the Sabbath with cream so thick you could cut it with a knife."

Her eyes looked far away like in a dream.

"When I'd go to a fair, everywhere I'd pass, people would draw their breath, they'd stop their bargaining and selling and stand back with sudden stillness, only to give a look on my face. See me only! Cheeks like red apples, skin softer and finer as pink velvet. Long, thick braids to my knees. Eyes dancing out of my head with the life in me. And such life as I once had! Wherever I gave a step, the whole earth burned under my feet, Give only a look on Mashah. That's the picture of me how I was. Only I was a hundred times healthier. In my face was all the sunshine and fresh air of the open fields."

I looked on Mother's faded eyes, her shape like a squashed barrel of yeast, and her face black and yellow with all the worries from the world.

"You looked like Mashah?" I asked.

"Where do you suppose Mashah got her looks? From the air? Mashah never had such colour in her cheeks, such fire in her eyes. And my shape was something to look on—not the straight up and down like the beauties make themselves in America."

The kitchen walls melted away to the far-off times

in Russia, as Mother went on and on with her fairy tales till late hours of the night.

"I was known in all the villages around not only for my beauty: I was the first dancer on every wedding. You don't see in America such dancing like mine. The minute I'd give a step in they'd begin clapping their hands and stamping their feet, the fiddlers began to play, and sing the song they played. And the whole crowd, old and young, would form a ring around me and watch with open mouth how I lifted myself in the air, dancing the *kozatzkeh*."

Once Mother got started she couldn't stop herself, telling more and more. She was like drunk with the memories of old times.

"When I got fourteen years old, the matchmakers from all the villages, far and near, began knocking on our doors, telling my father the rich men's sons that were crazy to marry themselves to me. But Father said, he got plenty of money himself. He wanted to buy himself honour in the family. He wanted only learning in a son-in-law. Not only could he give his daughter a big dowry, but he could promise his son-in-law twelve years' free board and he wouldn't have to do anything but sit in the synagogue and learn."

"When the matchmaker brought your father to the house the first time, so my father could look him over and hear him out his learning, they called me in to give a look on him, but I was so ashamed I ran out of the house. But my father and the matchmaker stayed all day and all night. And one after another your father chanted by heart Isaiah, Jeremiah, the songs of David, and the Book of Job.

"In the morning Father sent messengers to all the neighbours to come and eat with him cake and wine for his daughter's engagement that was to be the next day. I didn't give a look on your father till the day of the engagement, and then I was too bashful to really look on him. I only stole a glance now and then, but I could see how it shined from his face the high learning, like from an inside sun.

"Nobody in all the villages around had dowry like mine. Six feather beds and twelve pillows. I used to sit up nights with all the servants to pluck the down from the goose feathers. So full of down were my pillows that you could blow them away with a breath.

"I went special to Warsaw to pick out the ticking for my bedding. All my sheets had my name embroidered with a beautiful wreath of flowers over it. All my towels were half covered with red and blue embroidery and on each was some beautiful words embroidered such as, 'Happy sunshine,' 'Good-morning!' or 'Good-night!'

"My curtains alone took me a whole year to knit, on sticks two yards long. But the most beautiful thing of my whole dowry was my hand-crocheted tablecloth. It was made up of little knitted rings of all colours: red, blue, yellow, green, and purple. All the colours of the rainbow were in that tablecloth.

It was like dancing sunshine lighting up the room when it was spread on the table for the Sabbath. *Ach!* There ain't in America such beautiful things like we had home."

"Nonsense, Mamma!" broke in Mashah. "If you only had the money to go to Fifth Avenue you'd see the grand things you could buy."

"Yes, buy!" repeated Mother. "In America, rich people can only buy, and buy things made by machines. Even Rockefeller's daughter got only store-bought, ready-made things for her dowry. There was a feeling in my tablecloth——"

"But why did you leave that rainbow tablecloth and come to America?" I asked.

"Because the Tsar of Russia! Worms should eat him! He wanted for himself free soldiers to make pogroms. He wanted to tear your father away from his learning and make him a common soldier—to drink vodka with the drunken *mouzhiks*, eat pig, and shoot the people. . . .

"There was only one thing to do, go to the brass-buttoned butchers and buy him out of the army. The *pogromshchiks*, the minute they smelled money, they were like wild wolves on the smell of blood. The more we gave them, the more they wanted. We had to sell out everything, and give them all we had, to the last cent, to shut them up.

"Then, suddenly, my father died. He left us all his money. And your father tried to keep up his business, selling wheat and wine, while he was singing himself the Songs of Solomon. Maybe Solomon got himself rich first and then sang his Songs, but you father wanted to sing first and then attend to business. He was a smart salesman, only to sell things for less than they cost. . . . And when everything was gone from us, then our only hope was to come to America, where Father thought things cost nothing at all."

Chapter III

THE BURDEN BEARER

B ut Mother did not dream always about how good she had it as a young girl. If she had less to worry for the rent, so she had more time to worry for a man for Bessie, who was already nine years older than Mother was when she got married. And there was no sign of a man yet. And no dowry to help get one.

What Muhmenkeh said about the boarders didn't turn out that way, because all the boarders, the minute they gave a look at Mashah, fainted away for her. And they didn't see at all Bessie, who carried the whole house on her back. Their eyes turned only on Mashah and their ears didn't hear anything but what Mashah said.

The men didn't know that if Mashah was always shining like a doll, it was because Mashah took first her wages to make herself more beautiful and left the rest of us to worry for the bread and rent. They didn't know that Mashah, on her way home from work, always looked on the shop windows for what was the prettiest and latest style. They didn't know that all her time home, instead of helping with the housework, Mashah was always before the mirror trying on her things, this way and that way, so as to make them more and more becoming to her, while Bessie would rush home the quicker to help Mother with the washing or ironing, or bring home another bundle of night work, and stay up till all hours to earn another dollar for the house.

The men didn't know that Bessie gave every cent she earned to Father and had nothing left to buy herself something new. All they saw was that Mashah was a pleasure to look on, while Bessie was so buried, with her nose in the earth helping the family, that they had no more eyes on her than on Mother.

Even Fania, the third sister, got herself a young man before Bessie did. In the airshaft, facing our kitchen, he lived. He was a boarder with Zalmon, the fish-peddler. Once, when Fania put her head out of the window to dry her hair, the young man began to talk to her. Then he told her about the night school where he was going and he showed her the books he took from the free library.

And soon, every evening, Fania began to go to the same night school where the young man went. And he began writing her every day love poems, such grand, beautiful thoughts that read like from a book. And sometimes, Fania would read the poems the young man sent her to the girls on the stoop. And nobody would believe that such burning high thoughts came from that pale-faced, quiet-looking man that lived in that dark airshaft hole with Zalmon the fish-peddler, and who was only a sweeper and cleaner in the corner drugstore.

And so the neighbours saw Mashah always with a bunch of men, buzzing around her like flies around a pot of honey. They saw Fania go to the night school and to the library with the writing young man. But Bessie had nobody. And you could see it in her face, how it ate her heart to have the younger sisters go out with men, and she had nobody. Nobody.

And then it happened!

Once, when it was the night for the wages, Bessie came home with three packages, a new oilcloth for the table, a remnant from a lace curtain to tack around the sink, to hide away the rusty pipes, and a ten-cent roll of gold paper for the chandelier to cover up the fly dirt that was so thick you couldn't scrub it away.

Mashah wanted to go to hear the free music in the park, but Bessie begged her to stay home. "Help me only, this once, to shine up the house a little. You, too, will feel good if somebody should come in and find the house looks decent, like by other people."

And so excited was Bessie to clean up the house that she made us pull out everything to the middle of the room and scrub out the corners and under the bed. And when we packed all the junk away where it wouldn't show itself, the crowded kitchen got bigger and there was more room to move around without knocking things over.

And when we tacked the lace curtain around the sink, and fixed fancy the chandelier with the gold paper, and we spread out the new, white oilcloth on the table, it looked like a new house.

We were sitting like company, taking pleasure in our new, cleaned-up kitchen. *Ach!* I was thinking to myself, if only we didn't have to pull out the torn bedding from its hiding place to sleep—the rags to dress ourselves—if only we didn't have to dirty up the new whiteness of the oilcloth with the eating, then it would shine in our house always like a palace. It's only when poor people begin to eat and sleep and dress themselves that the ugliness and dirt begins to creep out of their black holes.

Just then, Mother came in. She looked around, her eyes jumping out of her head. "What happened!" she cried. "Gold shines in our house! Lace hangs on our walls!" Then she touched the white oilcloth on the table as if she was afraid to touch it with her hard-worked hand. "White marble to eat on!"

"It's too grand for every day. Quick only! Let's cover up the oilcloth with newspapers and save the lace curtain for company."

"No!" Bessie stamped her foot like a new person. "We won't cover up the beautiful whiteness. Now that we're working ourselves up, let's have it beautiful for ourselves, not only for company."

"*Nu—nu*—don't fly away with yourselves in fairy-land," laughed Mother. "We're poor people yet. And poor people got to save——"

"Save—save!" cried the new Bessie. "I'm sick of saving and slaving to choke myself in the dirt. I want to live while I'm yet alive."

We opened wide our eyes to give a look on Bessie. What had suddenly happened to her? Father called her the burden-bearer, because she was always with her nose in the earth slaving for the family. And now she suddenly wanted to lift up her head in the world and live.

Mother threw her hands up. "Have it your way! American children always want things over their heads."

The next evening, when we came home, Mother was away at a sick neighbour's that was dying. And Father was yet in the synagogue. Fania never had time to wait for supper on the evenings she went to night school. So she grabbed a piece of bread and herring and, still eating it, hurried downstairs, where her young man was waiting for her to take her to school.

Bessie hurried to get the supper and rushed Mashah and me to eat it quick. I was wondering why Bessie was so excited to get the supper, as if she was starving hungry, and yet didn't eat much herself. All the time she gave quick glances on Mashah and quickly turned her eyes away when Mashah looked up.

"I'll wash the dishes, Mashah, if you want to get out," said Bessie, the minute we were done eating.

"But it's raining," said Mashah.

"Then why don't you go to the Grand Street vaudeville?"

"I haven't the money."

Then think only! Bessie took from her stocking a quarter. "Here, you got it."

Mashah tool the money and stared on it hard, as if to see if it was lead. Then looking upon Bessie with her innocent, wondering eyes, she asked, "What makes you so good to me all of a sudden?"

"Oh well——" Bessie got red and looked away. "Oh, well—you stayed in last night to help fix up the house, so I thought you'd want to go somewhere."

Mashah didn't need to be begged to go to the theatre. She grabbed her hat and coat and out she went.

The minute the door was closed behind Mashah, Bessie pushed the dirty dishes under the sink behind the curtain. With the quickness of a cat she jumped on the bed. She grabbed the hanger with Mashah's pink dress, that was covered around with a white sheet, like a holy thing. Crazy with excitement, she pulled off her skirt and waist. And, like lightening, the pink princess dress was over her head.

"Quick, Sara," she called, "help me. I can't squeeze my arms into the sleeves."

"*Oi weh!* Mashah will kill us," I cried.

"I got to have it. I got to look nice to-night. Somebody—a man is coming."

The dress that slipped on so easy on Mashah's thin shape stuck on Bessie in the middle. But somehow, by the two of us pulling it together she could squeeze her arms through the tight sleeves.

"Hook it only faster," she begged.

I tried to push together the hooks, but they were too far apart.

"It'll choke you to wear it," I said, work out from pulling. "Can't you see it ain't big enough?"

"It's got to be big enough." And Bessie stood up on her toes and blew out all her breath, and she squeezed herself with her hands till I could pull together the hooks one at a time. But it was so tight, where every hook was came a wrinkle. It made her shape stick out so funny that I begged her: "Better put back on your old skirt and waist that you wear to the shop, because in this tight dress it sticks out so your fatness."

"But every day he sees me in the shop, in that same old skirt and waist. I want him to see me in something different. I want to brighten myself up to him."

"But it don't brighten you like Mashah because Mashah got red cheeks and——"

Bessie pushed me aside, and ran over to Mashah's looking-glass, and began fixing her hair. But she was so nervous and excited the comb fell out from her hand. And when she bent down to pick it up—

crack! burst open the seam on the side of the pink dress!

Just then was a knocking on the door. And Bessie ran into the bedroom to pin together the ripped seam.

When the knocking came again, I opened the door. There was a man. He had a starched shirt on, with a white starched collar on his neck, and a gold chain across his checked vest.

"Is Bessie Smolinsky here?" he asked.

"Right away she'll come!" I said. And I showed him to Father's chair with a cushion to sit on.

Then Bessie came out, her eyes burning out of her head, her cheeks redder than Mashah's, and her right arm held to the side, like pasted there, to cover up where she pinned herself together.

She shook hands with the man from only her elbow. But the man didn't notice anything, he looked as mixed-up and excited as Bessie herself.

First I went to the bedroom, so they could talk to themselves. And I was thinking to put on my shawl and go out in the street. Then I remembered that Bessie was like lame, with her arm pasted to her side to cover up the rip in her pink dress. And I began looking around, all over the house to find where Mother hid away the jelly for company.

While I was yet looking for the jelly, Father came in. His face lighted up with gladness to see company. And the young man got up from his chair and shook hands with Father. Bessie was so excited, she stood there red in her face and moving her lips like a *yok,* unable to open her mouth and let out a word how to make the introduction.

"*Nu,* Bessie?" asked Father. "What's this man's name? Who is he?"

"Berel Bernstein," came out the words from her choked neck. "He is the cutter from our shop."

Father shook hands with him again. "Berel Bernstein, from where do you come?"

"My village was seven miles from Grodno," said Berel Bernstein.

"Is your father also in America?"

"No, he's in Russia yet."

"How long are you here?"

"Ten years already."

"Do you still pray every morning?"

The man got red and looked down on the floor. "Sometimes, when I get up early enough, I pray. But I keep all the holidays."

"How much wages do you earn?"

"Eighteen dollars a week." And he stuck out his chest a little from his bashfulness.

"How much do you save each week from your eighteen dollars?" questioned more Father.

"Sometime six, sometimes seven dollars," said Berel Bernstein.

"What! On yourself only, you spend eleven twelve dollars!" Father looked him over from his patent-leather shoes to the gold horseshoe pin shining on his red necktie. "A whole family could live already on what you spend on your one self."

Berel Bernstein got red as fire. "I got to eat my meals in the restaurant where it costs you twice so much as it would cost home. I think like you say, a married man could live cheaper as a single one. If a man could only have a wife to cook for him and wash for him. That's why——" He stopped and couldn't go on what he had to say.

Father gave a quick, sharp look on the man, and then his eyes went on Bessie, like she had brought a thief in the house. But he didn't say anything. And it got so still in the house, everybody looking away from each other, that I brought in the tea and jelly.

As soon as they began drinking tea, Father loosened up his hard look and began again his questions. "You got something already in the bank?"

"Sure, I got money saved. For years already I lived for a purpose. I know inside the whole clothing trade. I was working already as a baster, a presser, and an operator. And now I'm already the head cutter. And I'm thinking to start myself a shop."

"So you'll be a manufacturer yet, in America," said Father. "Have more jelly in your tea. And how soon will you open yourself up a factory?"

"First I'm thinking to get myself married."

"That's good sense. A business man needs himself a wife. She could run him the home cheaper, and maybe help him yet in business, if she's got a head."

"That's just what I'm looking for," said Berel Bernstein. "I like a plain home girl that knows how to help save the dollar, and cook a good meal, and help me yet in the shop. And I think...your daughter Bessie is just fitting for me."

Father pushed back his glass of tea, and stood up, looking on the man. "Daughters like mine are not found in the gutter."

"Sure! Don't I see Bessie in the shop, every day how she knows more about the work as the forelady? I could get plenty of girls with money. But I want to take your daughter, like she is, without a dowry."

"Why don't you ask me first what I want?" cried Father. "Don't forget when she gets married, who'll carry me the burden from this house? She earns me the biggest wages. With Bessie I can be independent. I don't have to grab the first man that wants her. I can wait yet a few years."

"You can wait! But your daughter is getting older each year, not younger. Do you want her to wait till her braids grow gray?"

"Look at Weinberg's daughter!" said Father. "She is thirty years already, and she's still working for her father. Has a father no rights in America? Didn't I bring my children into the world? Shouldn't they at least support their old father when he's getting older? Why should children think only of themselves? Here I give up my whole life, working day and night, to spread the light of the Holy Torah. Don't my children owe me at least a living?"

"But Bessie must get married some time. And you can't get such chances like me every day."

"Don't forget it that you're only a man of the earth. I'm a man of God. Wouldn't Bessie get a higher place in Heaven supporting me than if she married and worked for you?"

"The cheek, from a beggar who dreams himself God!" Berel's voice grew loud, like a fish-peddler's. "I'm a plain 'man of the earth.' You can't put none of your Heaven over on me."

"But I ask you only, by your conscience, what should I do without her wages? The other children don't earn much. And they need more than they earn. They'd spend every cent on themselves if I'd only let them. But Bessie spends nothing on herself. She gives me every cent she earns. And if you marry her, you're as good as taking away from me my living—tearing the bread from my mouth."

Till now Bessie sat still, mixing her tea with the spoon, not tasting it. But now, as Father's bargaining over her got louder, she ran into the bedroom. She stood beating her breast with her clenched fist. Then she sat very still and the tears kept running silently down her cheeks. I couldn't stand to look on her. Tears came into my eyes. So I ran out of the bedroom to the kitchen, not to cry.

"I want a wife for a purpose."

"So you don't want me yet?" cried Berel Bernstein. "Do you know who I am? Matchmakers are running after me—girls with a thousand and two thousand dollars dowry. You ought to see their pictures! Young—beautiful—good family—everything a man can only want. They, begging themselves by me. But I don't even give a look on them. I like your girl better. I don't want those dressed-up dolls, to spend my money on them. I look ahead on the future. I want a wife for a purpose. I must open myself a shop. And Bessie could help me with the 'hands,' while I do the cutting. And we could work ourselves up—and——"

"*Nu,* if you want her so much, why don't you look on my side a little?"

"What more do you want me to do? Ain't I taking her from your hands without a cent?"

"Taking her from my hands! Only girls who hang on their father's neck for their eating and dressing, that the father has to pay dowry, to get rid of this burden. But Bessie brings me in every cent she earns. When a girl like mine leaves the house the father gets poorer, not richer. It's not enough to take my Bessie without a dowry. You must pay me yet."

"Pay you? Why and for what?"

"If Bessie get married, you got to pay all the expenses for the wedding and buy her clothes. I need a new outfit myself. You see what's on me is all I have. These things I wear are from Russia yet.

Give a look on my shoes! Wouldn't it be a shame for the world if Reb Smolinsky, the light of the block, the one man who holds up the flame of the Holy Torah before America, should come to his daughter's wedding in such shoes? You yourself don't want the bride's father to come to your wedding feast dressed in rags, like a beggar. I got to begin with a new pair of shoes, and everything new from the head to the feet. And all I ask more, is enough money to start myself up some business so I could get along without Bessie's wages."

Berel Bernstein hit the table with his fist till the tea glass jumped. "I should set you up in business yet!" he hollered at my father. "I'm marrying your daughter—not the whole family. Ain't it enough that your daughter kept you in laziness all these years? You want yet her husband to support you for the rest of your days? In America they got no use for Torah learning. In America everybody got to earn his living first. You got two hands and two feet. Why don't you go to work?"

"What? I work like a common thickneck? My learning comes before my living. I'm a man of brains. In a necessity I could turn to business. I have a quick head for business. If I only had money, I could start myself selling wine and schnapps, or maybe, open myself an office for an insurance agent or matchmaker, and hold on to my learning at the same time."

While Father was yet talking, Berel Bernstein began muttering to himself, "What I dreamed last night, and this night, and the night before should fall on his crazy head." Then he began shouting. "So it ain't enough for you that I take your daughter without a dowry? You don't want it yet? Me? Me? Berel Bernstein! Instead of grabbing me with both hands and thank God for the good luck that fell on you, for taking your daughter away without a cent, you want me to weigh you yet in gold? You think I got Rockefeller's millions to throw away? I got to sweat for every penny I earn. I'm no greenhorn. I'm no cow you can milk. If you don't want it yet, then good-by and good luck."

And he rushed to the door and slammed himself out without saying good-by to Bessie.

The next evening, Berel Bernstein brought Bessie home from work and stood talking to her on the stoop.

"Your crazy father got me so mad, I was too excited to say anything to you. I think more of you as your own father. Your father keeps you only for your wages. I would take you without a cent and make yet for you a living. And we would work together for a purpose, to save the dollar."

Still Bessie couldn't speak, but stood clenching and unclenching her fingers and staring down on the ground.

"This is America," Berel Bernstein went on, "where everybody got to look out for themselves.

Together, we'd have a future before us—our own shop—our own business. We could live yet in our own bought house. I already saw in the pawnshop the diamond ring I want to buy you. What will you have by living with you father? All your life you'll have to give away your wages, and he'll suck out from you your last drop of blood like a leech. . . . "

"I couldn't leave my father. He needs me. . . . "

Berel Bernstein shook Bessie by the arm. "But you got to think of yourself. Even in the Torah it says, leave your father and mother, and follow the man. Better listen to me. Come, let's get married in court."

Bessie shook her head, and tears began coming down her cheeks. "I know I'm a fool. But I cannot help it. I haven't the courage to live for myself. My own life is knocked out of me. No wonder Father called me the burden bearer."

"That's just what you are, a 'burden bearer.' Here you got the chance to life your head and become a person, and you want to stay in your slavery."

"But you see, Father never worked in his life. He don't know how to work. How could I leave them to starve?"

"Starve? He won't starve. He'll have to go to work. It's you who are to blame for his laziness and his rags. So long as he gets from you enough to eat, he'll hang on your neck, and bluff away his days with his learning and his prayers."

Bessie stopped crying and looked straight at Berel

Bernstein. "I couldn't marry a man that don't respect my father."

"You want me to respect a crazy *schnorrer* like your father?" He laughed hard into her face. "What I see plain is that you don't love me. Did you think you could rope me in for a fool, to support your whole family? The time I wasted yet on you, when I could have had the forelady who is crazy for me."

Bessie reached out to touch his hand. "Berel, I'll . . . "

"Yes. I see what you'll do. Lucky yet I got my sense back in time. I'll get a wife for me, myself, and not one to hang a whole beggar family on my neck." And he turned from her and rushed down the street, never once looking back.

Bessie stood very still. She looked after Berel Bernstein till she couldn't see him any more. She didn't say anything. But I could see her sink into herself as if all the life went out of her heart and she didn't care about anything any more.

I walked in after Bessie and hid myself behind the door of the bedroom and I cried and cried.

Six weeks later, we heard that Berel Bernstein was going to be engaged to the forelady who lived on the first floor of Muhmenkeh's house. As they told Bessie the news, she got twenty years older in that moment. She grew black and yellow, with all the worries of the world in her face, like Mother.

All my sadness for Bessie suddenly blazed up in me into wild anger. I could have choked Berel Bernstein with my bare hands.

In one breath, I ran the whole block and upstairs where the engagement was. In the hall I was stopped by the crowd of relations from both sides. I couldn't see Berel or his bride, but through the crack of the door, I saw big plates of sponge cake and raisins and nuts and bottles of wine. I was just going to give myself a push in when Berel Bernstein's mother grabbed me by the braids and shoved me out. "You little devil! Who asked you here?"

I walked down wilder than a mad cat. "I'm going to say my say to Berel Bernstein even if I got to set the house on fire." And suddenly, it came to me. I rushed like lightning into Muhmenkeh's house, then up the fire escape.

With his back to the window stood Berel Bernstein talking to his bride. And before anybody could stop me, I dashed open the window, rushed over to him and shook him, crying, "You—you——! For shaming my Bessie—you'll yet eat dirt before you die!"

Chapter IV

THE "EMPTY-HEAD"

Something happened in our house again!

Mashah, the "empty-head," showed signs that there was something in her. She was no more just a doll in a show window. She was no more just something lost in the looking glass of her pretty face.

For the first time in her life, Mashah showed signs of interest in someone outside herself. No longer was the one reason for her living to make prettier her pretty face. Now it was a man that was the beginning and end of her existence.

The man put new light in her eyes, new life in her face, and such a wonder-working joy in her heart that it changed the "empty-head" into a singing sunshine. The pretty doll became overnight a feeling person—a person with a heart.

We still didn't believe it—the miracle! Mashah in love!

His name was Jacob Novak and he was a piano-player. He lived in the first-floor front room of a private house on the corner. His rich father paid ten dollars a lesson a week to a professor up town who was teaching him and getting him ready for a concert, to play it all by himself for a hall full of people.

One day, as Mashah passed the corner private house, she heard playing such as she never heard before. She stood looking up at the open window from where the playing came, even after the music stopped. Then a face came to the window. It was a young man's face. Music was in his eyes and high feeling breathed from his face.

"Play again," Mashah begged.

The man looked on Mashah, and then he went back and played more beautifully than before. This time when Mashah still looked up after the music stopped, the man himself came out.

And that's how Mashah's love began.

Mashah had always liked to hear free music in the park. Now she was all music herself. It sang itself from her, the music of love, from the time she got up in the morning till she went to bed at night.

New life hummed in our house. Every day the house was swept from out of the corners and from under the beds. Before the rest were up, Mashah had scrubbed the house as for a holiday.

Before, Mashah was interested only in hanging up her own clothes. But now she told us that "Chairs were made to sit on, not throw things on." And she saw to it that everybody's clothes were hung up on hangers as good as her own.

In these days, when Mashah got home from work it was no longer to play with her pretty golden hair, combing it in a dozen different styles. Jacob Novak

His place at the table was set...

was expected for supper. And now she saw to it that his place at the table was set as perfect as in a restaurant. The tablecloth and napkins glistened with the fresh-ironed whiteness, as if just out from the store laundry. The steel knife and the tin fork and spoon were polished and polished till they shone bright as silver.

No longer were the cracked penny cups used for evening's tea, but whole cups with handles were taken down from the Passover set and used for every day. When Bessie was excited about a man, we thought it was riches to have white oilcloth for the table. When love came to Mashah, she covered the oilcloth with a real tablecloth. And more yet—when Mashah's lover came for dinner, he had to have a napkin because he always had it. And we each had to have a napkin also, so as not to make him feel funny with a napkin by himself alone.

When roses and lilacs became cheap, Mashah went without her lunch to buy flowers for the table, in honour of Jacob. She managed to find out just what eating he liked and just the salt and pepper to please his taste. Mother always said that, with her bitter heart, what were such little things as too much or too little salt in the soup. But now, because of Jacob, we all had food cooked and salted as it was never cooked and salted before.

Mashah found out that Jacob liked American cooking, like salad and spinach and other vegetables. And right away Mashah joined the cooking class in the settlement, one evening a week, to learn the American way of cooking vegetables and fixing salads. And soon we all had American salad and American-cooked vegetables instead of fried potato *lotkes* and the greasy *lokshen kugel* that Mother used to make.

Jacob had a tailor to keep fixed his clothes. But Mashah's eyes were so much on him that once she found a button loose before the tailor did. And after that, I believe yet, he worked the buttons loose on purpose, only to have the pleasure of Mashah's happiness when she sewed them on.

The bunch of other men that used to buzz around Mashah now dropped away when they saw how Mashah had fallen in love with Jacob Novak.

His father owned a big department store on Grand Street and Jacob looked like from rich people. It didn't shout from his clothes, the money they cost, as it did from Berel Bernstein. He did not wear a checked vest, nor on a red necktie a gold horseshoe pin. But it breathed from his quiet things, the solid richness from the rich who didn't have to show it off any more. Maybe that was the reason Father didn't question out Jacob as he did Bessie's man, because there was about Jacob Novak the sure richness of the higher-up that shut out all questions of how he spent his money. Or maybe Father didn't waste time asking the man, because Mashah always used out her wages on herself. Father said the sooner Mashah got married the better for us all. And there would only be more room in the house if she was gone.

Anyhow, Father only objected that he played the piano on the Sabbath. But he said he'd better wait till Jacob was tight married to the family before he'd begin to hold up to him the light of the Holy Torah.

One day, Mashah came home, all burning up with the great big news that Jacob's father, who had been away all this time to Chicago on business, was coming home. He was coming special to meet Mashah and us all because Jacob had written to him about us, and also he had to finish the arrangements of the concert that was to come off in a few weeks.

All day long, Jacob played on his piano, as long hours as other people work who have to go to work. And for years and years he had done this, to learn how to play so the whole world should listen to him. This concert was to show up all the long years of his learning that now he was ready for the ears of the world and no more to play only to the deaf walls of his room on Essex Street. This concert was to Jacob the great day of his life, the way the wedding day is to a girl in love.

"What is dearer to you, your music or me?" Mashah asked her lover once.

"I love my music more because of you, and I love you more, because of my music."

A vague, far-off sadness darkened Mashah's face.

"All these hours and hours that you practise your piano, you see nothing before your eyes but your notes. But no matter what I do, you are always before my eyes."

"You jealous dear." He kissed her eyelids tenderly. "Even my business-like father would have to love you."

"Yes, I am jealous—jealous of your music." Mashah's eyes burned into his. "The more you have to practise for that concert, the less time you have for me."

"But, dearest! My whole life hangs on this concert. Think what it has cost my father. I must at least show him what's in me."

At last it happened. Jacob came with his father.

The minute his father stepped in, we saw it was the richest man that had ever been in our house. From him it hollered money, like a hundred cash registers ringing up the dollars. The riches from his grand clothes so much outshined all the little riches that we shined up for him that in a minute it shrank into blackness the white tablecloth and the white napkins. And like a sun in the desert, the glitter of his diamonds withered and faded the poor little flowers on the table.

One look he gave on all of us. Then for a minute his eyes burned over Mashah. Even though his lips answered politely the introduction, we saw Mashah shrink and fade under his eyes as the flowers faded under the glitter of his diamonds. From Mashah, he gave the house another look over. And all Mashah's beauty couldn't stop the cash-register look in his eyes, that we and our whole house weren't worth one of his cuff buttons.

He didn't stop even to sit down in our house. But as quick as he could say it politely, he asked Jacob to go for a walk with him.

And he didn't ask Mashah to go along.

When Jacob didn't come back that evening, Mashah tried to push it aside and tell us it was so much business about the concert that he couldn't come back. But we ourselves had heard him tell her at the door that he would be sure back that evening. And we knew it was a bad sign if he didn't come.

The next evening was the evening of the concert. And Mashah rushed into the house with a frightened, worried look and asked anxiously if Jacob had come. She looked at the clock. From six it went over to seven and then to eight. As the hours passed, she grew more and more excited.

No Jacob. No letter. No message.

I had heard Jacob tell Mashah where he was to give his concert, and I stole out of the house and took the car to the concert hall. At the front door I stopped shaking with excitement. There was Jacob Novak's picture, as big as life, and under his picture, his name, in big print letters.

I had no money for the ticket, so I stood at the side of the man who was collecting the tickets, watching the crowd go in. When the first sounds of the music started, I ran from that place as one runs from a house on fire. The hurt of the great wrong burned my flesh. How could that concert go on and Mashah not there!

When I got back home Mashah was still waiting for Novak.

The clock went on ticking the seconds, the minutes, the hours. Everyone went to sleep. But still Mashah waited. At every sound, she listened for him.

It was midnight. But Mashah still sat waiting for Jacob to come. "He will come. He must come," she kept talking to herself.

Suddenly, when every one was sound asleep, a terrible cry tore through the air—the cry of somebody murdered with a knife—the choked bleeding wail of a dying, broken heart.

In one leap we rushed out of bed. We found Mashah with her head on the window sill, her whole body shaking with sobs—sobs that could not cease— and could not be consoled. Like dumb things, we all cried with her—all through the night.

With so many women weeping in the house, Father could not sleep any more.

"It's all because I let a man who plays on the Sabbath into my door that my house is so full of woe and wailing," said my father. And he opened his book of Jeremiah, and began chanting about the fall of Jerusalem.

Another day, and still another day, passed and Jacob did not come. And Mashah sat still, not stirring, not speaking. With glazed eyes she sat, as one watching her best loved one dead in a coffin.

Only when the whistle of the letter-carrier was

heard, Mashah stirred and asked in a voice that barely breathed, "Is there a letter? Is there a letter for me?"

But no letter came.

Three more days and three more nights passed. Mashah did not eat. Mashah did not sleep. Mashah just sat still in one place at the window with staring eyes that saw nothing.

Then she called me over and said, "Write for me a letter. My fingers can't write anymore." And so I wrote as she said it to me.

Jacob:

It's the last time you will hear from me. I'm not throwing up anything to you. I only wanted to tell you that you robbed me of my belief in love and truth. In you I believed. You I loved. You and your music were everything of truth and beauty there was in the world. And if you could leave me, then music is only ugly noise, and words of love, all lies. And there is no truth, no beauty, and no love in the world.

Mashah.

As soon as I wrote this letter, she sent me over with it to the place he lived.

I found him walking up and down his room, like something caged, his thoughts far away. "What a suffering face—what worried eyes," I thought, as I stood at his open door for some time, before he noticed me. Then he jumped at me and seized the letter I held in my hand.

"Oh, my poor dear Mashah!" he groaned, shutting his eyes with the hurt of his guilt. "I've been a brute—a criminal!"

Like one in a fever, he began talking to himself and fighting with the air around him.

"He'll not keep me from her another minute! To hell with Father! I will see her. How can a store-keeper's brain know her heart!" And grabbing me by the hand, he rushed with me to Mashah.

In the hall, he stopped, frightened. "Will she see me? Please ask her to come down," he begged like a child. "I'll wait here."

I bounded up the stairs and into the kitchen. It was like death in the house since Novak had stopped coming. And I thought my words would bring life back to Mashah's dead face. And she would run down to meet him as always before.

"He's waiting for you, downstairs," I gasped, breathless.

She drew herself up tall and proud as a queen. "I go to him? No——"

"But he must see you. He's afraid to come up. You ought to see him. He looks terrible."

Slowly she rose and came down. Cold as a stone statue, she looked at him. "What brought you here? Is it pity? I need no pity."

"Mashah!" His hands reached out to her, plead-ingly. "I've been a coward—bullied by my father. I listened to him because of the concert—but no more. You're everything to me!"

He drew her up in his arms and kissed her with burning lips.

"Mashah! Speak to me. Tell me only you forgive me. See how I suffered since I left you."

Come upstairs," she said, coldly.

Was this the same Mashah whose face lit up like a living sun at the sound of Jacob's footsteps? Where had gone the light of her eyes, the life that sang and danced when he was near? It seemed to me that something deep down in her had broken and it would never again be fixed. She was like something still and walking and talking, but inside she was frozen into something colder than death.

As they entered the house, his hand clinging to hers, Father came in.

"Empty-head!" shouted Father, tearing Mashah away from Jacob. "You yet speak to this liar, this denier of God! Didn't I tell you once a man who plays the piano on the Sabbath, a man without religion, can't be trusted? As he left you once, he'll leave you again."

"Listen to me just once, I beg you," Jacob pleaded. "It was the concert—my father——"

"I'll not listen to a *meshumid* who plays on the Sabbath!" Father pushed his hand from his arm. "It says in the Torah that when you see a *meshumid* drowning you must sink him deeper into the water. And if you see him burning, you must add yet fuel to the flames." Father opened the door and pushed Jacob out.

The next day, Jacob tried to see Mashah again.

And this time Father slammed the door in his face. Then he turned to Mashah.

"I give you the last warning, never to see that man again. If you do, I'll turn you out of the house. You must choose between that scroundrel and your father."

And so Mashah, weak, dumb, helpless with the first great sorrow of her life, gave in to Father's will. She let go her chance of fixing up her happiness because of Father's unforgiving pride. And Jacob was never seen in the house again.

Mashah went back to work. She still dressed neatly, and was even beautiful in her quiet silence. But she dressed mechanically. A sad, far-off look of something for ever gone had come into her eyes. She was like a bird with its song for ever stilled.

In her weakness and dumbness and helplessness, Father began letting out all his preaching on her poor head. "I always told you your bad end. I told you with your empty head and pretty face no good could come to you. Any man who falls in love with a pretty face don't think to marry himself. If a man wants a wife, he looks for one who can cook for him, and wash for him, and carry the burden of his house for him. I always told you that a man who plays on the Sabbath has no fear of God. And if he don't fear God, then how could you trust him anything he said?"

More and more I began to see that Father, in his innocent craziness to hold up the Light of the Law to his children, was as a tyrant more terrible than the Tsar from Russia. As he drove away Bessie's man, so he drove away Mashah's lover. And each time he killed the heart from one of his children, he grew louder with his preaching on us all.

We'd come home worn and tired from working hard all day and there was Father with a clear head from his dreams of the Holy Torah, and he'd begin to preach to each and every one of us our different sins that would land us in hell. He remembered the littlest fault of each and every one of us, from the time we were born. And he'd begin hammering these faults into us till it got black and red for our eyes.

Sometimes when I'd come home, the mere sound of Father's voice would get me so nervous that I'd want to scream and pull my hair and cry out like a lunatic, "I can't stand it! I can't stand it any more in this house!"

I began to feel I was different from my sisters. They couldn't stand Father's preaching any more than I, but they could suffer to listen to him, like dutiful children who honour and obey and respect their father, whether they like him or not. If they ever had times when they hated Father, they were too frightened of themselves to confess their hate.

I too was frightened the first time I felt I hated my father. I felt like a criminal. But could I help it what was inside of me? I had to feel what I felt even if it killed me.

I'd wake up in the middle of the night when all

were asleep, and cry into the deaf, dumb darkness, "I hate my father. And I hate God most of all for bringing me into such a terrible house."

More and more I began to think inside myself, I don't want to sell herring for the rest of my days. I want to learn something. I want to do something. I want some day to make myself for a person and come among people. But how can I do it if I live in this hell house of Father's preaching and Mother's complaining?

And when I get a lover I don't want Father questioning out his wages, or calling him a *meshumid* because he played the piano on the Sabbath.

And then I thought, what kind of a man could I get if I smell from selling herring? A son from Zalmon the fish-peddler?

No! No one from Essex of Hester Street for me. I don't want a man like Berel Bernstein whose head was all day on making money from the sweatshop. No, I wouldn't even want one like Jacob Novak, even if he was a piano-player, if he ate the bread of his father who bossed him. I'd want an American-born man who was his own boss. And would let me be my own boss. And no fathers, and no mothers, and no sweatshops, and no herring!

Chapter V

MORRIS LIPKIN
WRITES POETRY

We were sitting and eating our dinner when we heard the mail man's whistle and our name called.

I quickly ran downstairs and got a letter. It was for Fania. Many times before she had been getting them. But this was the first time that Father was around when one came.

"For whom is the letter?" asked Father, taking it from my hand.

"It's for Fania," I said.

"Who can be writing to such a child?" And he tore open the letter and read:

Beloved, Dearest One:
How I long to shout to the world our happiness. I feel that you and I are the only two people alive in the world—the only people that know the secret meaning of existence.

I have no diamond rings, no gifts of love that other lovers have for their beloved. My poetry is all I have to offer you. And so I dedicate my collected verses, "Poems of Poverty," to you, beloved.
                                                                Morris.

"Poems of Poverty!" cried Mother. "Ain't it black enough to be poor, without yet making poems about it?"

Father turned angrily on Mother. "Woman! Why didn't you tell me this what's going on in this house? A man writes letter to my daughter and I'm told nothing about it?"

"Is it my fault that you're away all the time, so busy working for God that you don't know what's going on in your own house? Are you a man like other men? Does your wife or your children lay in your head at all?"

Into this father-and-mother fight, Fania came in.

"Poems of Poverty!" Father shook the opened letter in Fania's face. "Who is this *schnorrer* who writes you love letters on wrapping paper?"

"My letter! Why did you open my letter? It's mine. You had no right to read it! It's terrible to have to live in a house where even a letter is not one's own." And she snatched it from Father's hand.

"Who is he? What is he? By what does he work?" Father demanded.

"He works for newspapers," Fania answered.

"And where does he sell them, from the sidewalk or has he a stand of his own?"

"He sell papers? Why, he's a writer, a poet."

"A writer, a poet you want for a husband? Those who sell the papers at least earn something. But what earns a poet? Do you want starvation and beggary for the rest of your days? Who'll pay your rent? Who'll buy your bread? Who'll put shoes on the feet of your children, with a husband who wastes his time writing poems of poverty instead of working for a living?" *hypocrit.*

Father, once started, went right on, like a wound-up phonograph that couldn't stop itself.

"Maybe you would like to go on working in the shop, to support your husband, after you're married? Do you know what black life is before you if you tie yourself to a poet?"

And then Father told us a Greek fairy tale he once read! The king of the gods wanted to divide up everything among those under him. To one he gave the sea, to another the stars, to another the earth, the sun, and so on. After everything was divided up, the poet woke from his dreams and asked for his part. "Where were you all this time, while everybody was fighting for his share of the world?" "I was in the heaven of my dreams," answered the poet. *"Nu,"* said the god. "If you can live in dreams, then you don't need the things of this world. Go back to your dreams."

Father looked around to see how we all listened with open mouths to his smartness. Only Fania, on whom he pointed his preaching, only she pushed away his story with a toss of her head.

"H'm! Only a fairy tale," she sniffed. "I'd rather have Lipkin and be poor, so long I have the man I love."

"How long will love last with a husband who feeds you with hunger? Even Job said, of all his sufferings, nothing was so terrible as poverty. A poor man is a living dead one. Even dead you got to have money. The undertaker wouldn't bury you, unless you have the price of a grave."

"Father!" I broke in, "didn't you yourself say yesterday that poverty is an ornament on a good Jew, like a red ribbon on a white horse?"

"Sure," added Mother, "aren't you always telling me that those whom God loves for the next world can't have it good here?"

"Woman! You compare a man who works for God, a man who holds up the flames of the Holy Torah before the world, to this *schnorrer*? Of what use are poets to themselves, or to anybody? Aren't there enough beggars——?"

"But didn't you say that the poorest beggars are happier and freer than the rich?" I dared question Father. "You said that a poor man never has to be afraid of thieves or robbers. He can walk alone in the middle of the night and fear nobody. Poor people don't need locks on their houses. They can leave their doors wide open, because nobody will come to steal poverty. . . . "

"Blood-and-iron! Hold your mouth!" hollered Father. "You're always saying things I don't ask you."

"But what will be the end of your driving men away from the house?" said Mother. "Do you want a houseful of old maids on your neck? If these men are not good enough, why ain't you smart enough to bring somebody better?"

Father's eyes suddenly lighted up with a new idea. You forgot how old was his *capote,* how threadbare his skullcap, so shining with young joy was his face.

"I'll show how quickly I can marry off the girls when I put my head on it."

"Yah," sneered Mother. "You showed me enough how quickly you can spoil your daughters' chances the minute you mix yourself in. If you had only let Mashah alone, she would have been married to a piano-player."

"Did you want me to let in a man who plays on the Sabbath in our family? A piano-player has no more character than a poet."

"*Nu*—Berel Bernstein was a man of character, a man who was about to become a manufacturer."

"But he was a stingy piker. For my daughters' husbands I want to pick out men who are people in the world."

"Where will you find better men than those they can find for themselves?"

"I'll go to old Zaretzky, the matchmaker. All the men in his list are guaranteed characters."

"But the minute you begin with the matchmaker you must have dowries like in Russia yet."

"With me for their father they get their dowries in their brains and in their good looks."

"*Yid!* You've forgotten already that I was the beauty of the village. What good looks the children got is from me," Mother laughed, straightening herself up and glancing toward the mirror.

"Woman! If not for your pretty face I wouldn't have now a houseful of females on my neck. But I'll show you how I can marry them off in one, two, three."

A few days after, as I came home, I saw a man talking to Fania. At first sight, I saw only his back, but I knew by the worn-out shabby coat and how his hair cried for a barber that it was Fania's poet, Morris Lipkin.

"I'll talk to your father," I heard him say to Fania. "I'll never give you up. He can't know the depth of our love. How our lives are bound in one another."

"You don't know my father," Fania whispered. "He'll never listen to us."

"He must listen. He shall listen." He put his arm around her. "Let me only tell him what our love is to us."

The stairs in the outside hall creaked under heavy shoes. Father with his pouncing footsteps was stamping ahead of another man.

"He's coming now!" Fania tried to draw away from Morris, but he only drew her closer.

"Darling! Together we can fight the world." His pale face, his burning eyes were aflame with the courage of his love.

The door was pushed open. Father stood before them.

Instantly Morris and Fania drew apart.

"Reb Smolinsky"—Morris came forward—"Fania

and I——" But the words died in his throat, for Father without looking at him stepped back and pushed another man into the room.

A big diamond was glittering from the man's necktie and diamonds hollered from the man's fingers.

"Mr. Moe Mirsky! These are my four daughters, Bessie, Mashah, Fania, and Sara," Father announced. "And over there, by the stove, is my wife."

Moe Mirsky bowed politely and began to fuss with his tie, dazzling us with the glitter of his shining wealth.

Father did not notice Lipkin any more than if the place where he stood was air.

"Bring only some tea and jelly for the company," Father ordered; his head high with pride at the rich company he brought. He himself handed around the tea that Mother brought over, and he passed Lipkin by as if he did not exist.

Whiter than death grew Lipkin's face. Stone-still he stood, his lids lowered over his shamed eyes. None of us dared look at him, but it burned through us, the hurt of his shame, and yet we too stood like helpless stone.

Setting his own glass of tea down on the table, Father pushed around the chairs for every one. And then he deliberately took Lipkin's chair away from the window where Lipkin was still standing and pulled it up to the table; and Father sat himself down in it, with his back toward Lipkin.

Through our half-closed eyes of shame, we felt, more than saw, Lipkin walk out stiffly like an unwanted ghost.

Moe Mirsky was quick to take in how the other man was frozen out by Father, but he pretended not to notice it. And as soon as the door closed behind Lipkin, Moe Mirsky gave us all a look over, and then his eyes lighted on Mashah, and he pushed his chair near her.

Father began to brag about our smartness the way he always did before strangers. And Moe Mirsky, warmed with the tea, or fired by Mashah's beautiful, sad face, laughed and entertained us all as if he had known us all his life. He told us about the different cities he travelled, the names of the grand hotels where he stopped at, the theatres he went to, and the big sales he made in diamonds. And before he left, he invited us all to go with him to Coney Island on Sunday.

As soon as he had gone, Father turned to Mother, "*Nu?* How would you like this diamond-dealer for a son-in-law?"

"*Ach!*" sighed Mother, a far-off look of longing gleaming in her eyes, "only to see my daughters settled in good luck! But what do you know about him? Who is he? What is he?" Mother clutched at Father's arm in excited eagerness.

"A diamond-dealer! What more can you ask? The riches shine from him. The minute I saw him by the matchmaker, I said: This is the man I want for my daughter. You can see for yourself this man is a person of the world, and not a pale, half-starved poet."

Fania could hold herself no longer. "Father," she burst out, "why were you so mean, so brutally cruel to Lipkin?"

"That poet would be the ruin of your life, and you wanted me to welcome him yet? Why, he hasn't the money to get himself a decent haircut. Starvation cries from his face——"

"Poverty is no crime. You had no right to insult him so before everybody, only because he's poor."

Father's eyes flashed with rage. "The impudence of that long-haired beggar—wanting to push himself into my family! I'm a person among people. How would I look before the world if I introduced such a hunger-squeezed nobody for a son-in-law?"

"That diamond show window that you brought into the house can't hold a candle before Lipkin's brains. You think Lipkin will be poor always? You ought to see how hard he works by night and day at his writing. How can you tell what Lipkin's future might yet be?"

"A father knows the future because he is older." His strong hand pushed back and beat down all contradictions. "I can see your bitter end if you marry such a *schnorrer*."

"I know what I want for my happiness."

"Either you listen to what I say, or out you go of this house!" Father pounded the table with his fist. "Such shameless unwomanliness as a girl telling her father *this* man I want to marry! *Rifkeh!*" He turned to Mother. "Did we ever know of such nonsense in the old country? Did you even give a look on me, or I on you till the wedding was all over?"

Mother shook her head at Father with a funny smile.

"Maybe if I had the sense of my daughters in America, I would have given you a good look over before the wedding."

In the stillness that followed Mother's words, I was thinking: Suppose Mother had not felt like marrying Father, then where would all of us children be now? And here, in America, where girls pick out for themselves the men they want for husbands, how grand it would be if the children also could pick out their fathers and mothers. But my foolish, flying thoughts were stopped by an angry cry from Fania.

"I'll sooner go out of this house than go to Coney Island with your walking jewelry store!"

"I certainly won't go," said Bessie. "He didn't even give a look on me."

"Only let me go," I cried. "I never yet seen Coney Island."

"Blood-and-iron!" Father pushed me aside. "You think because he's a gentleman and invites the family for politeness that he has time to waste with children? If Fania don't want to grab this chance, then you go with him, Mashah."

Mashah looked with her cold, tired eyes at Father.

"One man or another man, it's all the same to me now."

And so it was Mashah's luck to be the only one to go with Moe Mirsky to Coney Island.

The next week Moe Mirsky brought Mashah a pair of diamond earrings and a diamond ring.

"*Nu—Rifkeh?*" cried Father, examining the diamonds after Moe Mirsky was gone. "Am I a judge of people? Didn't I tell you from the first that I *know* how to pick out a man? With this diamond-dealer in the family, all our troubles are over. You'll see he'll cover Mashah with diamonds. And through her riches, all of us will get rich quick. Think only of the future for the other girls with a sister in the diamond business."

A few days after, Moe Mirsky told Mashah, "I got a chance to sell your diamonds at a big profit, and meanwhile I'll bring you yet bigger diamonds."

And so every few evenings Moe Mirsky kept changing Mashah's diamonds, taking the old diamonds one night and bringing other new diamonds the next night.

Before a month was up Mashah became engaged. She didn't care so much about Moe Mirsky or his diamonds. She didn't care about any man at all. But like all of us she was sick and tired from the house and crazy to get away.

Father was so excited with his success in getting Mashah engaged to a diamond-dealer that he wanted to show off more smartness.

"I'll show you how quickly I can get another rich man for Fania, now that my brain got started with matchmaking," he said to Mother.

Bessie was threading the beads she had taken home for night work. Suddenly all the beads in her lap dropped to the floor. "Let it all go to hell," she cried. "I'm sick of life."

Of late Bessie was getting more and more bitter, because it ate out her heart, when she saw that Father was thinking only of marrying the younger sisters because he didn't want to let go of her wages.

"Why do I kill myself for nothing?" Bessie went on, kicking the beads with her foot instead of picking them up. "Why should I be the burden bearer for them all?" And she began to weep.

"Old maid!" shouted Father. "Stop jumping out of your skin and making the whole house miserable with your salted tears."

Bessie ran into the bedroom and slammed the door, and Father kept right on. "It's only through me that Mashah got luck. If I put my head on it, I can just as quick get another man for Fania and show the neighbours that when Reb Smolinsky only wants, he can marry even two daughters in a day as easy as Rockefeller signs a check for a million dollars."

And so the next day, Father brought another man from Zaretzky, the matchmaker. His name was Abe Schmukler and he was in the cloaks-and-suits *he thinks he's doing such a great job but really they're only agreeing so they can get away from him...*

business. He came from Los Angeles, at the other end of America, to buy cloaks and suits for his stores and get himself a wife.

Abe Schmukler liked Fania at first sight. Fania wasn't stuck on him and his cloaks and suits any more than Mashah was stuck on Moe Mirsky with his diamonds. But how could the girls stop to think whether they liked the men, or didn't like the men, so long as they only got the chance to run away from our house, where there would be no more Father's preaching?

At first, we thought that Fania would never take to Abe Schmukler, because she was still in love with her poet, even thought he wasn't around since that night that he walked out of the house like a dead ghost. And then she knocked us all over with surprise by the quick way in which she turned from the poor poet to the rich buyer and seller of cloaks and suits, and went out every night to uptown theatres with Abe Schmukler. From the outside she looked all excited with happiness, because every day Abe Schmukler brought her new things: dresses, cloaks, suits, candies, and flowers, till all the girls on the block were green with envy.

Abe Schmukler had only a month's time in New York. Two weeks he already spent buying his cloaks and suits, and only two weeks he had left to get himself a wife. So he had to quicken his love with many presents.

And that's how Father's bragging that he could marry off his two daughters in one day really happened.

Every one knew that Mashah was not marrying Moe Mirsky for his diamonds. But Fania made all believe that she fell head over heels in love with her cloaks-and-suits millionaire. Only a night before the wedding, as Bessie, with biting envy in her eyes, watched Fania pack her trunk, Fania got into a nervous fit. She threw all her beautiful wedding presents down on the floor and burst out crying.

"My God! Bessie! You're cutting me with your eyes! What do you envy? A broken heart?'"

With her feet she stamped on a black lace dress, trimmed with gold, which Abe Schmukler had given her. "What do you envy? The shine of these gilded rags with which I choke my emptiness? I love Lipkin. And I'll always love him. But even if Abe Schmukler was a rag-picker, a bootblack, I'd rush into his arms, only to get away from our house. . . . If I seem so excited about Los Angeles, it's only because it's a dream city at the other end of the world, so many thousands of miles away from home."

But in the meantime, the whole tenement house where we lived, and every house on the block, the fish market, the butcher, the grocer, on the stoop and in the doorways, rang excited news, from lips to lips, like fire in the air, that there was to be a double wedding in our house.

Everywhere, I saw groups of people whispering

and looking after us, as though their eyes were tearing themselves out of their heads with envy. When Mother passed with her market basket, the neighbors stood back with choked breath, as though she was already Mrs. Vanderbilt, coming to give Christmas presents among the poor.

"*Ach!* How the sun shines for them!"

"Luck smiles on them!"

"For them is America a golden country!"

"A diamond-dealer and a cloaks-and-suits millionaire!"

"Music plays for them!"

"Life dances for them!"

"We must dry our heads worrying for bread, while they bathe themselves in milk and soak themselves in honey!"

It made me feel bad to see how everybody began to hate us because we had a little luck. Dogs envying another dog a bone. They were only bread-and-butter marriages, like in Europe, and all the neighbours eating themselves out with envy.

A month after the double wedding, we were seated at the table for dinner. Mother skimmed off the fat part of the potato soup, and carefully picked out all the little pieces of suet and fried onions for Father's plate, and handed it to him.

"Woman!" Father frowned. "Why have you no meat for my dinner this whole week? With the hard brain work I do day and night, I can't live on the flavour of onions!"

"But the meat went up a nickel a pound, and the two girls married, there are two wages less with which to buy."

"With one son-in-law a diamond-dealer and another a cloaks-and-suits manufacturer I ought to have at least one man's meal a day. If I were a butcher, a baker, a thickneck, a money-maker, if I did less for my children, then maybe they would have done more for me. But from the day they were born, I held up for them the flame of the Holy Torah. It was I, my brains, my knowledge of the world, that brought them such golden luck marriages—and see their gratitude!"

The door opened; Mashah, with a wild worried look in her eyes, entered, but Father was too excited with his wrongs to see her.

"Woe to a man who has females for his offspring," he went on. "The thanklessness of these daughters! Getting them such rich husbands—and they forgetting their father as though their luck dropped down to them from the sky. . . . "

He caught sight of Mashah, but he was too much in his thoughts to see how terrible she looked. "*Nu*, Mrs. Moe Mirsky," he reproached. "With a husband diamond-dealer, isn't it your duty to see that your father has at least meat—"

"Meat! I didn't even taste bread to-day!" The words tore themselves out of Mashah's throat. "Moe Mirsky, a diamond-dealer? Oh-h-h! The liar—the faker!"

She sank into a chair. What she had told had used up her last strength.

"Where are all the diamonds he gave you? Father stared with innocent eyes at her.

"Those diamonds weren't his. . . . "

"Not his?" A puzzled look came into Father's face. "Why, he said he was a dealer—"

"But he lied. He was only a salesman in a jewellery store." Her voice was faint with tiredness. "He lost his job—lost it—because he let me wear the diamonds he was sent to sell. . . . The day after the wedding, it happened. I was to shamed to tell you then. But now, I'm so starved, I could hold myself in no longer. I had to come for—for something to eat."

"Empty-head!" shouted Father. "Where were your brains? Didn't you go out with the man a whole month before you were married? Couldn't you see he was a swindler and a crook when you talked to him?"

"Couldn't I see?" cried Mashah. "I thought you said you saw. You said you knew yourself a person on first sight. You picked him out! You brought him to the house! I didn't care about any man any more. I only wanted to run away from home."

"You wanted to run away because you were a lazy empty-head. So now you got it for your laziness. I always told you your bad end. As you made your bed, so you got to sleep on it." I hate him.

For the week that Mashah stayed in our house,

not one day passed that Father did not remind her, over and over again, that there was no more hope for her, for this world or for the next. Never again would she be able to life up her head among people. But this time his preaching was in a whispering voice, because no matter how the shoe pinched us, we had to hide our shame from the neighbours.

At last, her husband came with the news that he got a job as a shoe clerk, so worn down was Mashah by Father's never-ending pictures of the hell that was waiting for her, that she was glad to leave our house, even though her diamond-dealer of a husband had come down to be a shoe clerk. So crushed, so broken was she, as she took her husband's arm, that Bessie, who was always jealous of Mashah because of her luck with men, Bessie took a dollar out of her purse and slipped it, unseen, into Mashah's empty one.

Now that the puffed balloon of Mashah's luck match crashed to nothingness, Father still fanned himself with pride in Fania's marriage. "At least one daughter takes after her father," he soothed himself. "At least one child listened to her father's wise words. One child has remained a credit to me."

For six months we didn't get any letters from Fania. She only sent us fancy postal cards with pictures of orange trees and beautiful bungalows surrounded with flowers that grew all winter. Then we got from her the first real letter. It told that Abe Schmukler was a gambler. He spent his nights in one poker game after another. So lonely did she get, that she wanted to leave all the riches of cloaks and suits, and the beautiful houses with fruits and flowers of that dream city, and come back to our black, choking tenements in New York, and go back to work in a shop if only Father would let her.

But Father answered her back a quick letter. "Don't dare come and disgrace me before the neighbors," he wrote. "You had a right to find out what kind of a man your husband was before you married him. The neighbours here wouldn't believe that you left him. They will say that he threw you out. And don't forget it, you are already six months older—six months less beautiful—less desirable, in the eyes of a man. Your chances for marrying again are lost for ever, because no man wants what another turns down. As you made your bed, so you must sleep on it."

"What are you always blaming everything on the children?" I burst out at Father. "Didn't you yourself make Fania marry Abe Schmukler when she cried she didn't want him? You know yourself how she ate out her heart for Morris Lipkin——"

"Hold your mouth!" And he walked away as if I was nothing.

"I'll never let no father marry me away to any old yok," I threw after him. And he made believe that he didn't hear me.

It was the same night that I found Fania's love letters from Morris Lipkin.

Father had gone to his lodge meetings as usual. I went to bed, but I tossed about in anger over Father. Then I thought that I couldn't sleep because the mattress was so lumpy. So I got up, lifted the mattress to turn it over. And there, spread out on the spring, were bunches of papers. They were covered with fine handwriting. I picked up one after another and began to read. . . . "Love of my heart.". . . Then I read one after another. "Dearest, loveliest! I feel you in my arms. I kiss you and press you close to my heart!" "Adorable precious one, you are the very breath of me. This day is blank with emptiness because I cannot see you. I can only soothe my aching heart reading poems of love. Here are words that might have rushed to you, loved one, out of my own heart:

> "Come to me in my dreams, and then by day
> I shall be well again,
> For then the night will more than pay
> The hopeless, hopeless longing of the day,
> The hopeless, hopeless longing of the day."

On and on, I read. I forgot everything until I heard the stamp of Father's footsteps. And I quickly hid the letters and jumped into bed.

All night long I dreamed of Morris Lipkin. It wasn't any more the Morris Lipkin whose hair was always crying for the barber. It was a new and wonderful Morris Lipkin. His eyes looked into my eyes. All those beautiful letters of love that he had written to Fania, I felt he had written to me. In

I forgot everything...

the morning, when I woke up, I found, crumpled in my hand, tight to my breast, the letter that said, "I love you. I love you. I love you!"

That morning, to work, Morris Lipkin was everywhere I looked. When I got to the shop, the clattering noise of the machines was the music of his words of love to me.

For days and weeks, I lived only in Morris Lipkin and in his letters. Noontime, when I was eating my lunch, I read them over and over again till I knew them by heart.

One evening, I couldn't help it anymore, I had to go to the library where Fania used to meet him. My heart stopped. There he was! What a pale face! What sad eyes! *Ach!* I knew what it was to be in love.

I took a book from the shelf and sat down near him. He was so beautiful. God, how I shivered. When he walked out, I followed him. I walked so near him!

"Fool! What are you so scared of—what are you so scared of!" I was pinching myself to speak to him. And there I let him cross the street to go into his house.

The next night, I fixed my hair just the way Mashah did and ran to the library. And all evening again I sat there like a *yok* with my heart in my mouth staring at him.

The library was already closing, and he was the last one out. He was still dreaming, his head in the air. He walked past me without even seeing me.

"Hello! Morris Lipkin!" I grabbed him by the

sleeve. And then I couldn't say another word more. We walked half the block and yet I couldn't speak.

"What do you want?" he asked.

Before I knew what I was doing, I was running away from him like a crazy.

"What a fool he'll think me!" I sobbed into my pillow half the night. As I quieted down with my crying, it became so clear in my head what I should have said to him: "I love you. I ask nothing. I want nothing. Only let me love you. I'll leave my father and mother and follow you to the end of the earth."

All by myself I poured out my love to him in the most wonderful words.

Then one day, going to work, as I turned the block, there! I ran right into him. All my thoughts and dreams from days and weeks stumbled out of me. "I—oh, Morris—I—I——"

He stared. "What's the matter with you?"

"Oh—Morris—I got to tell you—I love you."

"You silly little kid." He burst out laughing.

Something beautiful that had built itself up in my heart all these days and nights, weeks and months, had fallen on top of me and crushed me.

For a long, long time after, I could feel nothing but the hurt of his laugh. Then one night when the whole house was thick with sleep I jumped out of bed and tore up into nothing every one of those love letters, and as I stamped the pieces under my feet, I felt I stamped for ever love and everything beautiful out of my heart.

Chapter VI

THE BURDEN BEARER
CHANGES HER BURDEN

I worked in a paper-box factory, and I was the quickest "hand" on the floor.

"Give only a look on that little nothing!" the boss would whisper to those around. "Only skin and bones—but such quick hands! It burns in her an engine!"

I was the thinnest, smallest girl in our shop, and I earned by piecework bigger wages than the big women. And yet, when I'd bring home the wages to Father, he'd never let me have the money to buy myself something I needed.

A tenth of the children's wages Father always used to give to charity. And then he belonged to so many societies and lodges that even without our ever getting anything we wanted for ourselves, the money didn't stretch enough to pay for all the charities Father had to have.

"Gazlin!" cried Mother. "It's freezing cold and Sara got to get a warm coat for the winter. She's already a young lady. She can't wear a shawl any more. Suppose you stop for a while to do charity with the tenth of her wages and let her have her own money for the clothes she needs to go to work."

"Woman! Stop my charities! It's like stopping the breath of God in me. It says in the Holy Torah, 'No man is too poor to help those that are poorer than himself.' Can I shut my heart to the cry of those starving Russians when they send me those begging letters for help?"

"So with the blood money of your children's wages, you got to feed the starving Russians, thousands of miles away."

"Woman! I ask you by your conscience, who shall help the poor if not the poor?"

"*Nu,* if you got to feed the starving Russians, then stop at least to give away so much money on so many societies and lodges."

"Those societies I belong to are more to me than my life. I'm not living for myself. I have to go among people. Would you want me to stop my dues to the Convalescent Home that takes care of the poor sick from hospitals? Or the Old People's Home that is sheltering the poor homeless ones in their old age? Should I take my little mite away from the Free Day Nursery that is taking care of the little helpless babies whose mothers must go to work? Or could I stop my dues to the Free Hebrew School, the one place in America that keeps alive the flame of the Holy Torah?"

It was no use talking. Father was like stone in his high purpose of living for God and working for the good of the world.

And now in addition to holding up the flame of

the Holy Torah before America, Father got himself in the matchmaking business. People would pay him sometimes for matching them together. But before he got the money in his hand he already knew of some poor widow, or a helpless orphan, miles away, who needed it more than his own wife and children who were right under his nose, so close that he couldn't see them.

From the time he married his two daughters off in one day, all the people of the block looked up to Father as the smartest matchmaker of America.

Widows and widowers, young men who were looking for girls, and girls who were looking for men, fathers and mothers who had sons and daughters to get rid of, used to come to Father for advice.

Once Father wrote out his own "ad" in the *Ghetto News*, something like this:

> Reb Smolinsky, the old, reliable matchmaker. Girls and widows, with five hundred to five thousand dollars dowry. All kinds of men, doctors, lawyers, wealthy widowers. Put your future in my hands and I'll settle you with good luck for life.

When the wife of Zalmon the fish-peddler died and left him six children, he came to Father and said, "In another week, the thirty days after my wife's death will be up. So I could marry myself again. Have you got something good for me on your list?"

Father gave him a quick look over. His black, greasy beard was spotted with scales from the fish. He had a big wart on his nose and his thick red lip was cracked open in the middle. It smelled from him yards away, the fish he was selling. And he breathed quickly from stuffing himself with too much eating.

"Your wife ain't yet cold in the grave," said Father. "Why are you in such a hurry to tie yourself with another woman on your hands? Can't you have a little rest?"

"Well, I can't stand it any more from the children. They're always fighting and running wild in the streets. There wasn't a cooked meal in the house since my wife died. The dirt grows like yeast. The children eat only what you buy from cans. I eat in the restaurant. But I can't take the children with me. It would cost too much. I like it better to have my meals cooked for me, in my own house. So I got to have a wife."

"How much are you worth?" Father asked.

Zalmon the fish-peddler stuck up his chest. "I'm a rich man now. I got a thousand dollars from two lodges for my wife's death and I found $90 more tied up in her stocking. And my fish business is growing bigger every day. I no more sell from the pushcart. I got a basement store now. And a man to help me."

Father turned to the paper on the wall where he had written out the list of men and women that wanted to marry themselves.

"The horse-radish woman also got lodge money for her husband's death," Father said. "That's a fitting match for you. Horse radishes and fish would go well together."

"That old *yentch* for me? No—I want no old ones again. I had enough of it with the last one. May she rest in peace."

"How old are you yourself?"

"I'm fifty-six. But if I married the right woman for me, I'd throw off twenty years from my age. Maybe you could find me a girl."

Zalmon took out from his pocket a greasy roll of bills and gave one to Father. "Here's a little advance commission for you, so you should try your best for me. I'm not a stingy. I'll pay you well if you could find me a girl."

"With enough money, you could get even the President's daughter, in America."

"But she must be good-looking," said Zalmon. "And she mustn't be lazy and she mustn't curse. I had enough cursing with the last one. May she rest in peace.... The right woman would have a grand home by me. My wife used to get up four o'clock in the morning to help me with the pushcart. But now I got a man to help me and my new wife I could make for a lady with nothing to do but stay home and cook for me and clean the house and look after the children."

Zalmon snuffed tobacco in his nose and then handed some to Father. "My new wife could eat from the best—carp, flounders, pike—anything she could only wish herself to have she'd have by me.

I'd buy new furniture for the house and she'll have my wife's Sabbath fur coat and her gold watch and chain. You ought to see the heavy thickness of that chain." Zalmon took out from his pocket a pink satin box and, opening it, he lifted out a long, thick, shiny chain, on which hung a gold watch.

Father ran his fingers over the glittering gold; then he grabbed Zalmon with both hands by the front of his coat.

"Depend yourself on me, my good friend," he said. "I'll find the right woman for you quicker than any matchmaker in America. Give me only a few days and I'll settle you for life with good luck."

That very evening Father said to Mother: "Zalmon the fish-peddler is looking to marry himself to a young girl. With lodge money for his wife's death he's become a rich man now, and maybe this would be a good chance for us to get rid of our old maid."

Mother dropped the dishes she was washing back into the sink and turned upon Father. "On all my enemies your matchmaking! Didn't you show enough smartness picking out a crook for Mashah and a gambler for Fania? And now for Bessie you want an old fish-peddler with a houseful of children and a wife not yet cold in the grave."

"*Shah! Shah!* Woman! Zalmon is no crook. Zalmon is no gambler. I didn't know the other men from before. I depended myself on Zaretzky to give me a guaranty for their characters, when

Zaretzky himself is the biggest liar in America. But Zalmon we know, in and out, for years already. We know he's honest. He's religious. He's charitable. Everybody knows how he gives away all the leftover fish, on Friday, to the Orphan's Home."

"But he's an old man. And Bessie would have six children to cook and wash for."

"Wouldn't she have it better by Zalmon than working in the shop? She'd have a home, a husband. People would respect her and not point their fingers on her for a cursed old maid that no man wants. Besides, she'd be a mother to six orphans."

"These orphans are the worst gangsters of the block. They'll torture the life out of her."

"So you want the old maid to remain in my house and torture my life with her crankiness? She's not any more what she used to be. Before, she used to hand me her wages with the highest respect. But now, the devil got into her and she's jumping out of her skin finding fault with me. I'm not a good father to her. No wonder it says in the Torah, 'Woe to a man who has females for his offspring'!"

"And woe to us women who got to live in a Torah-made world that's only for men." Mother's eyes twinkled with fun even in anger. But Father never saw the joke on him, so full was he with man's troubles from women that the prophets foretold.

"Women were always the curse of men," he went on, "but when they get older they're devils and witches. That's why it says in the Torah that a man has a right to hate an old maid for no other reason but because no man had her, so no man wants her."

"Berel Bernstein wanted her," Mother flung at him.

"But that stingy only wanted a free hand for his shop. Now is her chance to get a real home, all waiting for her. Zalmon would give her everything a woman could only wish herself, a fur coat, new furniture for the house, and six children already there."

Mother gave Father a long, hopeless look. Then she pushed up her shoulders and, shaking her head, went back to the stove.

When Zalmon the fish-peddler came back in a few days, Father said, "I got a luck match for you, if you only want to pay the price. A girl—young, innocent, a picture for the eyes. She'd cook for you, and wash for you, and carry the whole burden of your house for you. Your children will have a mother and you will have a wife like in the good old days and not one of those new smart women that boss their husbands. She's quiet as a dove and she'll look up to a man with proper respect."

"Tell me only quick—when can I see her? Who is she?"

For a whole minute Father stared into Zalmon's excited eyes. He opened his lips to speak, but stopped silent for another minute, to dig into Zalmon the importance of his words.

"It's my—own—daughter—Bessie." Father stopped

between each two words, like an actor on the stage.

Zalmon's eyes jumped with gladness and he listened to Father like a thirsty man sipping wine.

"A golden child with a diamond heart," Father went on, "from the time she was no higher than this table she worked for me. To this day she hands me all her wages. A good daughter makes a good wife."

"Good luck on us all!" With great joy Zalmon shook Father's hand. "It's an honour for me to be your son-in-law. Your daughter made a name for herself how she worked the nails off her fingers for your family."

Father beamed with the bigness of charity on Zalmon. "See what I'm giving up for you! And all I ask from you is a little money to start myself a business, so as to let go her wages."

"Sure. If it's only a matter of a few hundred dollars, I'll do the right thing by you."

They shook hands again and wished themselves again good luck for settling the match so quickly. "It's a great honour for me to be your son-in-law," Zalmon said, over and over again.

"You hear it, woman?" Father called to Mother. "You hear only what Zalmon says? My own wife and children don't appreciate me. It's only strangers that know themselves on my good heart."

Bessie had no sooner come home from work than Father said to her, "Zalmon the fish-peddler wants to marry himself to you. You'd have a good home and you wouldn't have to work any more in a shop. His wife's gold watch and chain and her Sabbath fur coat will be yours, and——"

"Don't," cried Bessie, shuddering. "I hate Zalmon. I hate the smell of fish. If he were the last man on earth I wouldn't marry him."

'So this is the thanks for all I've done for you? This is how you thank me for getting you a man when you're such a dried-up old maid that no one wants to give a look on you. But this much I'll warn you! If you don't grab this chance quick, you're lost for ever. Now you're so old and cranky, even from the shop they'll throw you out."

Bessie got into a nervous fit, crying and tearing her hair and cursing the day she was born. But the next evening, when she came home, there was laid out on the bed a new velvet dress, richer than anything she had ever seen. It looked like a fifty-dollar dress from Fifth Avenue. Father had spent all afternoon, bargaining for the $20 Zalmon had given him, the finest dress in the Grand Street show window.

Bessie's eyes lighted like a young girl's at first sight of the new dress. But her face got old again when she realized that it was only to show herself off to Zalmon.

"Dress myself up for him—no!" said Bessie. "Only once I dressed myself up for a man. But then I loved him."

While she was yet talking, the door opened and a smell of perfume filled our kitchen. A man entered. He held in his hand a big box tied with red ribbon. He wore a new black suit and looked just like those wax figures in the show windows where they have clothes to hire for weddings. Above the white starched collar was a young, clean-shaved face. Only by the thickness of his bushy eyebrows, and the wart on his nose, did we begin to recognize that this new-shaved man was Zalmon, the old fish-peddler, without his beard.

For a minute, Father and Mother stared in silent wonder at him. He put down his box, puffed out his starched shirt front, smiling, much pleased with himself, into Father's and Mother's bewildered eyes.

"Is this you, your own self?" Father rushed forward and kissed Zalmon's clean, new-shaved face on both cheeks. "You look more'n twenty years younger already. I'd never recognize you for the same man."

Mother wrung her hands in make-believe worry. "Woe is me! A millionaire is in our house, and no carpet on the floor, no wine on the table!"

She pushed forward Father's chair with a back and a cushion to sit on, and began dusting it with her new blue-checked apron. "Here's our best chair! My Rockefeller prince! Do us the honour to sit yourself down on it."

Father and Mother kept touching Zalmon's new clothes with the tips of their fingers, and staring at him as though to make sure he was real. With his beard off, his new-bought bridegroom clothes, and his hair barbered short and pasted down with vaseline, and soaked in perfume in place of the old fish smell, Zalmon really shined like a rich Grand Street millionaire. No one could believe how this old fish-peddler could make himself such a dressed-up American man. But Bessie would not even look at him. She stood with her back turned and gazed down the open airshaft, an expression on her face of a person ready to jump out of the window and make an end of life.

"Here, Bessie my child! Why so bashful?" Father jerked her arm and gave her a pull forward. "Company came for you."

Bessie stood like wood as Zalmon put his box on the table, and with both hands on his heart he bowed before her, as if she were a queen. No sooner had Zalmon seated himself than Father walked over to the door and, with a wink to Mother, he said, "I suppose the young people would like to talk themselves out alone," and he went out with Mother and closed the door.

"I brought you here my wife's fur coat," said Zalmon, pushing the box to Bessie across the table. "My daughter Yenteh has eyes on it, so I quickly brought it here for you. I would rather see the coat on you. It costs me enough money."

Bessie did not even look up, but kept braiding and unbraiding the fringes of the tablecloth.

"My wife, may she rest in peace, didn't wear it more'n a few times for the Sabbath only. But you, you could wear it for every day."

"I don't like fur coats. You better give it to your daughter Yenteh." Bessie slapped the words at him, but he licked them up like honey.

"You good heart! I know how you always like to give away everything. But you shall have not only the coat. But I even brought you my wife's gold watch and chain." And he spread his present on the table before her.

Bessie drew back as though there was a catching sickness in the touch of the dead wife's things.

"I don't care for jewellery." The words dropped from her throat like chunks of ice, but Zalmon melted her frozen words in his craziness to get himself married again.

"Ach! You golden goodess!" Zalmon reached out to grab Bessie's hand, but she quickly hid her hands under the tablecloth. "My old wife, may she rest in peace, was only happy when she could shine up the street like a walking jewellery store. Only to spend and to spend, lay in her head. But you are only to save and to save, just like a savings bank . . . .

"I will give you a grand life by me. I'm a good man. I got a soft heart. A young wife could do anything she wants with me. If I give her money to buy anything, she don't have to tell me how much change she got left. I will hold you like a crown on my head. Anything you only wish yourself you'd have."

Still Bessie sat cold as stone. And I was wondering, how could a grown-up man, like Zalmon, who had sense enough to sell fish—how could he be so foolish about a woman. How could a man smart enough to tell a carp from a flounder go on showering love bargains on a woman without seeing that his grand words are like galling poison to her bitter heart. But the poor innocent Zalmon went blindly on, talking his head off until Father and Mother came back to see how things were going on.

One look at Bessie, and Father saw how all the chickens he had been counting from the money that Zalmon was to give him were not yet hatching in the icy air of Bessie's coldness.

"Daughter mine!" cried Father, giving her a pinch in the arm. "Why don't you serve some tea and jelly for the company?"

Glad for the chance to turn her back on Zalmon, Bessie rushed to the stove and began to prepare tea.

"*Nu,* Zalmon," said Father, in a loud whisper. "Isn't she a light for the eyes! And quiet as a dove. And looking up to a man with that highest respect as only women in the good old days used to have."

"Her cooking! You ought to taste her *gefülte* fish! Her *tzimes!* It melts in the mouth with a thousand tastes of Heaven. Her fried potato *lotkes*—in the dearest restaurant you can't buy anything so grand!" Mother piled up Father's praises till the tea was brought.

Father and Mother kept laughing and talking and singing Bessie's praises as they drank the tea. Only Bessie couldn't speak. Only she kept silent and miserable with the tortured frightened eyes of a person torn on a rack by the hair and by the feet.

Father patted Zalmon by the shoulder and beamed on Bessie as though she were the apple of his eye.

"My dear daughter worked so hard till the last minute, she didn't have a chance to put on her new dress. . . . Go, put on your new dress," urged Father, stroking Bessie's head, as if his old maid was his one and only young child.

Bessie kept mechanically stirring the tea that she could not drink.

"Come, daughter mine," Father went on, spreading his sweet salesman's talk so thick that I was afraid that even Zalmon would see through it. "Let our guest see that he's not the only one with new clothes in this house. Show him how you can shine in something new."

"Oh, I can't! I can't!" came from Bessie's tight throat.

"Sure you can," Mother insisted. "Zalmon dressed himself up all in your honour, and you got to do him the honour back."

To escape again from Zalmon's eyes, Bessie went

into the bedroom and put on her new dress with unwilling, dead hands. She dropped down wearily on the bed, unable to drag herself back to the kitchen where they were waiting for her.

"*Nu*, little heart, why does it take you so long to dress?" Father called.

With biting, angry lips Bessie arose and returned to her seat at the table.

But Father insisted that she stand up in front of them and turn herself around like a dancer, so that Zalmon could see all the fancy stitches and every bit of the gold braid that trimmed the dress.

"You see how she could shine and make herself for a fine lady if she would only not be so bashful." Father laughed into Zalmon's admiring eyes.

"And she sewed it up all herself, every stitch of it," lied Mother. "Such golden hands is like money in the bank. Think only how much money you can save if your wife can do her own sewing."

Bessie's face grew red with shame at the fake talk they were making to sell her over to Zalmon. But at last there came an end to the lies that Father and Mother could think of. And Zalmon had already said out all the love-bargaining speeches to Bessie. He couldn't think of anything more to say. His eyes began to grow red and heavy with drowsiness and he jerked himself up from a sleepy nod and rose to go.

"From now on, you must make yourself at home by us," said Mother.

"Don't keep yourself for a guest." Father shook

Zalmon's hand warmly. "I already feel you're one of our own."

No sooner had the door closed after Zalmon than Father turned on Bessie hot with anger.

"Old maid!" he cried. "Why did you sit there like a lump of ice? If not for me and your mother coming in on time, the whole play would have gone to the devil. Why are you holding yourself up with pride, that your hair is turning gray, that your face is growing black and yellow with age? It's only because Zalmon is such an innocent, good heart that he takes my word for the lies of praise I tell about you. . . . "

"Give only a look on this!" Mother picked up the gold watch and chain with one hand and with the other she reached for the coat. "Red-silk lining and sealskin fur. What more do you want from a man?"

"Fish—fish—three times a day, carp, flounder, pike." Bitterly Zalmon's promised bill of fare dropped from Bessie's tight lips. Then she ran into the bedroom and slammed the door behind her.

And all that night, long after Father and Mother were asleep, Bessie sobbed into my arms. "I can't stand it any more at home, and I can't stand Zalmon the fish-peddler."

A few nights after, Zalmon came again. He wore the same hired bridegroom's suit. But this time, clinging to his long coat-tails, was little five-year-old Benny, his youngest child.

"He ran after me so wild that he fell and hurt himself." Zalmon pointed to the scratch and smear of blood on the boy's knee. "So, I had to bring him to you. Maybe you would tie up his hurt."

Benny looked up with wide, innocent eyes at Bessie.

"I lost my garter by the bed and I can't find it," he said, pulling at his loose stocking.

Only the front of his face was washed. The neck and the ears streaked with dirt. But there was something so fresh, so beautiful inside him that it shone out of his eyes. You could not help loving him. Bessie sat little Benny on the table and washed off the scratch on his knee and then looked about in the scrap bag for a piece of elastic for a garter. As soon as she fixed his stocking in its place she found a rip in the child's sleeve that was tied up with safety pins and she took off his little jacket to mend it.

"Who'd believe that this suit was once new," said Zalmon, watching Bessie sew. "He used to wear it only for the Sabbath, and last week I let him wear it once, and all the dirt off the gutters is on it now, because he's always running wild in the streets."

"I'm always waiting in the street for my mamma to come home," said Benny, "but she don't come back. They put her in a box and she can't come out."

With a sob in her throat, Bessie's arm went out to the child and she drew him up to her lap and held him tightly against her heart. Little Benny began to prattle about his childish joys and woes. He showed her the gold ring on his dirty little finger which he had found that day in a penny bag of candy, and the blue mark on his arm where Yenteh, his big sister, had pinched him. And then, as his voice trailed off in drowsiness, Bessie began humming and rocking him to sleep.

The child seemed to put new life into her. A young, rosy look came into her gray face, as though all the frozen ice in her heart melted in the sunshine of a new spring.

Zalmon watched, silently, Bessie with the sleeping child in her arms. He forgot the stupid love-bargaining of the first night, he forgot to complain of the selfishness of his old wife, and the woes of his motherless house. Into his ox-like eyes came a new light of human understanding.

When little Benny had run after him that evening, he tried to push him back, afraid the child would be in the way of his courting. And here, before his eyes, he saw the child unlock the love that his fur coat and the gold watch and chain and all his thought-out love-bargaining speeches had failed to do.

But after that night, Zalmon didn't bring Benny, and the hardness came back into Bessie's eyes. She went about, white-faced and scared, as if she had been caught in a trap and couldn't get out. At night she twisted about on the mattress, unable to let go of her pain. Even in her sleep, she moaned like an animal hurt to death.

The while Father went around boasting to the neighbours that he was going to marry away his oldest daughter to Zalmon, who had already a bank book with thousands to his name. There was much coming and going in our house. One after another came to wish Bessie good luck. No one seemed to notice her white face but me.

The wedding day was coming on, nearer and nearer. It was after supper. Father had gone to the lodge and Mother to the market. Bessie looked at me for some minutes with her stone face that hurt worse than pain.

"Come walking with me," she said. "I can't stand it in this house. Soon the neighbours will be coming to wish me more joy and good luck. . . . Oh, God!" She covered her face with her hands. But she could not cry. She only shuddered in horror of her black wedding day.

In the street she began to talk. Her words clicked hard and cold and sure. "I'll not marry him. Never! I wanted to throw myself from the roof, or dash myself under a car. But I haven't it in me to kill myself. I'm going to run away to another city."

We hurried on, not seeing, not hearing anything around us. All at once Bessie jerked my hand. "See!" she said. "That's what I'm running from." And she pointed to the fish-peddler's house on the opposite side. Then she fled from the place as if it was a ghost.

"Hello!" Zalmon's boy, Dave, nudged my arm. "Where are you rushing so fast?"

"How's everybody?" I answered.

Bessie pulled me to come faster, but we heard Dave call out, "Benny is awful sick."

My sister stopped, turned around and looked at Dave. Then she walked right back to him. "What's the matter with Benny?" she asked, in a low voice.

"He's awful sick here." Dave put both his hands on his stomach. "Before, he yelled so, but now he's so white and still."

Bessie stood very still, staring at Dave. "Who's taking care of the child?" she asked.

"Yenteh. But she got so scared maybe the kid was dying, she ran out looking for Father. And I ran out to see what's keeping her so long."

"Come," was all that Bessie said. Right back to Zalmon's home she went. Without knocking, she opened the door and walked in.

The child was alone in the room, lying on a tumbled bed of rags.

"Poor little heart! Motherless lamb!" Bessie sobbed, rushing over to him. He lay back so weak, his big, old eyes staring at the ceiling. Suddenly, he screamed, clenched his little hands, and drew up his knees in pain. Then he straightened and lay stiff and still, like one dead.

Bessie put her hand on his face. "He's burning with fever. Quick, run for the doctor," she cried.

When I got back with the doctor, Bessie had

straightened the bed and was bathing Benny's head with her handkerchief. She had taken off his dirty little things and covered him over with her own petticoat, with the crochet trimming.

Bessie and the doctor were still working over the child when Zalmon came in. At sight of her in his house, he jumped with gladness. "You golden heart! You're sent from Heaven to my sick child," he cried, grabbing her arm.

Bessie shuddered from his touch as if a snake had bitten her. But when she bent over Benny, to make him take the medicine, she was all tenderness again.

"Mother—are you my mother?" whispered Benny, putting his arms around her, and in his weakness trying to hug her.

"Your child has been eating food that poisoned him." And the doctor pointed to an opened can of beans on the table.

"They won't have to live on canned eating any more," said Zalmon, winking at the doctor and snuffing tobacco up his nose. "She's coming to cook for me and take care of my house."

The doctor didn't speak. He only looked at Bessie, and there was understanding on his quiet face. . . .

From that evening on, a change came over Bessie. She never could warm up to the fish-peddler. But she stopped fighting Father in his plans for the marriage. When the wedding day came, she went quietly from our house to Zalmon's—the burden bearer had changed her burden.

Chapter VII

FATHER BECOMES A BUSINESS MAN IN AMERICA

"In America, a man can get rich quick if he only has a head for business," said Father, as he counted out the five hundred dollars that Zalmon the fish-peddler had given him.

"A head for business in America," Mother laughed into Father's face, "is the same head you got to have for business in Russia. You showed me enough already how smart you are. Why not better earn a living by what you know, get a job as a Rabbi in a synagogue? Religion is your business."

"What! Sell my religion for money? Become a false prophet to the Americanized Jews! No. My religion is not for sale. I only want to go into business so as to keep sacred my religion. I want to get into some quick money-making thing that will not take up too many hours a day, so I could get most of my time for learning." And rolling up the bills, he pushed them into his pocket.

"The while put the money in the bank," Mother begged.

"I got to have the cash ready in case I see some good bargain to buy quick." And out he went.

An hour later, Father came back, waving a fresh printed copy of the *Ghetto News*.

"Here's the bargain I've been looking for." And he read:

> "A BARGAIN FOR CASH. Leaving for Europe to-morrow, must have cash to-day. Will sell my long established grocery, in Elizabeth, New Jersey, worth four thousand, for four hundred dollars. Only the man with ready cash need come."

Father squared his shoulders and grew tall with joy. "I'm off to seize my luck by the horns."

He slapped the bulging roll of bills and laughed to himself, his chin in the air. "In America, there is no need to be poor, if you only got brains and money to begin something."

He held up the sheet to see again the address. "In America the bargains are so thick the newspapers are all full of them. Other people have made fortunes in America. Why shouldn't I? It's only fools who remain poor. I'll go at once and see the place."

But Mother dragged him back. "Let me only go along. Two heads are better than one."

"But, woman, I must first find out what there is to buy."

Mother clutched at both his hands. "In God's name, let me only hold the money. In my stocking it is safer than in your pocket."

He pushed her back and started for the door. "*Yideneh!* Does a man of brains need a woman's stocking to hold his money for him?"

"Promise me only," wailed Mother, running after him, down the stairs. "Promise me that you won't pay out the money till I come to see what you buy."

"Sure," he called back, over the banisters, "if it's only the bargain it says, I'll send quick for you," and hurried on, his face shining, his head in the air, as though Rockefeller's millions were already burning in his pockets.

We just sat down to eat our supper when the boy from the drugstore came.

"Mrs. Smolinsky," he said, "your husband 'phoned you should come to this address." And he handed us a paper containing the street number and how to get there.

We were too excited to eat another bite. We left the food standing on the table, hurriedly dressed our-selves, and went to Elizabeth.

It was eight o'clock when we got there. The store was lighted in great style. The outside of the windows were full of sales signs and the place hummed with business. Customers were going in and customers were going out, loaded with groceries. Father stood near the cash box, rubbing his hands with joy, as the owner took in the money for the sales.

After a while, Father introduced us to the owner of the store. The man bowed quickly and went on waiting on customers.

"Two hands are not enough," he said. "I could use two more clerks."

"Well, I'll have my wife and girl to help me," answered Father.

Mother kept gazing around the store, drinking in the full-packed shelves of cereals, canned goods, soap, and washing powder. The place seemed over-flowing with goods.

"Does he really ask only four hundred dollars for all this?" Mother whispered to Father. "Ask him to give you a pencil and paper so I can begin to count up all the goods there is in stock."

"Can't you see he's too busy with the customers to stop for such things now? Wait till after closing time."

"Such a smart business man he looks," Mother went on. "And the store hums with trade. Why does he let go such a good thing?"

"He wants to go back to the old country, to see his relations and show off to the neighbours how much money he made in America," answered Father.

The customers kept coming and coming, pushing and elbowing each other to be waited upon first. But at nine o'clock by the watch, the man refused to sell any more.

"Come again to-morrow," he told them, as he pushed them out and locked the door. Then he went back to the cash box to count the money.

"Seventy-eight dollars and eighty-nine cents." The man smilingly put the money in his pocket. "Not so bad for a plain Monday, eh?"

"Do you still take in more on other days?" began

Father. But Mother jerked him by the sleeve, not to talk how good the bargain was, for fear we should lose it.

"My man tells me you are giving up the business to go to Russia."

"That's it," the man nodded.

"Four hundred dollars you want for the store?" questioned Mother. *"Nu,* let us first count up the stock and see what you offer to sell."

The man opened his eyes on Mother. "Sell! offer! I've got nothing to offer. I sold this store to your husband, at five o'clock, with the agreement that he was to take possession of it at nine."

"So," breathed Mother in astonishment. "The store is ours already!"

"It sure is," answered the man, as he quickly unlocked the door, threw the key to Father, and walked out.

"So you bought the store already without asking me," cried Mother, hitting Father on the head playfully. "For once in your life you had more luck than brains."

"What a wife! Even when I show her I got brains she is so jealous she calls it only luck."

"Nu, my smart man, call it brains. But why didn't you let you own wife have the pleasure of buying together our new business? You could have waited till I came."

"Wait! I wanted to wait, my woman who bosses me! I wanted you to see for yourself with what a quick head I can make a big business deal. But if I would have waited, the bargain would have been snatched out of my hands. For when I came here, there was another man to buy the store. He was here before me and also with cash in his hand."

"Then how did you get ahead of him?"

"Because the other man was an Italian, and the owner sold me the bargain only because I was a Jew...."

Father began dancing around the store crazy with joy. "And such a bargain! Look only around this full-packed store! Who would not grab such a chance, quick? Think only! Seventy-eight dollars and eighty-nine cents in one day! In one week, seven times seventy-eight dollars and eighty-nine cents. *Shah!* We will have to hire a bookkeeper to count up for us all our profits a year."

"*Gott sei dank!* Tears of thankfulness blurred Mother's eyes. "The sun is beginning to shine for us. After all our black years, we lived to see our own bought store in America!" And in her excitement, she threw her arms around Father's neck and kissed him on both cheeks.

"*Ach!* We'll yet be people in this new world!" Gladness flowed from Mother to Father like a living sun. "We're going to save a penny to a penny and a dollar to a dollar, so that, a year from now, we'll have the money for our own bought house, with steam heat and hot running water and a white marble sink."

Higher and higher flew her happiness. "And I'm going to show you how well I know what beautiful is. I'll fix up the parlour with carpet on the floor, and a red-velvet set, and lace curtains, tied on the side with red-satin ribbon."

"But first we must buy a golden wineglass with silver candlesticks for the Sabbath." Father stroked Mother's hair with new tenderness. "Woman who bosses me! Don't you think the first hundred dollars we ought to take to give away to charity, so as to thank God for our luck?"

Mother pushed back Father's hand in playful affection.

"*Meshugener Yid!* You with your charities! Why can't you let the money warm itself by us a little? How can you every become a business man, in America, if the minute you get a few dollars in one hand, you want to give it away with the other to charity?"

As I looked at Father and Mother playing with the joy of a business of their own, I thought to myself, "If only there was plenty of money between them, how happy they would be together, fighting in fun, instead of nagging and galling each other fighting over pennies."

And I thought to myself, "Now all the food we'll need will be right with us in the store and Mother wouldn't have to eat out her heart bargaining at the pushcarts and spend hours in the market to save a few cents. And she'll stop her worries, stop her cursing and hollering, and be a mother like other mothers."

I looked about me. *Ach!* What plenty to eat! My mouth began to water at sight of a whole tubful of butter, all our own. Butter for bread day and night, and the best of eggs from now on.

"And with seventy-eight dollars and eighty-nine cents coming in every day, we'll soon be able to buy a piano and I'll begin to take piano lessons. And if I were a piano-player instead of a shop hand, I wouldn't have to marry myself to a common man like my sisters. I'll try to catch on to a doctor, or a lawyer, or maybe an actor on the stage. And if my husband were an actor, then I could go to the theatre free every night."

Full of my dreams I stepped over to the window. There was a great pile of oatmeal boxes that had been stacked up to make a fancy pyramid. But the man selling them off had broken into it and spoiled the even lines on both sides. So I started to fix it up again in proper shape. But reaching over, some way, I knocked the whole pile down and it tumbled to the floor and the boxes went rolling everywhere.

"Crazy, what have you done!" cried my mother, and both she and Father bent down to pick them up.

Mother and Father raised themselves up with boxes in each hand. On Mother's face came an expression as if she held something bewitched. Slowly she lifted the boxes up and down. Then she turned on Father.

"Business man, what are you holding in your hands?"

Father stared puzzled at the boxes, as if to read the label.

"It says it's oatmeal, but it must be marked wrong. Maybe it's that feathery puffed rice."

Mother shook her box close to her ear.

"Business man! What have you? You got air in your hand," and she tore open the box and held emptiness before Father's eyes.

"How could they be empty?" said he, puzzled. "Didn't I see him selling them?"

"Fool!" Mother turned upon him. "Couldn't he have had full ones on the top of the pile to sell from?" And she kicked the boxes on the floor till she found one with something in it. "See, here is one more he could have sold. One more has oatmeal in it."

Father began to try each empty box, in the hope of finding another one with something in it.

"Blind *yok!*" shrieked Mother. "Stop playing with air. Let's at least see what a great bargain you grabbed." And she and I began tearing around the store to examine the stock, while Father stared blankly at us.

The shelves had goods only in the front row. The whole space behind was empty. Mother stabbed a knife into the tub of butter and hit into hard wood beneath the thin spread which had been plastered against the fake wooden bottom.

I picked up the top layer of a newly opened case of eggs and found only empty paper fillers beneath.

Beside the almost empty barrel of sugar stood another sugar barrel, not yet opened.

"What's this?" asked Mother.

"It's sugar." Father came forward hopefully. "I pushed it myself to see it was full."

"Full of what?" Mother glared at him.

I knocked it open with a hatchet. A barrel full of sawdust stared up at us. I dug into the barrel and pulled out a brick.

Half the night we worked to see the extent of the great business deal that Father snatched with such mad haste. Not only were the shelves faked with emptiness, the windows full of dummies, but worse yet! We began to read the signs on the windows that shouted aloud bargains in the store, in red and black letters. But only now, we had sense enough to put two and two together, and saw that oatmeal was marked two boxes for fifteen cents when one alone cost ten cents. Ketchup, seven cents, when it should sell for fifteen cents. Eggs that even on the pushcart sold for thirty cents were, in that grand bargain window, marked a quarter.

"No wonder the customers pushed on each other rushing to buy in this store," Mother wailed. "What women would not kill each other crowding to a store where they could get ketchup for seven cents when it cost fifteen cents? The wonder by me is that my smart husband didn't give that swindler the chance to take in the cash for another day when he could have sold the empty boxes full of air for oatmeal, and the barrels full of sawdust for sugar."

"And such a born gentleman he looked! And so smart he talked!" Father stared with his innocent eyes into space.

"A gentleman!" shrieked Mother. "A crook, a thief, a rattlesnake! Why are we standing around here like fools? Aren't there policemen, judges, courts of justice in America? We'll arrest the robber. Where does he live? What's his name?

"Name? Live?" Father opened his innocent wide eyes like a child. "I paid him cash, because he said he had to go right away to Russia."

"Justice in America!" sighed Mother. "There is justice nowhere for a fool. A fool they whip even in the Holy Temple."

We did not go home, but slept that night in the room in back of the store. In the morning we took out the signs that were marked down below cost. Father stood himself at the empty cash box ready to ring up the cash and Mother and I stood ready to wait on customers. At last a customer came! A woman for a bag of salt! And then came a little girl for a box of crackers. But she didn't buy them, for her mother had given her only four cents, and we had marked the crackers back to five cents.

About nine o'clock, a young man walked in and looked about with a funny smile on his face.

"Good morning, mister! I'm glad you came,"

said Father, extending a friendly hand to the visitor. "I had news and maybe I'll have to go soon to my daughter in California."

"Well," replied the man, "there's not much to keep you here."

"Of course I could leave my wife and daughter in the store. But you know women have long hair and small brains. It needs a man's head to run a business. If I had a good customer, I think I'd rather sell my store. So if you're still looking to buy it——"

"Me?" The man pointed to himself. "Me buy this store? What kind of a sucker do you think I am?"

"But only yesterday you had the cash in your hand and you were so anxious to buy, only that man didn't want to sell to an Italian. I'm not so narrow-minded. I'll sell to any gentleman with cash."

"You won't sell it to me, Uncle Aby." The man laughed into Father's face. "The roll of one-dollar bills that I had yesterday with a fifty on the outside belonged to my late employer—the gentleman who sold you this store. I offered to buy it and displayed this roll six times yesterday, before you came. But you were the man we had been waiting for all day. I wouldn't be telling you all this, but the dirty skunk double-crossed me and beat it last night without giving me my share."

"*Oi weh!*" Mother dug her hands in her hair wildly. "We're robbed! Swindled! Our blood, our life, all our money gone!" And then at sight of the man puffing his cigarette so calmly, she rushed at him:

"Quick! Sara! Run for a policeman to arrest this crook."

I started for the door, but the young man pushed by me, bowing politely. "Don't bother, little girl. I wouldn't have come here if the cops could have anything on me. I was only a clerk and I had to do what the boss told me."

He tipped his hat and walked away like he owned the earth.

We stood staring after him, dumb with helplessness. With drawn face Mother turned back to the store where Father sat with his hands folded, a look of childlike bewilderment in his wide, innocent eyes.

"Woe is me! Bitter is me! We're ruined!" Mother shook her fist in Father's face. *"Gazlin!* That's what you get for not listening to me. If you had only let me go along as I begged myself by you, you would not be mooning now over a cash box as empty of cash as that sawdust barrel was empty of sugar."

"We live to learn," said Father, hopefully. "Next time I'll know better."

"But you never learn better. You only learn to be a worse fool."

"How could I dream that the man was such a crook? He made me feel such faith in him, I was ready to give him not only the $400, I would have given him $4,000 if only I had it. I would have given him my whole life.

"Why do you never trust you own wife? Why do you only trust strange people?"

"You think I'm like you, mistrusting everybody? I trust people. The whole world is built on trust. The bank, the mines, the Government could never exist unless people trusted each other."

"Oh-h-h-h! Of all the troubles on earth, is there anything so terrible as to have to live with a fool?"

For a moment Father dropped his head, almost touched by Mother's cries. Then he pushed up his shoulders and shook off his sadness.

"There's nothing so bad that maybe it couldn't yet be worse. Maybe instead of losing the money I could yet have broken my leg or got myself killed. Maybe God let me off with the mere loss of money to spare me a worse misfortune. . . . Woman! If only you had a little understanding of life, you would thank God for His mercy on us——"

"Listen to him only!" Mother's cries shook through the house. "All our money gone. Starvation stares us in the face. And yet he wants me to thank God for His mercy on us."

In her excited anger, she grabbed Father by the front of his coat, trying to shake him out of his calmness. "*Gazlin!* Now that the girls are married and no wages coming in, what shall we live on?"

But Father, calmer than ever, gently loosened

Mother's hands. "The God that feeds the worms under the stone, and the fishes in the sea, will He not feed us? Always you tried to frighten me with your hollering 'Wolf!' but the wolf never came. Sometimes we had a little less to eat, sometimes a little more. But we haven't starved yet. The wheel of life is always turning. What is down to-day will turn up to-morrow."

Mother rocked, her head in her hands. "How can the lost four hundred dollars ever turn up again? A fool throws a stone in the water and ten smart men can't fish it out. To whom will you now turn for help?"

Father's face became alive with light. He towered over Mother like an ancient prophet that had just stepped out of the Bible. "Have you forgotten the undying words of our race: 'The Lord is my shepherd, no want shall I know'? . . . When all other human help is gone, then God Himself steps out of His High Heaven, to help us. This man who robbed me only pushed me closer into the arms of God. Now I know that everything that happens to us is from God, for our good."

"And that is why I'm so deeply buried in the ground by you," wailed Mother, "because you turn all your worries on to God."

Mother began hitting her head against the wall and crying, "I can't stand it from him any more. I can't. I can't." And Father rushed over to her and tried to quiet her.

"Foolish *yideneh!* Why are you getting yourself so excited over nothing? What's loss of money anyway? You know the old saying, 'Money lost, nothing lost. Hope lost, all is lost.' The less money I have, the more I live on hope. And hope is the only reality here on earth. It's hope that makes people build cities and span bridges and send ships from one end of the earth to another. Even dying, man plants his hope on the next world."

"My gall is bursting! My flesh is falling from me in pieces, listening to him! A man lets himself be swindled of his last penny and he throws yet salt on his own wounds, talking on hope."

"Nag! *Noodnik!*" Father turned upon Mother. "Stop making me miserable. You were always looking for worries, so now you got something to worry about. God sends always to the spinner his flax, and to the drinker his wine, and to the woman who is looking for worries something to worry about."

"*Gevalt!* To whom can I go with my bitter heart? I'm living with a madman that ought to be tied up with ropes——"

"Stop your yelling!" commanded Father. "*Ishah Rah!* Worry yourself in your own head. Don't holler on me. I know the money is lost. Do I need yet a steam whistle to shout this to me? Suppose Rockefeller or Morgan would stop to worry every time they made a little mistake in business? Big men grow wise through their mistakes. It's only women who have nothing to think about who waste themselves tearing their hair over little losses that are past and done with. If you don't stop this nagging this very minute, I'll leave this house and never come back again."

"Go—go!" shrieked Mother. "Never come back to darken my days. At least a few years before my end I want to be free from you. If I were only a widow, people would pity themselves on me. But with you around, they think I got a bread giver when what I have is a stone giver. Go—go from me—blind lunatic—you haven't sense enough to tie a cat's tail."

But Father made no move to go. Instead, they went right on arguing and shouting at each other. And even long after Father was asleep, Mother kept on wringing her hands and going over and over our terrible loss.

Chapter VIII

THE HARD HEART

How could we help ourselves? All we had was sunk in this empty fake of a store. Still it was a place to start with something. And so we moved to a lonesome street, at the edge of a dead town, and lived out there, at the back of the store. Hoping with nothing to hope with, our fainting hearts still prayed for a miracle to save us.

While I was busy fixing the place, Mother was out bargaining with the wholesalers to trust her with enough goods to restock the store. Always she managed to push by the little people and get herself into the private office of the big man at the head of the business. Catching hold of the man's hands, in the fire of her great need, she clung to him till he heard out all her troubles of an empty store. And so she burned into a man's eyes her pleading to be trusted, that one after another gave her goods on time.

After a while, it seemed that Father and Mother could make a go of the store. But how could I stand the empty deadness of the place?

Ach! The loneliness of that little town! And the cold, stiff people there. It was like living among walking chunks of ice. The each-for-himself look froze me to the bone.

Hours passed before a customer would step in for a bar of soap or a loaf of bread. As I listened to the ticking of the clock, each minute of each hour seemed like the ashes of a thousand years slowly smothering me.

I wanted back the mornings going to work. And the evenings from work. The crowds sweeping you on, like waves of a beating sea. The shop. The roar of the rushing machines. the drive and the thrill of doing things faster and faster. The pay envelope. The joyous feel of money where every little penny was earned with your own hands.

What would become of me if I remained out here, day in and day out, without friends. My arms would wither at my sides. I'd forget how to shake hands. My tongue would grow dumb in my mouth. And all my longing for people would shrink in my frozen heart.

Mother had just come back from New York, loaded with packages. Till the goods would be sent, she had grabbed from the wholesalers a few samples of everything she could possibly carry. She tossed the things on the counter and dropped into a chair by the window. She lay back, closed her eyes, and a grateful, rested look came into her face. "God should only be merciful and help us work up the store," she gasped, mopping her face with a corner of her shawl. "After all, it's the first time since we came to America that we have a little light and air. When I look out of the window, it's not into a black airshaft. I see a tree, the sky, green grass."

"There's a lot of grass in the cemetery, too," I cried.

But Mother was so drunk with the green grass and the blue sky, she was deaf and blind to my bitterness.

"Once we only get the goods we need, people will come running to us, as to a bargain counter," she said, softly, as if she were floating on air.

"*Nu,* so Father will have more money to pay to his lodges and to send to the starving Russians, while we'll be slaving away for him."

"*Shah! Shah!*" Mother shook her head at me.

"How could you have married such a crazy lunatic as Father?" I burst out.

"A daughter to talk that way of her own father?" She stared in horror at me. "Even if he was a drunkard and a card-player, you owe him respect."

"I can't respect a man who lives on the blood of his wife and children. If you had any sense, you'd arrest him for not supporting you."

"Arrest a man who is the light of the world? A man innocent as a child and harmless as an angel?"

Our arguing was cut short, as a customer came in. He was a wooden-faced American farmer, with sunburn on his cheeks and neck, and the smell of the barn on him. We leaped forward in one breath and asked what he wanted.

"A pound of coffee," he ordered.

Then he asked for a loaf of bread. And we put it beside his coffee.

"A bag of sugar."

A worried fear came into Mother's face. "Oh, sugar?" she hesitated. "We're out of sugar just now. It hasn't been sent yet."

"All right," said the man, grouchily. "Give me a gallon of syrup."

How could we tell the man that we hadn't such things in stock? We stared at him like guilty criminals. At last I found my voice and said, fearfully, "We're out of syrup, too."

With a black frown, he pushed back the packages. "I have to get everything in one place," he growled.

All the air of hope went out of our hearts as the man turned and walked away. We just wilted into silence, unable to meet on another's eyes.

After a while, another man entered. Again hope rose in us. But he was only a passer-by who came for a match to light his pipe.

Mother busied herself dusting the poor little stock, set in front of the empty shelves, while I yawned and waited in maddening idleness. Then a little boy trailed in and asked for a penny lollipop.

"Mother will pay you after," he said, shoving the candy into his mouth. So dull with discouragement was I, that I even forgot to ask him who his mother was till he was out of the store. And when I ran after him, he pointed to a woman coming toward us with a basket.

I smiled my best welcome to the new customer. But she pushed by me stiffly and, with a scolding face, threw on the counter a package of oatmeal that was mouldy, and ketchup and canned milk that had gone bad.

"I got them at your cheating bargain sale," she cried. "Give me my money back or new goods."

The store had not been ours when she had bought her things. But we got so scared at the woman's railing, fearing she would drive away other customers, Mother gave her fresh goods.

It was lucky that the woman got out just before Father came in. Shining with godliness from his day of prayer, he went straight to the cash box to count out the money we had taken in. Carefully he folded every paper dollar and put it in his pocket, leaving only pennies and nickels for change.

I wondered had Mother seen, but she went on busily, filling small paper bags with salt. Turning to Father, she asked him to weigh them out.

As he lifted with his butter fingers the first bag, to put it on the scale, the paper burst and the salt spilled to the floor.

"*Ach!*" He kicked the salt with his foot. "The grocery business is only for thicknecks and truckdrivers. Such long hours of brainless drudgery is only for grubby grinds who have no high thoughts to think out."

He looked far out into space, and almost a sadness came into his eyes. "I'm sorry I didn't go into the banking business," he sighed. "A banker works only from ten to three. The rest of the time I'd have for thinking out the thoughts in my head."

"Lunatic!" shrieked Mother. "You, without a shekel to your name! Why do you only want to be a banker? Wouldn't it be better if you tried to make yourself for the President of America?"

"Woman! How do you suppose Rockefeller, or Morgan, or any of those millionaires made their start in America? They all began with empty hands. Their only capital was hope, courage to work out their ideas. I got a million burning ideas flying through my head. But I'm cursed with a wife who hangs like a stone on my neck—a nag, a *noodnik* that blots out my sunshine."

But Father's face brightened as a customer entered, a young, college-looking fellow. Father pushed Mother and me aside and came forward to the man. He liked to show us how to wait on customers.

"A box of bran, please," said the man.

"Bran? For what do you need such a thing?" asked Father, bossily.

"Breakfast-food bran," the man answered coldly.

"Bran for breakfast? Such things you only hear in this crazy America." Father began to preach his smartness into the man's neck. "By us home, in Shnipishock, they gave bran to horses and cattle. But Americans are such fools, they make eating out of it. This is a sensible store. We don't keep such nonsense."

Mother stood there, holding her breath, her eyes jumping out of her head toward Father. Then, turning quickly, she rushed forward with a package of bran. But the insulted man had already gone.

Mother shook the bran in Father's face. "Woe is me! My eyes dry out of my head till I see a customer come, and you drive them away like a madman."

"You want to teach me how to talk to people? Woman! Stay in your place. You're smart enough to bargain with the fish-peddler. But I'm the head of this business." With his big finger, he pointed to the kitchen. "Go back to your cook-stove. I'll run this store."

While Father was preaching Mother back into her place, a girl came in for a pound of rice. When she went to pay, she had only ten cents.

"The rice is twelve cents," I told her.

"Can I have it now? I just live next door and I'll bring back the two cents later."

I handed Father the ten cents, saying it was for a pound of rice.

"Crazy! Where was your head? Don't you know yet, rice is twelve cents?"

"I trusted her the two cents——"

"Without asking me? I'm the one to decide who is to be trusted."

"But you're never here. You're away praying most of the time."

"Hold your mouth! You're talking too much."

"Why do you make such a holler on me over two cents, when you, yourself, gave away four hundred dollars to a crook for empty shelves?"

"Blood-and-iron! How dare you question your father his business? What's the world coming to in this wild America? No respect for fathers. No fear of God." His eyes flamed as he shook his fist at me. "Only dare open your mouth to me again! Here I struggle to work up a business and she gives away all the profits of my goods. No heart. No conscience. Two cents here and two cents there. That's how all my hard-earned dollars bleed away."

Oh, God! *Two cents!* My gall burst in me! For seventeen years I had stood his preaching and his bullying. But now all the hammering hell that I had to listen to since I was born cracked my brain. His heartlessness to Mother, his pitiless driving away Bessie's only chance to love, bargaining away Fania to a gambler and Mashah to a diamond-faker—when they each had the luck to win lovers of their own—all these tyrannies crashed over me. Should I let him crush me as he crushed them? No. This is America, where children are people.

"I can't stand it! I can't!" I cried, rushing to the back of the store. "Two cents! Two cents! All that cursing and thundering over two cents!"

Blindly, I grabbed my things together into a bundle. I didn't care where I was going or what would become of me. Only to break away from my black life. Only not to hear Father's preaching voice again.

As I put on my hat and coat, I saw Mother, clutching at her heart in helplessness, her sorrowful eyes gazing at me. All the suffering of her years was in the dumb look she turned on me. Bending over, she took out from her stocking the red handkerchief with the knot that held her saved-up rent money. And without a word, she pushed it into my hand.

As I came through the door with my bundle, Father caught sight of me. "What's this?" he asked. "Where are you going?"

"I'm going back to work, in New York."

"What? Wild-head! Without asking, without consulting your father, you get yourself ready to go? Do you yet know that I want you to work in New York? Let's first count out your carfare to home every night. Maybe it will cost so much there wouldn't be anything left from your wages."

"But I'm not coming home!"

"What? A daughter of mine, only seventeen years old, not home at night?"

"I'll go to Bessie or Mashah."

"Mashah is starving poor, and you know how crowded it is by Bessie."

"If there's no place for me by my sisters, I'll find a place by strangers."

"A young girl, along, among strangers? Do you know what's going on in the world? No girl can live

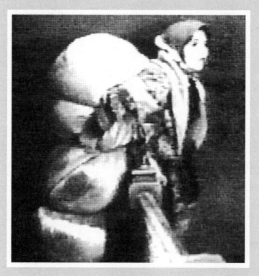

I grabbed my things together into a bundle.

without a father or a husband to look out for her. It
says in the Torah, only through a man has a woman an
existence. Only through a man can a woman enter
Heaven."

"I'm smart enough to look out for myself. It's a new
life now. In America, women don't need men to boss
them."

"*Blut-und-Eisen!* They ought to put you in a mad-
house till you're cured of your crazy nonsense!"

Always before, when Father began the drum,
drum of his preaching on me, my will was squelched.
But now he saw the stony hardness of my eyes. And
suddenly his whole face saddened with the hurt of a
wounded martyr, suffering his righteousness.

"Is this your thanks for all your father did for
you?" he pleaded, with the gentle patience of a holy
one. "Where do you find a poor father who has done
for his children as much as I? I didn't cripple you. I
didn't give you consumption. I didn't send you to work
at the age of six like some poor fathers do. You didn't
start work till you were over ten. Now, when I begin to
have a little use from you, you want to run away and
live for yourself?"

"I've got to live my own life. It's enough that
Mother and the others lived for you."

"*Chzufeh!* You brazen one! The crime of crimes
against God—daring your will against your father's will.
In olden times the whole city would have stoned you!"

"Thank God, I'm not living in olden times.

Thank God, I'm living in America! You made the lives of the other children! I'm going to make my own life!"

"You hard heart! You soul of stone! You're the curse from all my children. They all honoured and obeyed their father."

"And what's their end? Look at them now! You think I'll slave for you till my braids grow gray—wait till you find me another fish-peddler to sell me out in marriage! You think I'm a fool like Bessie! No! No!"

Wild with all that was choked in me since I was born, my eyes burned into my father's eyes. "My will is as strong as yours. I'm going to live my own life. Nobody can stop me. I'm not from the old country. I'm American!"

"You blasphemer!" His hand flung out and struck my cheek. "Denier of God! I'll teach you respect for the law!"

I leaped back and dashed for the door. The Old World had struck its last on me.

Chapter IX

BREAD GIVERS

A ll the way on the train to New York, Father's curses still rang in my ears. The flame of his eyes scorched their bitter wrath into my eyes. The hand with which he struck me still burned on my cheek.

"New York! All out!" The conductor shook my arm and shouted in my ears, "All out!"

I stared about. The train was nearly empty. Oh, I'm here, already, in New York. . . . I tried to pull myself up from my thoughts. . . . Bessie! I was going to Bessie. . . .

It was nine o'clock when I got to Zalmon's fish store. The shouting and bargaining for the holiday fish were enough to burst the ceiling. Zalmon stood on one side, surrounded by a crowd of women. Bessie on the other side, with another crowd. Sweat streamed from Bessie's and Zalmon's twisted faces, as they fought for their life with the bargaining *yentehs*.

"Robber!" cried an old, wrinkled woman with a shawl over her head. "Ten cents you ask for carp! By Cohen's it's only nine cents."

"Not such goods like by me." Zalmon lifted a

fish in his black, hairy hand, and waved it before the woman's eyes. "Give a look only on my beautiful carp! It jumps with life yet."

"But, swindler! My husband sweats blood for every penny. Why do you squeeze from me the last cent?"

"You think I steal my goods? And I got to pay rent."

"*Nu*, have a little mercy in your heart." The woman clutched at his arm wildly. "Twenty-eight cents for three pounds?"

"Twenty-nine cents and not a penny less." He put the fish on the scale and quickly tried to throw it into the woman's basket.

"Thief!" she shrieked. "You're skinning me in the weight."

"*Kooshenierkeh!* Out from here. Worms should eat you." And he turned from her to another customer.

I elbowed my way to where Bessie was. Her thin arms were covered with the gummy scales of the fish. Her face, her hair, and her apron were thick with it. So buried to the neck in fish was she, that she couldn't hear me or see me.

"Only another little fish yet for good measure," pleaded a woman, snatching up a squashed flounder. "I have eleven hungry mouths to feed."

"It's already over the weight," cried Bessie, tearing the fish out of the woman's hand. "Go to the charities, if you want fish for nothing."

The woman moved away, muttering curses. There was such famine-squeezed emptiness in her eyes that it hurt to look at her. I could stand the bargaining no longer and walked to the back of the store. But even in the far room, I could hear the haggling and the cursing, the tearing at each other's throats for pennies.

I looked about me, at the grand, married life that Father had grabbed for Bessie. Five boys sleeping on one mattress on the floor. Yenteh, on a narrow lounge. That place in the corner, with the ragged green curtains, Zalmon's and Bessie's bedroom. No place for me here, but I was so tired, my eyes could hold open no longer. Leaning my head over my hands on the table, I fell asleep.

"What's this? What brought you here?" I opened my eyes and saw Zalmon and Bessie standing over me.

"I left home," I blurted out, now wide awake.

"What?" Zalmon yawned into my face. "You'd better go right straight back, then. A girl's place is under her father's hand."

"*Shah!*" Bessie put herself between him and me. "It's too late to go back to-night."

"Then right back in the morning. A nice example you'd be for my daughter," and he stumbled away to the bedroom.

Bessie put her hand over my shoulder. "Go to sleep with Yenteh and to-morrow we'll talk." Her head dropped to the side and her body seemed to double over, as she dragged herself to bed.

I looked at the fat Yenteh on the narrow lounge. I could see no room for me. But I was so thin. And I crawled up to the edge and slowly worked a place for my feet to rest. But I scarcely had fallen asleep when I was dumped to the floor as Yenteh turned over with a sleepy grunt. There was no use to try the lounge again. I sat down wearily on a chair.

Bessie tiptoed over to me. With her finger on her lips she motioned for me to follow. Out of doors, we sat down on the step.

"What happened?" she whispered, slipping her hand into mine.

"Father. I couldn't stand him any longer."

"Thank God you had the courage to break away. If I'd had your sense, I wouldn't have sunk into Zalmon's fishwife."

"But where could I find a place to live? I'm so burning to get on my own feet!"

Bessie dropped her face in her hands. "*Ach!* I haven't even a little corner for my own sister," she groaned. "But Mashah has no fish store. She has no stepchildren. Among your own you can always squeeze yourself together."

"Don't worry for me. I'm free from Father's preaching. The rest will go like flying."

We fell into a silence. The air was full of voices. Great hopes beat in my heart like wings of flying things. But Bessie's sadness stopped the joy in me.

"Many times I wanted to run like you," she sighed. "But there's Benny."

So much I had to say to Bessie, but soon her head began to nod and we went in. Zalmon was snoring so sound that we quietly stole a blanket from his bed, and Bessie and I slept together on the kitchen floor.

The moment it was light a worse yelling that that of the *yentehs* grabbing for fish broke loose in that house. Five boys fighting each other, all trying to wash at the sink at one time, roused me from my dead sleep.

"You little mut! Give me that soap!" shouted Sol.

"It's mine. I had it first."

Sol snatched the soap out of Benny's hand, giving him such a push with his elbow that he went sprawling on the floor. At this, big Dave kicked them out of his way, and spread himself before the whole sink. He began splashing water on his face, humming a song from the street.

Bessie put her hand to her ears, adding her shrieking to the noise. *"Oi, oi, oi!* Every morning I'm yelling at them. 'Wash yourself two at a time.' But they all rush together like wild animals. In our house we also had only one sink, but we didn't kill each other to be first."

Zalmon ran in. "Devils! Stop this, or I'll break the bones in your bodies and kick you out in the street."

He sat down and his angry eyes bulged at me. "Right after breakfast, home you go."

"I'm not going home," I said without looking up.

"But you'll not stay here." He pointed to Yenteh, tying a red ribbon on her hair. "I got enough trouble on my hands with my own girl going wild! I don't want another *Americanerin* in my house."

"Drink your coffee," Bessie urged, her eyes going out with her heart to me. But my throat closed up. I couldn't swallow another drop of Zalmon's food.

Oh, how glad I was to get out of that house! Mashah's clean little home flashed before me as I hurried away. There, there would be no fighting, no yelling, no Zalmon and no fish smells. Only Mashah's own little children, Danny, Ruthy, and the baby, to light up and make more beautiful the beautiful place. I pushed on through the crowd, so anxious to get to Mashah that I saw nothing until someone stepped in front of me.

"*Nu*, little sister! What a grand young lady you're getting to be!" And there was Moe Mirsky, Mashah's husband, in a new checked suit, with a carefully folded, blue-bordered handkerchief sticking out of his breast pocket. His freshly ironed trousers were turned up at the bottom, showing his silk socks and new patent-leather shoes. Such a grand gentleman!

"I'm going to Mashah," I said, hurrying on.

At Mashah's open door stood a milkman arguing with her.

"You didn't pay last week's bill, and if you can't pay now, we'll have to stop the milk."

He lifted his rack of bottles and turned to go, but Mashah grasped his arm imploringly. "I've got to have milk for my babies."

"I'm sorry, ma'am, but I got babies of my own. If I don't turn in this collection, I'll lose my job."

"I'll surely pay you next week."

"You said that twice before. What's the matter? Ain't your husband working?"

Mashah's pale face turned red with guilt. Dumb with the shame of her poverty, her eyes dropped and then lifted, begging pity. But the milkman had already turned his back on her.

Mashah stared blindly into the dark hall, so stunned by her worries that she did not even see me.

To think that Moe Mirsky could shine like a prince of plenty while my sister's face was so black with want! There flashed before me a picture of her when she was a young girl, standing proud in the power of her beauty. And here she was slapped in the face by an unpaid bill. And I had come hoping to make a home with her!

"Is Moe out of work again? When I met him at the corner he was blowing from himself like a millionaire."

At the sound of my voice, Mashah looked up.

"Sara—you here? And you heard it all?"

I nodded. Then I asked her again what her husband was doing.

"Moe is working all right. But he bought himself a new suit last week and a new overcoat this week, so there wasn't anything left for the house."

I followed Mashah through into the kitchen. The gas was burning, although outside was still bright sunshine. The one window was close up to a jammed-in tenement that shut out all light. But Mashah had lit up the dingy darkness with her love for beauty. With her own hands she had patched up the broken plaster on the walls and painted them a golden yellow. The rotten boards of the window sill and the shelves were hidden by white oilcloth and held in place by shining brass tacks. The stove was painted silver. White curtains of the cheapest cheesecloth were on the one window, but hung with that grace that Mashah put into anything she touched.

"What patience you still have to keep things so beautiful," I said, gazing in wonder at the bright corner behind the silvered stove where the scoured pots and pans from the Five- and Ten-Cent Store hung in orderly rows from behind the polished brass hooks. And even her bits of wood from the broken boxes were laid in such an even orderly pile that not a splinter shone on her spotless floor.

"I couldn't stand it if I had to live in the dirt like the women around me. It's bad enough they shut out the light and let in the smells. But at least I can keep my own house clean."

Mashah sank wearily on a stool and pointed to a

chair for me to sit down. And now as I looked at her I saw what bloody toil it had cost to turn the dirt of poverty into this little palace of shining cleanliness.

Beauty was in that house. But it had come out of Mashah's face. The sunny colour of her walls had taken the colour out of her cheeks. The shine of her pots and pans had taken the lustre out of her hair. And the soda with which she had scrubbed the floor so clean, and laundered her rags to white, had burned in and eaten the beauty out of her hands.

"Don't stare at me like that!" cried Mashah. "I know how I look. Tell me better about yourself. How do you come here, so early?"

I told her how I suffered through the night at Bessie's and that I left home.

"Where will you live? What will you do? With Moe for my bread giver I'm too dirt-poor to help you."

"You think I've come to hang myself upon your neck? I can get a job quicker'n lightning. If I stay with you, I'll pay for my eating."

Mashah's face brightened. "Maybe your coming will give me the chance to tear myself out of the house some Sunday. Since the babies came I'm like in a prison. And yet, come see how lucky I am, they are so good."

We went into the other room. Danny and Ruthy were playing on the floor, happily tearing up an old newspaper.

Mashah sat down to feed the baby, Danny and Ruthy cuddled against her knees, playing with the baby's feet. Gone werc the worry and fear from Mashah's eyes. It breathed from her, the pride and the joy that these three were born of her, fed by her, living and breathing because of her being.

Sunshine flowed out of her eyes over her children. "When I have them like this, I feel I'm holding the riches of heaven in my arms."

The room darkened. The gas jet began to flicker and go out.

"Oh, my God!" Frightened worry came back into Mashah's face. "The gas is going out. It's a quarter meter. What shall I do? Where shall I borrow now?"

Mashah thrust the children on the floor. "Such a miserable existence! I wish they were never born. Can I never run away from this money—money—money!"

The children got so scared, they all began to cry.

"Why do you leave out your misery on their innocent heads?" I scolded Mashah.

"It's their innocence that chains me to this misery. I'm insulted by the milkman, shamed by the grocer, kicked like a dog by their father, all on account of them."

While Mashah tore at her hair, cursing the bitter luck of her poverty, I took a quarter out of my counted pennies, climbed on a chair, and put it into the meter.

The room grew light again. The children stopped

their crying. But Mashah no longer had patience to look at them. She turned to the tub full of soaking clothes. "I've got to get all this out on a line, the dinner cooked, and the children in bed before Moe comes."

Savagely, she clapped a shirt on the washboard. Her back humped like an angry cat's as she flung into the tub. Again the grind of poverty hardened her face. Again the crazy, wasting hurry to beat the race of hours—forcing her two thin hands to do the work of a steam laundry.

Toward evening, I put the children to bed while Mashah rushed to get the dinner ready. And then for half an hour the eating stood on the table and Moe didn't come. At last, Mashah got tired of watching the clock and we sat down to eat.

We had no sooner finished washing up the dishes when the bread giver came in, smiling, carefree, blowing his chest with pride and pleasure in himself. The sight of his piggish face and new-bought clothes got me so mad that I fled to the next room.

"How you look!" Moe's voice was full of disgust. "The janitress is more decent dressed."

"Why didn't you come home for dinner?" asked Mashah, with the patience of long-suffering. "I waited for you again."

"I have to have peace to think out my business worries."

"But it cost you so much to eat out."

"What do you think, I depend on what you cook

for me? For my dollar I can go to the finest restaurant, and I'm served like a king."

"I'm going crazy from the bills, while you—"

"Who tells you to make bills? If you have no money, then don't buy anything."

He drew a cigarette from his silk vest, lit it, and then, through the smoke, he eyed her coldly. "You're nothing but a worn-out rag."

"How can I take time to look decent, with all the work and worry on my head?"

"If it would be in you, you'd find time. With your worn-out face, nice clothes would be wasted on you."

Mashah sank into a chair, her drawn lips whitened with pain. Moe glanced at her swollen ankles. "Always there's something the matter with you. I hate sick people. You're just like a horse. You work, work, till you can't move. You don't know when to stop till you drop. If I'd ever go out with you now, people would only wonder how such a nice man come to have such a worn-out rag for a wife."

I had been trying to control myself. But now I could hold in no longer. I rushed into the kitchen.

"If you were my husband, I'd kill you. I'd scrub floors sooner than live with a thing like you."

"You would, eh?" His eyes reddened with rage as he glared at me. "I'm not your husband. And the way I run my house is none of your damn business."

"It is my business. Mashah is my sister. How

dare you eat yourself in a restaurant while the children's milk bill is unpaid? You married Mashah because she was beautiful, then you piled your children on her neck, starved her, wore her out. You spoiled her beauty. Then you blame her for losing it."

"Get the hell out of here! If I put my hands on you, I'll break your neck. The idea of a little skinny runt telling me how to run my home!"

Even in my fury I saw the hopelessness of trying to take Mashah's part when she hadn't the grit to stand up for herself. I stepped into the next room, seized my hat and coat, and walked out.

BOOK II

Between Two Worlds

Chapter X

I SHUT THE DOOR

Turning me out in the street like dirt! The heartlessness! Moe Mirsky! He'll yet suffer for my suffering. I'll yet show him, and show Zalmon, and show them all who I am. *Ach!* Only to make myself somebody great—and have them come begging favours at my feet.

And then it flashed to me. The story from the Sunday paper. A girl—slaving away in the shop. Her hair was already turning gray, and nothing had ever happened to her. Then suddenly she began to study in the night school, then college. And worked and studied, on and on, till she became a teacher in the schools.

A school teacher—I! I saw myself sitting back like a lady at my desk, the children, their eyes on me, watching and waiting for me to call out the different ones to the board, to spell a word, or answer me a question. It was like looking up to the top of the highest skyscraper while down in the gutter.

All night long I walked the streets, drunk with my dreams. I didn't know how the hours flew, how or where my feet carried me, until I saw the man turning out the lights of the street lamps. Was it already morning? The silence woke up from the block. There began the rumbling of milk wagons, the clatter of bottles and cans, and the hum of opening stores, peddlers filling their push-carts with fruit and loaves of bread. I wasn't a bit tired, but I was starving hungry, and I walked into the nearest bakery for a cup of coffee with two rolls, for ten cents.

As I sat there, in the stillness of the morning, I realized that I had yet never been alone since I was born. This was the first time I ate by myself, with silence and stillness for my company.

At home, when they sat down to eat, all my sisters were talking everything at once. I remember one night, coming home from the shop, my bones cracking from tiredness. I crawled into the bedroom and tried to close the door.

"What is the matter? Are you sick?" they asked.

"No. I only want a little quiet in me. I only want to be alone."

"Look only the princess!" My sisters dragged me back to the noisy kitchen. "Crazy! Ain't we good enough for you any more?'

Even after my sisters were married, mealtime was when Mother let out her bitter heart of worry and father hammered out his preaching like a wound-up phonograph. In the shop, the girls were talking all at once, clothes, styles, beaux, and dances—each one trying to out-yell the other. Perhaps in this same bakery it would be full of noise in an hour or two.

But now, thank God, it was still. And I was alone in that stillness.

How strong, how full of life and hope I felt as I walked out of that bakery. I opened my arms, burning to hug the new day. The strength of a million people was surging up in me. I felt I could turn the earth upside down with my littlest finger. I wanted to dance, to fly in the air and kiss the sun and stars with my singing heart. I, alone with myself, was enjoying myself for the first time as with grandest company.

In this high-hearted mood I began to look for a room where I could be alone. All the room-to-let signs that I passed seemed like so many doors opening to a new life. The first house I tried, the to-let room was on the top floor. I flew up the five flights of stairs on wings.

"You have a room?" I asked, my eyes laughing and my voice singing the joy in me.

A hard, mean look hit me in the face.

"I don't take girls." And the woman slammed the door.

In the next house, I walked up a little slower, and my voice had a quietness not like my own. A washed-out, thin-lipped woman with little suspicious eyes examined me. "No girls," snapped this one, too.

"Why no girls?" I dared ask the skinny tsarina.

"I want to keep my house clean. No cooking, no washing. Less trouble, less dirt, with men."

My heart sank to my feet. But I forced myself to hunt on. I had to find a place to live.

In the rear basement, a fat *yenteh*, in a loose wrapper, showed me a little coffin of a room, dark as the grave. "I've got three girls sleeping here already. And there's yet a place for a fourth in the bed. I charge only three dollars a month."

"I want a room all alone to myself."

"You? A room alone?" She gave me one fierce look till my cheeks began to burn. "This is a decent house. I'm a respectable woman."

On and on I searched. . . . Each place took it out of me more and more. For the first time in my life I saw what a luxury it was for a poor girl to want to be alone in a room.

My knees bent under me. I was ready to drop from weariness when I saw a crooked sign, in a scrawling hand, "Private Room, A Bargain Cheap."

It was a dark hole on the ground floor, opening into a narrow shaft. The only window where some light might have come in was thick with black dust. The bed see-sawed on its broken feet, one shorter than the others. The mattress was full of lumps, and the sheets were shreds and patches. But the room had a separate entrance to the hall. A door I could shut. And it was only six dollars a month.

"This is just the thing for me," I cried. "I'll clean it up like a little palace."

Through half-shut eyes the woman examined me. "Can you pay on time?" she asked.

"Of course I can pay." I drew myself up, tall as the ceiling.

"By what you work?"

"I'm not asking for any charity that I should have to tell you my business."

"But I got to know if you're working steady, to pay me my rent."

"You won't have to worry. I'm working by day and studying for a teacher by night."

She drew back as if I was about to rob her. "My gas! My gas bill. What I'd get from your rent, I'd lose on the gas. I already had an experience with one like you. She took out books from the library. And in the middle of the night, I could see by the crack in the door that she was burning away my gas, reading."

I looked at the room. A separate door to myself— a door to shut out all the noises of the world, and only six dollars. Where could I get such a bargain in the whole East Side?

Like a drowning person clinging to a rope, my tired body edged up to that door and clung to it. My hands clutched at the knob. This door was life. It was air. The bottom starting-point of becoming a person. I simply must have this room with the shut door. And I must make this woman rent it to me. If I failed to get it, I'd drop dead at her feet.

"Look only on me!" I commanded her. "You're a smart woman. You ought to know yourself on a person, first sight. Here, I give you a month's rent in advance." And I pushed the six dollars into her hand.

Her whole face lighted up with friendliness. She counted the money. Then kissing each dollar for good luck, she handed me the key.

At last alone, in my room. I let go everything, the weight of my body falling against the closed door. The aloneness was enough for me, and in a moment it sank me to sleep.

The first thing when I opened my eyes, I counted out the money I had left in my little knot. Only three dollars and sixty-five cents between me and hunger. A job. And I must get it at once.

It was slack season in the factories. I walked the streets, wondering where to turn for work, when I passed a laundry. A big printed sign was in the window: "Ironer wanted."

As I opened the door, a blinding wave of heat struck my face. The air was full of the sweaty smell of washing clothes. At the back, girls could scarcely be seen through the clouds of steam. Hair was sticking to their faces. Necks streamed with sweat.

A huge, bulgy-faced man sat on the counter, marking collars.

"Do you need an ironer?" I asked.

He looked at me from his big height till I felt like a speck of dust under his feet. With a grunt, he went on marking the laundry.

I put my courage into my teeth and faced him. "You got a sign out, 'Ironer wanted.'"

"Yes, but not you," he growled. "I want someone who can swing an iron." And he pointed with his thumb to a husky German woman with giant, red arms, who ironed a white dress with big, steady strokes. "That's the kind I need for an ironer."

"But let me only show you how good I can iron," I begged. "I was quicker than the big ones in my shop."

He tried me with an iron at an empty board with a small lot. But though I put all my strength into it, I was so nervous with him watching me, I thought the job was lost. But the man nodded kindly as I handed him the ironed apron. "You got guts all right," he chuckled. "I'll start you at the mangle for five a week, and later I'll break you into an ironer."

By the evening, I was so tired that I walked into the Grand Street Cafeteria for something to eat. I had read about the place in the paper. Kind, rich ladies had opened it for working girls, to have their meals in beautiful surroundings and cheap.

It was good to see flowers on the table. And the clean, educated face of the lady manager who sat by the desk. I needed something beautiful to look at after that hard day in the laundry. The portions were a little skimpy. But the white curtains and the clean, restful place lifted me with longing for the higher life.

Great dreams spurred my feet on my way to night school.

"What do you want to learn?" asked the teacher at the desk.

"I want to learn everything in the school from the beginning to the end."

She raised the lids of her cold eyes and stared at me. "Perhaps you had better take one thing at a time," she said, indifferently. "There's a commercial course, manual training——"

"I want a quick education for a teacher," I cried.

A hard laugh was my answer. Then she showed me the lists of the different classes, and I came out of my high dreams by registering for English and arithmetic.

Then I began five nights a week in a crowded class of fifty, with a teacher so busy with her class that she had no time to notice me.

The first morning in my room, I awoke very early. My head was clear, and I looked with full eyes on the thick dirt that I had grabbed in such anxious haste. There were only a few rusty nails on the door for my clothes. The table was shaky and the one chair was patched with boards.

Against this heart-choking dinginess flashed Mashah's shining little palace. Her place was once worse than this, and she polished it up. Why can't I? A pot of paint, a little white oilcloth with brass tacks, a scrubbing brush with soap. But first of all, I thought, if only I could wash away the mud of ages from that window, it would make it lighter in the room.

When my landlady saw me start on my cleaning, she cried warningly: "I never washed the windows since I lived here, not even for the holidays, because the upstairs tenants—a black year on them—are always throwing down things. Their hands should only fall to their sides."

But I wouldn't listen to her, and began to wash the window. The minute I stuck my head out, a bunch of potato peelings fell on me. I shook off the peelings and went on with the washing. Someone began shaking a carpet. Then a shower of ashes blinded me.

I sank on the bed, all the strength out of my arms and fingers. The deadening dirt! How could I ever do anything in this airless gloom? If I open the window the dirt will be flying in. If I keep it closed, how can I breathe?

I don't ask for fancy furniture, but only a little light for the eyes, only a clean window such as Mashah has in her blackest poverty.

The sound of the factory whistle brought me to my feet. Already seven o'clock. My fussing over the window made it too late for me to start cooking my coffee for breakfast. I grabbed a slice of black bread and ate as I hurried to the car. . . . Fool that I am, trying to imitate Mashah, her cleanliness. Ten hours I must work in the laundry. Two hours in the night school. Two hours more to study my lessons. When can I take time to be clean? If I'm to have strength and courage to go on with what I set out to do, I must shut my eyes to the dirt.

That evening, after night school, I spread my books out on my table and began to hammer into my thick head the difference between a noun, a verb, and a preposition. Oh, the noise around me. But I tried to struggle on with the lesson. . . . "A noun is the name of anything . . . ? A verb is the predicate of action . . . ? A preposition connects words . . . ?"

The more I repeated the definitions the more mixed up I got. It was all words, words, about words.

Maybe it was the terrible racket that was muddling my brain. Phonographs and pianolas blared against each other. Voices gossiping and jabbering across the windows. Wailing children. The yowling shrieks of two alley cats. The shrill bark of a hungry pup.

The jarring clatter tore me by the hair, stretched me out of my skin, and grated under my teeth. I felt like one crucified in a torture pit of noise.

Then I clasped my hands over my head and began talking to myself: "Stop all this sensitiveness, or you're beaten already before the fight is begun. . . . You've got to study. As you had to shut your eyes to the dirt, so you must shut your ears to the noise."

A quietness within me soothed my tortured nerves. I turned to my books on the table, and with fierce determination to sink myself into my head, I began my lessons again.

Chaper XI

A PIECE OF MEAT

By the whole force of my will I could reason myself out of the dirt and noise around me. But how could I reason with my hungry stomach? How could I stretch my five dollars a week to meet all my needs?

I took a piece of paper and wrote it all down. A dollar and a half for rent. Sixty cents for carfare. I couldn't walk that long distance to work and back and have time for night school. No saving there. And I must put aside at least fifty cents a week to pay back Mother's rent money. What is there left for food? Two dollars and forty cents. That means thirty-four and two-sevenths cents a day. How could I have enough to eat from that? But that's all I can have now. Somehow, it's got to do.

But whenever I passed a restaurant or a delicatessen store, I couldn't tear my eyes away from the food in the window. Something wild in me wanted to break through the glass, snatch some of that sausage and corned-beef, and gorge myself just once.

One day in the laundry, while busy ironing a shirt, the thought of Mother's cooking came over me. Why was it that Mother's simplest dishes, her plain potato soup, her *gefülte* fish, were so filling? And what was the matter with the cafeteria food that it left me hungrier after eating than before?

For a moment I imagined myself eating Mother's *gefülte* fish. A happy memory floated over me. A feast I was having. What a melting taste in the mouth!

"Hey—there!" cried the boss, rushing madly at me.

Oi weh! Smoke was rising from under my iron.

"Oh, I'll wash it out," I gasped in fright, as I lifted the iron and saw the scorched triangle.

But the boss snatched the shirt away from me. "Three dollars out of your wages for this," he raged.

Not a word could I say. Either it was to lose my job or pay. And I could not lose my job.

Three dollars out from my wages, when every fraction of a penny was counted out where it had to go. Maybe for weeks I'd have to live on dry bread to make up the loss. I got so frightened, from weakness I longed to throw myself in some dark corner, only to weep away my bitter luck. But I dared not let go. The boss was around. I picked up the iron again, though I could hardly shift the weight back and forth.

A terrible hunger rose up in me—a hunger I had been trying to forget since my lunch of two stale slices of bread and a scrap of cheese. Just when I had to begin saving more from eating, the starvation of days and weeks began tearing and dragging down

I couldn't tear my eyes away from the food . . .

my last strength. Let me at least have one dinner with meat before I begin to starve. For that last hour of work, I saw before my eyes meat, only meat, great, big chunks of it. And I biting into the meat.

Like a wolf with hunger, I ran to the cafeteria. From the end of the line, I saw the big, printed bill of fare:

>Roast beef, 25c.
>Roast lamb, 30c.
>Beef stew, 20c.

My eyes stopped. Over the word stew, I saw big chunks of meat, carrots, and peas, with thick brown gravy. I reached for the tray, and took my place on the line. I was like a mad thing straining toward the pots of food, and the line seemed to stand for ever in one place. A big, husky, fat man stood behind me. He held his tray so that the end poked into my ribs every time he shuffled on his feet. But, thank God, the line began to move up, slowly nearer the serving table.

My anxious eyes leaped to the faces of the servers. I tried to see which one of them served the stew. My portion depended on her mood of the minute. If I'm lucky to strike her when she feels good, then the spoon will go deep down into the pot and come up heaping full. If she feels mean, then I get only from the tip of the spoon, a stingy portion. God! She holds in her hands my life, my strength, new blood for my veins, new clearness in my brain to go on with the fight. Oh! If she would only give me enough to fill myself, this one time! . . .

At last I reached the serving table.

"Stew with a lot of meat in it."

Breathlessly, I watched how far the spoon would go into the pot. A hot sweat broke over my face as I saw the mean hunks of potato and skinny strings of meat floating in the starched gravy which she handed me.

"Please, won't you put in one real piece of meat?" And I pushed back the plate for more.

I might as well have talked to the wall. She did not see me or hear me. Her eyes were smiling back to the fat man behind me who grinned knowingly at her.

"Stew," was all he said.

She picked up my plate, pushed the spoon deep down into the pot and brought it up heaping with thick chunks of meat.

"Oh, thank you! Thank you! I'll take it now," I cried, reaching for it with both hands.

"No, you don't." And the man took the plate from the server and set it on his tray.

Speechless, bewildered, I stood there, unable to move.

"I asked for stew—*stew!*"

"I gave you some and you didn't take it." She sniffed.

"But you didn't give me as much as you gave him. Isn't my money as good as his?"

"Don't you know they always give men more?" called a voice from the line.

"It takes a woman to be mean to a woman," piped up another.

"You're holding up the line," said the head lady, coming over, with quiet politeness.

"I want stew," came again from my tight throat.

"She gave you a fair portion."

"But why did she give more to the man just because he was a man? I'm hungry."

All the reply I got was a cold glance. "Please move on or step out of the line."

People began to titter and stare at me. Even the girl at the serving table laughed as she put on a man's plate a big slice of fried liver, twice as big as she would have given me.

"Cheaters! Robbers!" I longed to cry out to them. "Why do you have flowers on the table and cheat a starving girl from her bite of food?" But I was too trampled to speak. With tight lips, I walked out.

In the street, there was no cheap restaurant in sight. I had a dreary feeling that it was the same in every other place. Since I must starve next week, I might as well begin now. I went home boiling with hate for the whole world.

In my room, I found the tail end of a loaf of bread. Each bite I swallowed was wet with my tears.

It was so cold that night that in every tenement people huddled into their beds early and put all their clothes over themselves to keep warm. So cold it was, even the gas froze.

I stuck a candle into a bottle, took up my grammar struggling to forget my bitterness, studying. Everything I had I wrapped around myself and, buried in my thin bedclothes, I held on to my book.

My feet were lumps of ice. How could I study? But I would. I must. I forced myself to keep to my lessons like one forcing himself awake when he's falling asleep.

A rap came to the door. It was repeated over and over again before I could drag myself out of my coverings to see who it was.

"Mother!" I cried. Yes, there stood my mother, a shawl over her head and a big bundle on her back. She threw her arms around me and kissed me hungrily.

"In a night like this, I thought you'd need a feather bed," she said, throwing her bundle on my cot. Her face was stiff with cold, and she blew on her half-frozen fingers.

"All the way from Elizabeth for you to carry it," I cried. In the sputtering light of the candle, her sunken eyes gleamed out of their black sockets with a dumb, pleading love that made me hate myself for my selfishness. It seemed to me I never knew till now how close to my heart my mother was.

"Here's a jar of herring that I pickled for you," she said, unwrapping it from an old newspaper. "A

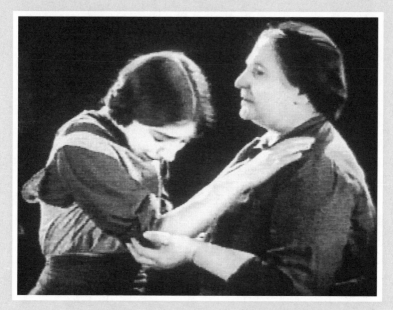

"Mother! You're so good to me."

piece of herring on bread, and you have already a good meal."

Her goodness hurt so that I began talking fast to keep back the tears in my throat.

"How is Father? How is business? How could you get away from the store?"

"It's lodge night, and your father will be away till late. With all my hurrying it took so long to get here, that I'll have to go back in a few minutes to be home before he comes."

Hours she travelled, only to see me for a few minutes. God! How much bigger was Mother's goodness than my burning ambition to rise in the world!

"Mother! You're so good to me. What can I do back for you?" I said, feeling small under her feet with unworthiness.

"Only come to see me soon."

"I'd do anything for you. I'd give you away my life. But I can't take time to go 'way out to Elizabeth. Every little minute must go to my studies."

"I tore myself away from all my work to come to see you."

"But you're not studying for college."

"Is college more important than to see your old mother?"

"I could see you later. But I can't go to college later. Think only of the years I wasted in the shop instead of school, and I must catch up all that lost time."

"You're young yet. You have plenty of time."

"It's because I'm young that my minutes are like diamonds to me. I have so much to learn before I can enter college. But won't you be proud of me when I work myself up for a school teacher, in America?"

"I'd be happier to see you get married. What's a school teacher? Old maids—all of them. It's good enough for *Goyim,* but not for you."

"Don't worry. I'll even get married some day. But to marry myself to a man that's a person, I must first make myself for a person."

Mother shook her head. "*Ach!* Already I must go." But her feet stuck to the floor and her hands clung to me for many minutes before she could tear herself away. Long after she had gone, I felt her still in the room.

As I tucked my shivering bones under the feather bed, I felt that nothing on earth was as warm as Mother's love. Gone was the rankling hurt I had suffered at the cafeteria. I forgot to hate even the fat man and the head lady with her cold, low-voiced politeness. All the bitterness of my heart was forgotten.

I laughed when I thought of poor dear old Mother—coming so far with that big feather bed on her back. . . . How warm I am. . . . If only I had time to go to see her. . . . To-morrow, I'll sit up in bed, warm, for once, and study my grammar.

Chapter XII

MY SISTERS AND I

I stood in my room, stirring the pot of oatmeal with one hand, and with the other I held on to my history book. I always had to read while cooking to make myself forget the dreary little meal I had to eat all by myself. I hated my stomach. It was like some clawing wild animal in me that I had to stop to feed always. I hated my eating. And yet I could hardly wait till my oatmeal was finished. I kept swallowing spoonfuls while it was still cooking.

I glanced at the boiling pot.... I don't have to share it with anyone.... That's what made it so hateful. A longing came over me for the old kitchen in Hester Street. Even in our worst poverty we sat around the table, together, like people. Even Father's preaching and Mother's worrying made mealtimes something higher than mere eating and filling the stomach.

How long since I ate Mother's meals with the family! How far away they all seemed! How torn apart and divided! When will I have time to see them again?

Before I had a chance to put the pot back on the stove, who should burst in but Fania and Bessie.

"You here—Fania?" I cried, as we hugged and kissed each other.

"Just got off the train," put in Bessie, excitedly. "And I brought her to you, before she even saw Mother."

They sat down on my cot. What a picture of poverty and riches! Bessie in her old fish-store clothes, a ragged *kooshenierkeh;* Fania, like a Queen of Sheba, shining with silks and sparkling with diamonds. Fania looked scornfully around my dingy room.

"How can you bury yourself alive in such a black hole? How do you ever breathe here? A girl like you, if you'd come with me to Los Angeles, you'd live and laugh."

"I'll live and laugh after I pass my college examinations."

"For what does a girl need to be so educated? You can read and write. You know enough. But look at her, Bessie. Ain't it a shame to let herself go down like this?" Fania picked at the patched elbow of my worn-out serge. "You're a young girl yet, Sara; why don't you put on a little style?"

"I haven't time or money for the outside show."

"The outside show? What else do people see?"

I glanced at my stylish sister. Was this dressed-up, grand lady the same Fania who was once loved by the poor poet Lipkin? Gone was the innocence of young dreams from her eyes. Good eating, good sleeping, and the sunshine of plenty breathed from her face. And she held her head high, as if she didn't come from the same family as the rest of us. But for all her shine, I could see in the shadowy places under her eyes thready lines of restlessness.

"Are you at least happy with your riches?" My hand touched her shoulder as I searched her face.

"Why shouldn't she be happy?" said Bessie. "Look at her, only! Like a born Mrs. Vanderbilt! Her husband must be rolling in money, and he gives it all to her. And she has no stepchildren like me, either."

Fania did not answer. The satisfied look suddenly faded from her face, leaving her eyes hard and stony. Then her lips began to work and she burst into bitter weeping.

"Gives it all to me," she sobbed, wiping her wet face. "He wants me to be dressed in the latest style, yet he kicks I'm spending all his money. He wants everything grand but cheap. When I pay a hundred dollars for a suit, I've got to tell him it's fifty. To keep his mouth shut and not to have any fights, I feed him with lies. Getting money from him is like pulling teeth. These diamonds that you see on me, that's his saving bank. He buys me jewellery, only to show me off to his friends that he's so rich."

She covered her face with her hands, struggling to control her unhappiness. "Where I live, I haven't a friend to talk to. All they do out there is play cards. And I play with them, only to forget myself. I can't stand it to be alone."

"Why don't you read the way you used to when you were home?" I asked.

"I can't look at a book. My head stopped with my troubles. *Ach!* How can you people know what it is to be miserable as I am."

The proud grand lady crumpled before my eyes into nothing but an East Side *yenteh*, with a broken heart.

So this is what it was to be the wife of a cloaks-and-suits millionaire!

"But, thank God, you look so well." I tried to find some bright spot to encourage her.

"It's only fat you see on me. And this is just paint," she said, pointing to her cheeks.

"Don't sin," warned Bessie. "You're better off than me. You got a servant to do your work, so you got time even to paint your face."

"Why shouldn't I have a servant? Abe can lose five hundred or a thousand dollars playing poker in the wink of an eye, so why should I be slaving in the kitchen?"

She leaped up from her chair, as though to tear herself from her chains. "What eats out my heart worst of all is when I begin to look back what my life might have been with Morris Lipkin."

"Father didn't bury you so deep under the ground as me," sighed Bessie. "What have I from my life? Carp, flounder, pike, morning, noon, and night."

Poor Bessie! With her pitiful thin face squeezed dry of hope or happiness. Older, more life-weary than Mother she looked, in her old, crushed hat and her big, coarse shoes.

"Let me tell you it's terrible to be a stepmother," she wailed. "At first I sewed and scrubbed and killed myself cooking for Zalmon's children. But you can never do enough for them. . . . The first dance Minnie ever went to with a young man, I bought her a grand piece of pink silk for a dress. I stayed up half the night sewing, but before it was half done, she said I didn't have any style. She had to take it to an uptown dressmaker. When she began finding fault with my work I got so choked that I began to cry and pull up my hair. Nothing I do for these children is right for them."

"Then I'm better off than you married people!" I exclaimed. "It's not a picnic to live alone. But at least I've no boss of a husband to crush the spirit in me."

"But who wants to be an old maid?" cried Fania. "Some day you got to get married. Better come with me to Los Angeles. I've a wonderful young man for you out there. He and Abe are going into a partnership, and I can easy rope him in for you."

"I'll tell you the truth, Fania, the kind of a man that could be partners with Abe is not the kind that could love me, or that I could love. Besides, I don't want to get married. I've set out to do something and I'm going to do it, even if it kills me."

"It may not kill you. But if you're left an old maid it's worse."

She seized me by the arm. "Put on your hat and coat and come with us to Mother."

"If you only knew what a big bunch of lessons I've got to cram into my head in this one little day."

"But this is Sunday. Even the schools are shut down to-day."

"My work goes on Sundays and holidays. I'm like a soldier in battle. I can't stop for visiting, even with my own family."

"You hard heart!" Fania threw up her hands at me. "Come, Bessie. Let's leave her to her mad education. She's worse than Father with his Holy Torah."

Chapter XIII

OUTCAST

Noontime in the laundry. All the girls were together giggling and laughing and enjoying themselves as they ate their lunch. Only I was alone in the corner, cramming my grammar. A longing to join the crowd and be happy with them came over me. So I closed my book and moved my stool nearer, to hear what the fun was all about.

"You think that was bad," Minnie Feist was saying. "Gee whiz! That was nothing. You should have seen what I seen in Coney Island on the beach." Then a loud whisper and with meaningful glances she started to tell a coarse, funny story. I grew hot and cold with shame as they burst out in shouts of laughter.

Instinctively, I moved my chair back to my own place.

Daggers shot at me from all eyes.

"Give only a look on her, *the lady!* Who does she think she is?"

"Huh! That thing blows yet from herself."

"Pure she is! Innocent! Pfui! Leaves a father and mother for God knows why."

"I ask you only, why does a girl go to live alone?"

How their words stabbed me.

"We know, kid. Can't fool us, baby!"

"What's his name? And she puts on airs yet like a holy one."

Angry jabbering pelted me till the whistle for work put an end to further insults.

After that I was shut out like a "greenhorn" who didn't talk their language. When they gossiped beaux, or dances, or the latest styles, their mouths snapped tight when I got near. When they planned any picnics or parties, I was left out.

Hurt to the bone, I sank into a shell of stiff pride. I pretended not to see, not to hear the slights heaped on me. Lunchtime I was always apart in my corner, my head buried in a book. But often when I seemed to be reading, I longed to throw myself at the feel of the girls and cry out to them, "Say anything you like. Do anything you like. All right—hurt me. But don't leave me out. I don't want to be left out!"

Even in school I suffered, because I was not like the rest. I irritated the teachers, stopping the lessons with my questions. A bored weariness fell over the whole class the minute I started to speak. They'd begin to nudge each other by the sleeve and whisper, "Oh Lord! That bug! Again showing off her smartness!" They didn't hunger and thirst for knowledge, they weren't excited about anything they were learning, so it jarred on them that I was so excited. To them I was only a selfish grabber of their time because I was so crazy to know too much.

One evening, the teacher was reading to us the list of subjects we'd have to pass to enter college.

"Who are those bosses of education who made us study so much dead stuff?" I asked.

A frown of annoyance wrinkled the teacher's face. The other began to wink and smile at one another, but I couldn't help myself. My thoughts pushed themselves out of me. "I only want to know what interests me. Why should I have to choke myself with geometry? How can those tyrants over the college force all kinds of different people to stuff their heads with the same deadness that we all got to know alike? I want the knowledge that is the living life. . . . "

Loud laughter fell like a chilling shower on me. Even the teacher joined in the fun. After that, they never called me by name. The minute I came they grinned and tittered, "There goes the living life!"

Maybe if I could only live like others and look like other, they wouldn't pick on me so much, I thought to myself. I studied myself in the mirror. I examined, one by one, the features that gazed back at me. Tired eyes. Eyes that gazed far away at nothing. A set sadness about the lips like in old maids who'd given up all hope of happiness. A gray face. A stone face. Turned to stone from not living. A black shirt-waist, high up to the neck. Not a breath of colour. Everything about me was gray, drab, dead. I was only twenty-three and I dressed myself like an old lady in mourning.

I began talking to the gray face in the mirror. What had I done to myself to make myself look so old and ugly? Other girls as plain as I, why do they look attractive? When they have no colour, they put on colour. That's what I must do. Why not? I want to be looked at, longed for, followed. . . . I hate my goodness. The only sin on earth is to let life pass you by. . . .

The next day, I took my little penny savings, and during lunch hour I went to the nearest department store. I bought lipstick, rouge, powder. A lace collar for my waist. Even red roses for my hat.

Late into the night I spent fixing myself up, pinning the roses on my hat, trying on my lace collar this way and that, to show off the whiteness of my throat. A wildness possessed me to make up for the pale, colourless years. I saw myself in bright red and dazzling green and gold. I could beat them all if I only let loose the love of colour in me. My fingers trembled, and my eyes burned through the mirror as I began daubing on lipstick and rouge.

I looked in the glass at the new self I had made. Now I was exactly like the others! Red lips, red cheeks, even red roses under the brim of my hat. Blackened lashes, darkened eyebrows. Soft, white lace at my neck. Ah! What a different picture! No old maid here! A young girl in the height of her bloom! . . . But my excited happiness soon sank down. I felt funny and queer. Something was wrong. As if my painted face didn't hang together with the rest of me. On the outside I looked like the other girls. But the easy gladness that sparkled from their eyes was not in mine. They were a bunch of light-hearted savages who looked gay because they felt gay. I was like a dolled-up dummy fixed for a part on the stage.

"No—no! I will be like them!" I cried. "I'll go like this to work. I've as much right to be gay and draw men as they."

But next morning when I got into the street, I grew panicky with self-consciousness. Everybody seemed to be staring at me. I felt shamed and confused with my false face. It was as though the rouge had turned into a mask, and I could not breathe through the cover. I sneaked through the streets like a guilty thing. When I got to the laundry I hurried into the cloakroom to tear the roses off my hat and wash the paint off my face. But before I knew what or how, the girls crowded around me.

"Give a look, only! The lady!"

"Done it with a shovel!"

"So scared, she's got to scrape it off."

I turned to my work, raw with the shame that I had tried to be like the rest and couldn't

I threw myself more desperately than ever into my studies. My one hope was to get to the educated world, where only the thoughts you give out count, and not how you look. My longing for the living breath of a little understanding became centered more and more in my dream of going to college. Wherever I went, in the street, in the subway, by day and by night, I had always before my eyes a vision of myself in college, mingling every day with the inspired minds of great professors and educated higher-ups.

I had always before my eyes a vision of myself in college...

Chapter XIV

A MAN WANTED ME

At school one evening, the teacher returned my examination paper. One look and my heart stopped. I had failed in geometry. How I had forced myself to study it! But the screw for figures seemed missing in my head.

A terrible doubt got me. Maybe I wasn't smart enough to swallow all that dry learning you had to swallow to enter college! Maybe I could never pass the entrance examinations!

At this time of discouragement, a letter came from Fania:

Max Goldstein, the man I told you about, is coming special to New York to see you. From what I told him about you he thinks you're just the wife he needs. I only hope you'll be lucky enough to get him.

Think only! You'll have your own house and garden. Your own car. You'll have servants do all your work for you. You'll be able to wear the best stylish clothes that money can buy. You'll lift up your head and know what life is.

What have you, shutting yourself up in your black hole, not fit for a dog? You don't live. You don't eat. You don't dress like a person. And for what are you wearing out the best years of your youth? To work yourself up to be an old maid school teacher?

I was too impatient to read on and threw away the letter.

It was Sunday afternoon. No work and no school. It was always my best time for lessons. And now I had to begin studying all over again the geometry I hated. The books were before me on the table. The pencils, the papers, but I could not touch them. I had no heart to begin.

Outside in the street it was sunshine. It was spring in the air. Other girls were enjoying themselves with their young men. The whole world was alive. Only I was shut out of life. Living people want to live and I'm wasting myself with something so inhuman as squares and triangles. That is why I've grown dead and inhuman myself. What's all this book-learning compared to a free walk in the sunshine?

Maybe Fania was right. If I keep on wearing out my years stuffing dead ashes of learning in my tired brain, later, when I'll want to live and love, it will be too late. I'll be too old.

I used to say to my loneliness: If it will not kill you, it will be the making of you. All great people have to be alone to work out their greatness. But now all my high talk was hollow and unreal. The loneliness of my little room rose about me like a thick blackness, about to fall on me and crush me.

The minutes passed into hours. But I still could not force myself to begin my lessons. Never before did I let time go by me so wastefully. I hated the touch of the books before me as if they were living enemies. I hated the burdens I had put upon myself to get an education. I hated book-learning and colleges. All education was against life. I wanted to live and not stupefy myself with geometry.

It was evening. The room was as dark as my heart. I was too tired to light the gas. I was just about to throw myself on my cot with all my things on. I wanted to forget everything and sleep my life away.

Suddenly, a strong hand rapped my door.

"Come in," I yawned, turning on the light.

A man! A man entered. And I knew, by the positive way in which he stepped into the room, that this was the one my sister had sent.

"I know you better than your own sister, so much she's been telling me about you," he said, by way of introduction. "I'm Max Goldstein. Shake hands."

"Oh, yes—my sister wrote me.—But I did not expect you to-day.—My room is so upset."

He swept away my confusion with his hearty laugh. "What does the room matter? We're friends already, aren't we?"

And so it was. I liked him instantly. If only he were not looking for a wife. That made me shrink from him with self-consciousness.

"Your sister even told me how you won't doll yourself up for men," he laughed. "But I like you the way you are better than if you fixed yourself up in the grandest style. I like that part in the middle of your hair. No painted cheeks. No painted lips. You look just like those home girls with all their innocence from Europe yet."

"Is this the way you talk to girls the minute you meet them?" I laughed back at him.

With a swift glance he took in everything in my room. "Your sister was making excuses for the way you live. I think more of you for standing on your own feet. I lived worse when I ran away from home. You and I are so much alike, because I, too, wanted to make my own way in the world. And you remind me of my own beginning."

That man could wake the dead from their graves. Where was my discouragement now? My eyes could only follow his eyes. His slender body was all joyous youth. Full red lips. His hands and feet like wired electricity. I felt I'd be afraid to touch even the tips of his fingers for fear I'd get shocks.

"Tell me about your running away." I edged my chair nearer to him, in my excited eagerness.

His face was kindled with pleasure. It was like inviting him to a feast to ask him to talk about himself.

"I still see that first day when I got off the ship with my little bundle on my back. I was almost lost in the blowing snow of a freezing blizzard. Than I came upon a gang of men clearing the street with great shovels. At once, I saw that these men must be paid for their work. So I pushed myself in among them and begged for a shovel. The big, fat foreman looked down on the poor little greenhorn, wondering should he take pity on me. But before waiting for an answer, I snatched up a shovel from the stack and dug into the snow. At the end of the day, when I was paid a dollar, I felt the riches of all America in my hand. . . .

"This first money, I had to pay down for a week's lodging. The next day, there was no more snow shoveling. I was hungry. I had to get work, and I didn't know where. I just walked the streets, searching people's faces, driven by hunger. Then I saw an old man struggling with his pushcart over the frozen snow. I rushed up to him, begging him with my eyes and my hands to let me help him. So he gave me the job to drive his pushcart and holler for him, 'Pay cash clothes.'"

"How could you manage the English words that first day?" I asked.

A humorous twinkle leaped into Max's eyes. "That man knew as much about English as I. What I hollered was, 'Pay cats coals.' But my boss couldn't tell the difference. To me it was only singing a song. I didn't understand the words, but my voice was like dynamite, thundering out into the air all that was in my young heart, alone in a big city."

The rest of the story flowed on like magic. At the end of the week he was in business for himself. He cried the streets, "Pay cats coals," without even a pushcart. From all the windows, people began to look with wonder at the strange greenhorn singer. Every day he came back to his lodging loaded full with piles of old clothes. In a month, he had enough money saved to start a little stand of second-hand clothes in Hester Street.

"That day, I felt so happy with my riches that I danced and sang in front of my goods to make people come and buy," he went on. "Such a free theatre as I gave them! Hester Street never saw and never heard such acting and dancing and singing in their whole life. . . .

"Then a man from the crowd came over and said, 'Young man, you're too smart to waste yourself selling second-hand clothes in Hester Street. I'll make you for an actor. I'll give you twenty-five dollars a week to dance and sing on the stage in my theatre on Grand Street.' "

And so for a while he became an actor and earned a lot of money.

"But I began living a fast life, bumming around like a gay young feller with the women. One night, after a drinking party, going out from an overheated place, I caught cold. It went worse till it turned into consumption. The doctor told me I'd have to leave the stage and live outdoors if I wanted to save my life."

A new chance to get on his feet came to him in California. In a town near Los Angeles, he started a little stand of imitation jewellery. So he saved up enough to open a small general store. And now, after a few years, it has grown to be the biggest department store in the village.

Every step of his struggle to rise, he painted with such colourful pictures, it was like turning the pages of a wonderful book right there with him. By the time he had finished his story, I had forgotten all about myself. I gazed up at him feeling like a tiny ant at the feet of a great lion.

"Think, only, I never yet went inside a school or a college in America," he went on. "And I have American-born college men working for me as bookkeepers and salesmen. I can hire them and fire them, as it wills itself in me. Because with all their college education they haven't got the heads to make the money that I have."

I didn't like this last boast of his. But I was so carried away by the man himself that I wasn't aware how much I didn't like it.

He began telling me of his real-estate investments that he had scattered all over Los Angeles. He pictured the wonders of this city of his. Bungalows full of sunshine and flowers. Roses growing in January. People living in the open all the year round.

Suddenly, he looked straight at me. "Tell me," he asked, "is it true what you sister said, that after working all day in the laundry you go to school at night? We've got to bring you to Los Angeles. There you'll get the roses back into your cheeks."

He seized my hand in a flow of sympathy and stroked the callous rough spots the laundry had stamped on them. "These hands should be playing the piano, not ironing clothes."

Finer than silk and velvet was the touch of his hand on mine. I wanted to hold myself back from him, but everything in me rushed out to him.

"Let's go out," he said. "Where shall I take you?"

"Go on talking only."

"I talk enough all day, buying and selling. When I'm through with business I want to play and forget myself. How would you like a vaudeville show?"

He put his strong hands under my elbows. In a flash I was lifted out of my chair to my feet. That man was so full of compelling force when his eyes turned on me that I had to do what he wanted.

I found myself entering a vaudeville theatre. There was a chorus of dancing women. A disgusting-looking comedian with a false red nose wagged his finger and leered grossly at the shimmying shoulders. He was cracking jokes about the different women. And each time he came to the point of a joke, Max Goldstein clapped his hands and feet and shouted with laughter.

"Why isn't this funny to me? Am I so thick?" I asked myself. I felt like a mummy sitting there. At first I couldn't help myself. When Max turned to me to share his enjoyment, I tried to smile, but inside I felt sort of sickened. Max saw that his hearty laughter at the show shocked me and pushed us apart.

"Come on." He patted me indulgently. "I'll take you to something more your kind."

He put me into a taxicab and whirled me uptown among the glittering electric lights of Broadway. We stopped in front of a highly lighted place. Loud strains of music poured out as a man in uniform swung open the door for us. I was frightened about going in at first.

I thought it might be another foolishness like the vaudeville show. But the next moment I was in a dazzle of lights and bright coloured walls. The brass band lifted me fiercely out of myself and shook me to the roots. Crowds, what crowds of couples. Women's white shoulders against men's black coats. Women and men letting go toward each other, drunk with the fiery rhythm of jazz.

Ach! Just to dance! To lose myself in the mad joy of the crowd. Whirl away wild and free from all worry and care. This was the life. Worth everything to taste such a moment of happiness!

He took me into his open arms and off we went. Such a dancer as Max was! He glided over the floor, a thing of wings. Lost and forgotten were all thoughts of lessons. The joy of the dance burst loose the shut-in prisoner in me. I was a bird that had leaped out of her cage. Wild gladness sang in my veins, swept me up, up, away from this earth.

"I'll say you're some dancer!" cried Max, plumping me into a seat at one of the tables. "Say, you've come to life! I saw it was in you first sight off! But it's one o'clock, little *teacherin!* You must be starved for supper."

The very word one o'clock startled me. I suddenly felt tired and began to yawn. "Better take me home. I've never been out so late."

"Late?" Max scoffed. "Our best good time will just begin."

"No—oh, no," I insisted, "I've got to go home. I have work the next day."

His lips drooped sulkily as he looked into my eyes and saw the iron will in me.

I felt his chill at the door and wondered whether he'd come back to see me again. "But I'm a person with a mind as much as he," I said. "If there's anything real, deep between us, he'll come back. And if he doesn't, I don't want him."

I was too excited to sleep the few hours that were left of that night, after Max Goldstein left me.

When I glanced at myself in the mirror, I was amazed at my shining face. I was laughing in myself like one bewitched with happiness.

Overnight I had become a changed person. The weight of ages that had burdened me down since I was a child had dropped away from me. Overnight youth burst loose in me. And all because of a man. A man who took me out for one night's pleasure. A fierce desire for life was let loose in me. I had tasted pleasure. And it burned in me for more, more.

All day at the laundry, my head was flying away from me like a lost thing in the air. In the evening, I was wondering, should I be absent from school? Because I was too much on fire to come down to the

I was amazed at my shining face.

cold facts of lessons. And yet, I jollied myself that I didn't want him to come till I could calm down, back to common sense. I told myself I wanted peace and quiet after so much high-flying pleasure. But all the time, a thin, needle-like craving in me was wishing and hoping and aching for him to come. And when his knock came at my door, wild gladness leaped up in me and I rushed to let him in.

His eyes were dancing out of his head with happiness. He held a telegram in his hand which he waved in my face.

"Just got this wire from my agent. People offering me twenty thousand for a lot that I bought for five thousand. And think only! I wired back not to close the deal for less than fifty thousand. Real estate is booming in Los Angeles. The biggest boom in all America."

And he went on pouring out to me all his get-rich-quick schemes that would turn him into a millionaire. Last night his adventures were new and interesting. But now again his talking only about himself and his business began to get on my nerves. Why don't he ask how I am? Why isn't he interested in my school, my studies? Was the whole world only the boom, boom, boom, of his real-estate schemes?

"Come, get ready, my little *teacherin!* To-night we'll go to the Grand Street Theatre."

"I'm too tired after so much excitement last night. Wouldn't you like better a quiet evening in the park?"

"*Ach!* I couldn't sit still and be quiet five minutes. I've got to be on the go. I've got to see things
moving before my eyes. Excitement is like eating
to me. In my town, I belong to about a dozen
lodges. Every night I'm on the go to a different
meeting."

"Any one listening to you would think that lodge
meetings and money-making are the beginning and
the end of life."

"Sure thing. Money-making is the biggest game
in America. At the lodge meetings I combine my
business and my pleasure. It's meeting people.
Matching wits. If my luck keeps up, I'll have
enough in a few years to sit back and live on my
income."

He jerked about restlessly, telling me again of all
the real estate he owned and the lots he expected to
see, and those he sold at the beginning of his business career. His rushing torrent of money, money
beat down on me till I suddenly felt worn out. But
Max Goldstein took my hat and coat off my nail on the
door and threw them at me playfully. "If you hurry,
we'll have time enough to go to the restaurant before
the show."

"I'm no excitement eater like you."

"*Ach!* You talk just like an old maid. You ought to
get out into the world. Then you'd wake up."

I stared at him, hurt, frightened. Am I an old
maid? I set my teeth to hold back the bitter

thoughts crowding in my throat. How I hated
him!.... He and I? No. No.... I shivered at the
thought of it.... It could never be—he and I.
Never.... Then suddenly he became aware of my
silence.

"Come, come." He put his hand over mine and
stroked my fingers. His touch was like magic.
Feelings from under the earth blazed up in me. I
pulled my hand away, in fear of this power he had
over me.

"I'll tell you the truth, I like you more because
you're independent. There's a magnet inside of you. It
pulls me out of my senses. What's happening to me?
You're so different. You're so cold. You're only books,
books, books. I sometimes wonder, are you at all a
woman? And yet you set me on fire."

His eyes burned into mine. The next moment he
was like a child begging for affection. In a daze, I followed him.

I found myself sitting opposite him, at a little
table in a restaurant. The music. The lights. He and I,
alone together, in a corner all by ourselves. The very
air fanned the rush of feeling between us.

"What shall I order for you, little heart?"

"Anything! anything—you order." My hand ached
to touch the curly head bent toward me across the
table.

Food came. But I was too bewildered to know
what I was eating. His eyes, his voice, the near-

ness of him swept me out of myself with joy and longing.

With what innocent delight he watched me put every bite in my mouth. "Eat, darling, get a little fat on you." He poured sunlight over me with every breath. What did anything matter except this irresistible gladness that drew us toward each other?

Every evening next week he came to see me. One moment I loved him; the next moment I tried to resist him, wanted to be free of him. One moment he would say something that would rise up like a sword between us, pushing us apart; and then, at the touch of his hand, the look of his eyes, I forgot all his faults. My one need of needs, stronger than my life, was my love to be loved.

One evening, he was content to stay with me, in my room. I read to him a story, "The Pavilion on the Links." How delighted I was by the thoughtful face that listened to every word. So, at last, I got him excited about something outside of business. Love had opened this new soul in him. With a new feeling of closeness to him, my eyes looked into his as I shut the book.

"Finished?" he cried, eagerly. "You looked so beautiful while you were reading to me! Just like a picture! Now, listen to business, darling. I've been figuring out that I'd better cinch that offer of twenty thousand for my property. My agents are holding up the deal till I come."

I read to him a story...

God! So this was in his head when I thought he listened with such whole-hearted interest to my story! For the first time since I met him, I could see where he belonged. In silence, I looked at him, wondering how I could have been so carried away by a man who was such a stranger to me.

"The only thing that keeps me here is you, golden heart." He took my hand in both his own. "The first look I gave at you, I knew you were for me. . . . I know I'm a good catch. No wonder all kinds of women are after me"; he went on praising himself, as if he were goods for sale. "But I'm such a crazy, I want what I want, and I want you. So what do you say?"

He shoved aside the books that piled my table.

"What for should you waste your time yet with school any more? You're smart enough the way you are. Only dumbheads fool themselves that education and colleges and all that sort of nonsense will push them on in the world. It's money that makes the wheels go round. With my money I can have college graduates working for me, for my agents, my bookkeepers, my lawyers. I can hire them and fire them. And they, with all their education, are under my feet, just because I got the money."

The man seemed to turn into a talking roll of dollar bills right there before my eyes. His smile. He could buy everything. That's what laughed in his eyes. He could buy everything. To him, a wife would only be another piece of property. I grew cold at the thought how near I had been to marrying him.

A great calmness came over me. We were so far apart, it was as if someone else was talking for me. "I'm only happy alone. You were right once. I *am* an old maid."

For a long time, after Max left, I could not tear my eyes away from the chair where he had sat, from the spot on the floor that his feet had touched.... Max wanted to marry me. Me he wanted. Me....

I turned to the mirror and saw myself with new wonder. There was a glow in my face that was never there before. Gone was that vague gaze at nothing. My eyes had grown bigger and darker. They had become seeing eyes. I had seen and felt. I had tasted and known. And it shone there, in my eyes, and surged through my arms and fingers. I touched the hand he had touched, my face, my neck. There was a feel like new velvet on my skin. I knew now the meaning of a certain inner smile that I used to see in certain women's eyes. I felt that same smile in me. My head went up with a new pride. I had an assurance that I never had before. I was thrilled. Flattered. Ripened for love.

Then why did I let him go?

Hours I sat there, my head in my hands, wondering why. Slowly, one piece of a broken thought began to weave itself together with another. If I'd let myself love him, I'd end by hating him. He only excited me. But that wasn't enough. Even in the ecstasy of our kisses, I knew he was not my kind.

I looked at the books on my table that had stared at me like enemies a little while before. They were again the life of my life. *Ach!* Nothing was so beautiful as to learn, to know, to master by the sheer force of my will even the dead squares and triangles of geometry. I seized my books and hugged them to my breast as though they were living things.

Chapter XV

ON AND ON—ALONE

A sudden longing to see my father came over me. I felt that my refusal to marry Max Goldstein was something he could understand. He had given up worldly success to drink the wisdom of the Torah. He would tell me that, after all, I was the only daughter of his faith. I had lived the old, old story which he had drilled into our childhood ears—the story of Jacob and Esau. I had it from Father, this ingrained something in me that would not let me take the mess of pottage.

For the whole day after, I thought of Father. If I only could talk myself out to him. Now, I could love and understand him from afar as I had once hated him and could not bear him when near. I had broken away from him as a child only to be drawn to him now, in my great spiritual need, as a person is drawn to a person.

Some of his preachings came back to me: "Can fire and water live together? Neither can Godliness and an easy life." How rich with the sap of centuries were his words of wisdom! I never knew the meaning of his sayings when I had to listen to him at home.

But now it came over me like half-remembered, far-off songs, like music and poetry.

When I came back from work, I had a great urge to drop everything and take the train to Elizabeth and rush home to see him. Never since I was born did I feel such a great need for him and his wiser-than-the-world kind of wisdom. *She's becoming him,*

I still remember how I sat there in my room glued to my chair instead of jumping up to take the train as I wanted to do. Something was holding me back. And I always wondered whether it wasn't my instinct that he was even then coming down the block to me. He seemed coming closer and closer to me. And I was scarcely surprised, but only thrilled and happy, when I heard the familiar stamping of his feet. It was like the answering of a prayer, to see before my eyes my door open and my father standing there like a picture out of the Bible.

Had a miracle happened? My father come to see me? In a rush of gladness words from Isaiah flashed before me as in letters of fire: "I will join the hearts of the parents and the children."

Never had there been any show of feeling between Father and us children. Only once a year, on the Day of Atonement, he put his hands over our heads to bless us. Now, as I looked at him, he seemed to me like Isaiah, Jeremiah, Solomon, and David, all joined together in the one wise old face. And this man with all the ancient prophets shining out of his eyes—my father.

I longed to rush forward and fling my arms around his neck. "Father," I cried. And then my voice stopped. For I suddenly became aware of his cold, hard glance on me.

"Is it true what Max Goldstein said?" His eyes glared. "Is it true you refused him?"

My heart stopped. I just stared at him. Not a word could force itself out of my tight throat.

"Answer me! Answer me!" His voice grew louder and harsher.

"It wasn't the real love," I stammered, hardly aware what I was saying.

"Love you want yet? What do you know about love? How could any man love a lawless, conscienceless thing like you? I never dreamed that a decent man would want to marry you. You had a chance to make a good ending to a bad play, and you push away such a luck match with your own hands. I always knew you were crazy. Now I see you're your worst enemy."

All I could feel was the hurt of his beating me down. Just as I looked to Father for love, he rose up to stone me.

"This was the one chance of your life. Another chance to marry will never come to you. There are plenty of nicer girls than you. Younger, more beautiful. Home girls, those are the girls men want. What have you to show off to a man? The shame and disgrace that you heaped upon your old father?

A lawless daughter makes a lawless wife. No man wants to marry a girl who runs away from home."

Rage flamed from his eyes as he thundered at me, stamping his feet. "Pfui on your education! What's going to be your end? A dried-up old maid? You think you can make over the world? You think millions of educated old maids like you could change the world one inch? Woe to America where women are let free like men. All that's false in politics, prohibition, and all the evils of the world come from them."

I no longer saw my father before me, but a tyrant from the Old World where only men were people. To him I was nothing but his last unmarried daughter to be bought and sold. Even in my revolt I could not keep back a smile.

"It's no use talking to you. I see to my sorrow that my words won't help you. He who loses his understanding is like one spiritually sick. Right is wrong to him and wrong is right. It says in the Torah: What's a woman without a man? Less than nothing—a blotted-out existence. No life on earth and no hope of Heaven."

He drew himself back like a deposed king who had been wounded and dishonoured. There was a hurt, a sorrow in his eyes that hurt me and made me weak with guilt against him.

"It bleeds in me my heart when I see how you're

digging your own ruin and you won't listen to my warning. After all, you're my child, flesh of my flesh, blood of my blood."

My God! I am flesh of his flesh and blood of his blood. Why can't he understand me? Why don't we understand each other? Full of bitterness, I cried to him: "What do you want from me? Why do you torture me?"

"My child," he pleaded, "hear me. I'm an old man. I lived longer than you. I know what's good for you better than you know. Look around you. Nothing in nature lives by itself alone. Every tree has its little branch. Every branch has its little flower. God put people on earth to get married and have children yet. It says in the Torah, Breed and multiply. A woman's highest happiness is to be a man's wife, the mother of a man's children. You're not a person at all. What do you make from yourself? Why do you hold yourself better than the whole world? You hide yourself from people. Never go anywhere. Never see any one. Who ever heard of such madness? You're worse than an animal. Even animals live with one another. The birds in the air, the fishes in the sea, even the littlest worms under the stone need their own kind to fulfill themselves. You'll rot away by yourself."

Why does he throw yet salt on my wounds? The nails of my fingers dug into my palms trying to control myself. Why can't he see how my whole being cried out for love, for sympathy, for the living breath of any kind of people?

"Father!" I burst out. "I want love. I'd give my life away to love and be loved. I want a home, a husband and children. But——"

"But Max Goldstein, such a golden young man, he isn't good enough for you yet? You're yet blowing from yourself? Who do you think you are? Whom do you want? The President of America, maybe?"

I saw there was no use talking. He could never understand. He was the Old World. I was the New.

"I give you up!" He spat his rage in my face. "You're without character, without morals, without religion. What use are you to yourself or to the world? When you'll die, they'll bury you in Potter's Field, among all the bums and outcasts of America."

"I have to live and die by what's in me," I said, dully. "Preaching don't change me. Why don't you let me alone?"

"Wait! You'll see your bitter end when you'll begin to grow older. I warn you, your terrible selfishness. . . . "

"All my selfishness is from you." I was stung at last to hitting back at him. "What have you ever done for your wife and children but crush them and break them? I ran away from home because I hated you. I couldn't bear the sight of you."

"*Schlang!* Toad! Wild animal! Thing of evil!

How came you ever to be my child? I disown you. I curse you. May your name and your memory be blotted out of this earth."

He rushed from me, slamming the door, a defeated prophet, a Jeremiah to whom the people would not listen.

I knew now that I was alone. I had to give up the dreams of any understanding from Father as I had to give up the longing for love from Max Goldstein. Those two experiences made me clear to myself. Knowledge was what I wanted more than anything else in the world. I had made my choice. And now I had to pay the price. So this is what it cost, daring to follow the urge in me. No father. No lover. No family. No friend. I must go on and on. And I must go on—alone.

Chapter XVI

COLLEGE

That burning day when I got ready to leave New York and start out on my journey to college! I felt like Columbus starting out for the other end of the earth. I felt like the pilgrim fathers who had left their homeland and all their kin behind them and trailed out in search of the New World.

I had stayed up night after night, washing and ironing, patching and darning my things. At last, I put them all together in a bundle, wrapped them up with newspapers, and tied them securely with the thick clothes line that I had in my room on which to hang out my wash. I made another bundle of my books. In another newspaper I wrapped up my food for the journey: a loaf of bread, a herring, and a pickle. In my purse was the money I had been saving from my food, from my clothes, a penny to a penny, a dollar to a dollar, for so many years. It was not much but I counted out that it would be enough for my train ticket and a few weeks start till I got work out there.

It was only when I got to the train that I realized I had hardly eaten all day. Starving hungry, I tore the paper open. *Ach!* Crazy-head! In my haste I had forgotten even to cut up the bread. I bent over on the side of my seat, and half covering myself with a newspaper, I pinched pieces out of the loaf and ripped ravenously at the herring. With each bite, I cast side glances like a guilty thing; nobody should see the way I ate.

After a while, as the lights were turned low, the other passengers began to nod their heads, each outsnoring the other in their thick sleep. I was the only one on the train too excited to close my eyes.

Like a dream was the whole night's journey. And like a dream mounting on a dream was this college town, this New America of culture education.

Before this, New York was all of America to me. But now I came to a town of quiet streets, shaded with greens. No crowds, no tenements. No hurrying noise to beat the race of the hours. Only a leisured quietness whispered in the air: Peace. Be still. Eternal time is all before you.

Each house had its own green grass in front, it own free space all around, and it faced the street with the calm security of being owned for generations, and not rented by the month from a landlord. In the early twilight, it was like a picture out of fairyland to see people sitting on their porches, lazily swinging in their hammocks, or watering their own growing flowers.

So these are the real Americans, I thought, thrilled by the lean, straight bearing of the passers-by.

COLLEGE

They had none of that terrible fight for bread and rent that I always saw in New York people's eyes. Their faces were not worn with the hunger for things they never could have in their lives. There was in them that sure, settled look of those who belong to the world in which they were born.

The college buildings were like beautiful palaces. The campus stretched out like fields of a big park. Air—air. Free space and sunshine. The river at dusk. Glimmering lights on passing boats, the floating voices of young people. And when night came, there were the sky and the stars.

This was the beauty for which I had always longed. For the first few days I could only walk about and drink it in thirstily, more and more. Beauty of houses, beauty of streets, beauty shining out of the calm faces and cool eyes of the people! Oh—too cool. . . .

How could I most quickly become friends with them? How could I come into their homes, exchange with them my thoughts, break with them bread at their tables? If I could only lose myself body and soul in the serenity of this new world, the hunger and the turmoil of my ghetto years would drop away from me, and I, too, would know the beauty of stillness and peace.

What light-hearted laughing youth met my eyes! All the young people I had ever seen were shut up in factories. But here were young girls and young men enjoying life, free from the worry for a living.

College to them was being out for a good time, like to us in the shop a Sunday picnic. But in our gayest Sunday picnics there was always the under-feeling that Monday meant back to the shop again. To these born lucky ones joy seemed to stretch out for ever.

What a sight I was in my gray pushcart clothes against the beautiful gay colours and the fine things that those young girls wore. I had seen cheap, fancy style, Five- and Ten-Cent Store finery. But never had I seen such plain beautifulness. The simple skirts and sweaters, the stockings and shoes to match. The neat finished quietness of their tailored suits. There was no show-off in their clothes, and yet how much more pulling to the eyes and all the senses than the Grand Street richness I knew.

And the spick-and-span cleanliness of these people! It smelled from them, the soap and the bathing. Their fingernails so white and pink. Their hands and necks white like milk. I wondered how did those girls get their hair so soft, so shiny, and so smooth about their heads. Even their black shoes had a clean look.

Never had I seen men so all shaved up with pink, clean skins. The richest store-keepers in Grand Street shined themselves up with diamonds like walking jewellery stores, but they weren't so hollering clean as these men. And they all had their hair clipped so short; they all had a shape to their heads. So ironed out smooth and even they looked in their spotless, creaseless clothes, as if the dirty battle of life had never yet been on them.

I looked at these children of joy with a million eyes. I looked at them with my hands, my feet, with the thinnest nerves of my hair. By all their differences from me, their youth, their shiny freshness, their carefreeness, they pulled me out of my senses to them. And they didn't even know I was there.

I thought once I got into the classes with them, they'd see me and we'd get to know one another. What a sharp awakening came with my first hour!

As I entered the classroom, I saw young men and girls laughing and talking to one another without introductions. I looked for my seat. Then I noticed, up in front, a very earnest-faced young man with thick glasses over his sad eyes. He made me think of Morris Lipkin, so I chose my seat next to him.

"What's the name of the professor?" I asked.

"Smith," came from his tight lips. He did not even look at me. He pulled himself together and began busily writing, to show me he didn't want to be interrupted.

I turned to the girl on my other side. What a fresh, clean beauty! A creature of sunshine. And clothes that matched her radiant youth.

"Is this the freshman class in geometry?" I asked her.

She nodded politely and smiled. But how quickly

her eyes sized me up! It was not an unkind glance. And yet, it said more plainly than words, "From where do you come? How did you get in here?"

Sitting side by side with them through the whole hour, I felt stranger to them than if I had passed them in Hester Street. Wasn't there some secret something that would open us toward one another?

In one class after another, I kept asking myself, "What's the matter with me? Why do they look at me so when I talk with them?"

Maybe I'd have to change myself inside and out to be one of them. But how?

The lectures were over at four o'clock. With a sigh, I turned from the college building, away from the pleasant streets, down to the shabby back alley near the post office, and entered the George Martin Hand Laundry.

Mr. Martin was a fat, easy-going, good-natured man. I no sooner told him of my experience in New York than he took me on at once as an ironer at fifty cents an hour, and he told me he had work for as many hours a day as I could put in.

I felt if I could only look a little bit like other girls on the outside, maybe I could get in with them. And that meant money! And money meant work, work, work!

Till eleven o'clock that night, I ironed fancy white shirtwaists.

"You're some busy little worker, even if I do say

so," said Mr. Martin, good-naturedly. "But I must lock up. You can't live here."

I went home, aching in every bone. And in the quiet and good air, I so overslept that I was late for my first class. To make matters worse, I found a note in my mailbox that puzzled and frightened me. It said, "Please report at once to the dean's office to explain your absence from Physical Education I, at four o'clock."

A line of other students was waiting there. When my turn came I asked the secretary, "What's this physical education business?"

"This is a compulsory course," he said. "You cannot get credit in any other course unless you satisfy this requirement."

At the hour when I had intended to go back to Martin's Laundry, I entered the big gymnasium. There were a crowd of girls dressed in funny short black bloomers and rubber-soled shoes.

The teacher blew the whistle and called harshly, "Students are expected to report in their uniforms."

"I have none."

"They're to be obtained at the bookstore," she said, with a stern look at me. "Please do not report again without it."

I stood there dumb.

"Well, stay for to-day and exercise as you are," said the teacher, taking pity on me.

She pointed out my place in the line, where I had

to stand with the rest like a lot of wooden soldiers. She made us twist ourselves around here and there. "Right face!" "Left face!" "Right about face!" I tried to do as the others did, but I felt like a jumping-jack being pulled this way and that way. I picked up dumbbells and pushed them up and down and sideways until my arms were lame. Then she made us hop around like a lot of monkeys.

At the end of the hour, I was so out of breath that I sank down, my heart pounding against my ribs. I was dripping with sweat worse than Saturday night in the steam laundry. What's all this physical education nonsense? I came to college to learn something, to get an education with my head, and not monkeyshines with my arms and legs.

I went over to the instructor. "How much an hour do we get for this work?" I asked her, bitterly.

She looked at me with a stupid stare. "This is a two-point course."

Now I got real mad. "I've got to sweat my life away enough only to earn a living," I cried. "God knows I exercised enough, since I was a kid——"

"You properly exercised?" She looked at me from head to foot. "Your posture is bad. Your shoulders sag. You need additional corrective exercises outside the class."

More tired than ever, I came to the class next day. After the dumbbells, she made me jump over the hurdles. For the life of me, I couldn't do it. I bumped myself and scratched my knees on the top bar of the hurdle, knocking it over with a great clatter. They all laughed except the teacher.

"Repeat the exercise, please," she said, with a frozen face.

I was all bruises, trying to do it. And they were holding their sides with laughter. I was their clown, and this was their circus. And suddenly, I got so wild with rage that I seized the hurdle and right before their eyes I smashed it to pieces.

The whole gymnasium went still as death.

The teacher's face was white. "Report at once to the dean."

The scared look on the faces of the girls made me feel that I was to be locked up or fired.

For a minute when I entered the dean's grand office, I was so confused I couldn't even see.

He rose and pointed to a chair beside his desk. "What can I do for you?" he asked, in a voice that quieted me as he spoke.

I told him how mad I was, to have piled on me jumping hurdles when I was so tired anyway. He regarded me with that cooling steadiness of his. When I was through, he walked to the window and I waited, miserable. Finally, he turned to me again, and with a smile! "I'm quite certain that physical education is not essential in your case. I will excuse you from attending the course."

After this things went better with me. In spite of the hard work in the laundry, I managed to get along in my classes. More and more interesting became the life of the college as I watched it from the outside.

What a feast of happenings each day of college was to those other students. Societies, dances, letters from home, packages of food, midnight spreads and even birthday parties. I never knew that there were people glad enough of life to celebrate the day they were born. I watched the gay goings-on around me like one coming to a feast, but always standing back and only looking on.

One day, the ache for people broke down my feelings of difference from them. I felt I must tear myself out of my aloneness. Nothing had ever come to me without my going out after it. I had to fight for my living, fight for every bit of my education. Why should I expect friendship and love to come to me out of the air while I sat there, dreaming about it?

The freshman class gave a dance that very evening. Something in the back of my head told me that an evening dress and slippers were part of going to a dance. I had no such things. But should that stop me? If I had waited till I could afford the right clothes for college, I should never have been able to go at all.

I put a fresh collar over my old serge dress. And with a dollar stolen from my eating money, I bought a ticket to the dance. As I peeped into the glittering gymnasium, blaring with jazz, my timid fears stopped the breath in me. How the whole big place sang with their light-hearted happiness!

Young eyes drinking joy from young eyes. Girls, like gay-coloured butterflies, whirling in the arms of young men.

Floating ribbons and sashes shimmered against men's black coats. I took the nearest chair, blinded by the dazzle of the happy couples. Why did I come here? A terrible sense of age weighed upon me; yet I watched and waited for someone to come and ask me to dance. But not one man came near me. Some of my classmates nodded distantly in passing, but most of them were too filled with their own happiness even to see me.

The whirling joy went on and on, and still I sat there watching, cold, lifeless, like a lost ghost. I was nothing and nobody. It was worse than being ignored. Worse than being an outcast. I simply didn't belong. I had no existence in their young eyes. I wanted to run and hide myself, but fear and pride nailed me against the wall.

A chaperon must have noticed my face, and she brought over one of those clumsy, backward youths who was lost in a corner by himself. How unwilling were his feet as she dragged him over! In a dull voice, he asked, "May I have the next dance?" his eyes fixed in the distance as he spoke.

"Thank you. I don't want to dance." And I fled from the place.

I found myself walking in the darkness of the campus. In the thick shadows of the trees I hid myself and poured out my shamed and injured soul to the night. So, it wasn't character or brains that counted. Only youth and beauty and clothes—things I never had and never could have. Joy and love were not for such as me. Why not? Why not? . . .

I flung myself on the ground, beating with my fists against the endless sorrows of my life. Even in college I had not escaped from the ghetto. Here loneliness hounded me even worse than in Hester Street. Was there no escape? Will I never lift myself to be a person among people?

I pressed my face against the earth. All that was left of me reached out in prayer. God! I've gone so far, help me to go on. God! I don't know how, but I must go on. Help me not to want their little happiness. I have wanted their love more than my life. Help me be bigger than this hunger in me. Give me the love that can live without love. . . .

Darkness and stillness washed over me. Slowly I stumbled to my feet and looked up at the sky. The stars in their infinite peace seemed to pour their healing light into me. I thought of captives in prison, the sick and the suffering from the beginning of time who had looked to these start for strength. What was my little sorrow to the centuries of pain which those stars had watched? So near they seemed, so compassionate. My bitter hurt seemed to grow small and drop away. If I must go on alone, I should still have silence and the high stars to walk with me.

*   *   *

Never before or since in all my life had I worked as hard as during the first term. I was not only earning a living and getting an education, I was trying to break into this new college world.

Every week, I saved a bit more for a little something in my appearance—a brush for the hair, a pair of gloves, a pair of shoes with stockings to match. And now I began to work still longer hours to save up for a plain felt hat like those college girls wore. And the result of my wanting to dress up was that I was too tired to master my hardest subject. In January, the blow fell. On the bulletin board, where everybody could see, my name was posted as failing in geometry. It meant taking the course all over again. And something still worse. Two weeks later, the bursar sent me a bill for the same old geometry class.

I hurried to his office and pushed myself in ahead of the line of waiting students. "I want my money back for the geometry course that you didn't teach me," I cried. "I paid to learn, not fail."

The man gaped at me for a moment as if I had gone mad and then paid no more attention to me. His indifference got me into such a rage that I could have broken through the cage and shaken him. But I remembered the smashed hurdle and the kind dean. With an effort, I got hold of myself and went to this more understanding man.

"I didn't smash any hurdles, but I'm ready to smash the world. Why should I pay the college for something I didn't get get?" And then I told him how they wanted to cheat me.

This time, even the dean did not understand. And I had no new hat that winter.

I flung myself into the next term's work with a fierce determination to wring the last drop of knowledge from each course. At first, psychology was like Greek to me. So many words about words. "Apperception," "reflex arc," "inhibitions." What had all that fancy book language to do with the real, plain every day?

Then, one day, Mr. Edman said to the class: "Give an example from your own experience showing how anger or any strong emotion interferes with your thinking?"

Suddenly, it dawned on me. I jumped to my feet with excitement. I told him about Zalmon the fish-peddler. Once I saw him get so mad at a woman for wanting to bargain down a penny on a pound of fish that in his anger he threw a dollar's worth of change at her.

In a flash, so many sleeping things in my life woke up in me. I remembered the time I was so crazy for Morris Lipkin. How I had poured out all my feelings without sense. That whole picture of my first mad love sprang before my eyes like a new revelation, and I cried, "No wonder they say, 'All lovers are fools'!"

Everybody laughed. But my anger did not get

the better of me now. I had learned self-control. I was now a person of reason.

From that day on, the words of psychology were full of living wonder. In a few weeks I was ahead of any one else in the class. I saw the students around me as so many pink-faced children who never had had to live yet. I realized that the time when I sold herring in Hester Street, I was learning life more than if I had gone to school.

The fight with Father to break away from home, the fight in the cafeteria for a piece of meat—when I went through those experiences I thought them privations and losses; now I saw them treasure chests of insight. What countless riches lay buried under the ground of those early years that I had thought so black, so barren, so thwarted with want!

Before long, I had finished the whole textbook of psychology.

"I'm through with the book," I said to Mr. Edman. "Please give me more work. I've got to keep my head going."

He gave me a list of references. And I was so excited with the first new book that I stayed up half the night reading it on and on. I could hardly wait for the class to show Mr. Edman all I had learned. After the lecture, I hastened to his desk.

"I'm all ready to recite on this new book," I cried, as I handed it to him.

"Recite?" He looked puzzled.

"Ask me any questions. See only how much I've just learned."

"I'm late to a class right now. I'm busy with lectures all day long."

"If you're busy all day, I'll come to you in the evening. Where do you live?"

He drew back and stared at me. "I'm glad to tell you what to read," he said, stiffly. "But I have no time for recitations outside of class hours. I'm too busy."

God! How his indifference cut me! "Too busy!" The miser. Here I come to him hungry, starving— come begging for one little crumb of knowledge! And he has it all—and yet pushes me back with, "I'm too busy!"

How I had dreamed of college! The inspired companionship of teachers who are friends! The high places above the earth, where minds are fired by minds. And what's this place I've come to? Was the college only a factory, and the teachers machines turning out lectures by the hour on wooden dummies, incapable of response? Was there no time for the flash from eye to eye, from heart to heart? Was that vanishing spark of light that flies away quicker than it came unless it is given life at the moment by the kindling breath of another mind—was that to be shoved aside with, "I'm too busy. I have no time for recitations outside class hours"?

A few days later, I saw Mr. Edman coming out hurriedly from Philosophy Hall. Oh, if I could only ask him about that fear inhibition I had read about. How it would clear my mind to talk it over with him for only a minute. But he'd maybe be too busy to even glance at me.

"How do you do, Miss Smolinksy!" He smiled and stopped as he saw me. "How are you getting on with those references I gave you?"

My whole heart leaped up in gratitude. "Oh, perhaps I bothered you too much."

"No bother at all. I only wish I had more time."

That very evening I overheard two tired-looking instructors in the college cafeteria.

"Maybe I was a fool to take this job. No sweatshop labour is so underpaid as the college instructor."

"How do they expect us to live? I get a thousand dollars a year and I teach sixteen periods a week."

"And look at Edman. He teaches eighteen periods and his pay is no more than ours."

So that was it. And I had thought I hated Mr. Edman for being so aloof, so stingy with his time. Now I understood how overworked and overdriven he was. How much he had taught me in that one little class! What a marvellous teacher he was! *Ach!* If one could only meet such a man outside of class, how the whole world would open up and shine with light!

Summer came. And when the others went home for their vacation I found a canning factory near the town. And all summer I worked, stringing beans, shelling peas, pulling berries. I worked as long hours as in the New York laundry. But here, it was in sheds full of air.

And as I worked, I thought of Mr. Edman and all he had taught me. His course in psychology had opened to me a new world of reason and "objectivity." Through him, I had learned to think logically for the first time in my life.

Till now, I lived only by blind instinct and feeling. I might have remained for ever an over-emotional lunatic. This wider understanding of life, this new power of logic and reason I owe to Mr. Edman.

How could I ever have been so crazy for a little bit of a poet like Lipkin? If I worshipped Mr. Edman, there would be some *reason* in my worship. Edman is not a silly poet like Lipkin. He is a thinker, a scientist. Through him I have gained this impersonal, scientific attitude of mind.

I returned to college a week before the new term started. I went to the post office to buy some stamps. There was Mr. Edman! He was giving the postman his new address. Tanned with the summer sun, he looked more wonderful, more distinguished than ever. "Eighteen Bank Street." The words burned themselves into me. "Eighteen Bank Street." So that's where Mr. Edman lived.

Turning from the postman, he looked up and saw me.

"Hello! What have you been doing?" was his friendly greeting.

"Working in a canning factory. But my head

was going over and over everything you taught me."

"That's splendid," he smiled. "I'm glad to find a student who takes psychology so seriously."

How kind, how wonderful he was! For a long time after he went away, I could only look and look after him. How that little bit of friendliness had changed the world for me! How I could be filled to the brim with happiness by the sound of a voice, the smile of a face!

Before I knew how or why, I found myself walking up and down the sidewalk of the house marked Eighteen Bank Street.

All at once I noticed the sign, "Room To Let."

My heart gave a sudden jump. I stopped still, almost without breath. Then I walked up the steps and rang the bell.

"May I see the room to let?" I asked of the woman who opened the door.

She led me up to the third-story hall bedroom. It was a dollar a week more than I could afford to pay. But even if I had to starve, I had to rent that room. What matter if my body starved as long as my soul would be fed!

"All my roomers are from college," she said, as I paid her a week's rent in advance. "Miss Porter, the art teacher, has my front parlour. And right below you is Mr. Edman, the teacher of psychology."

And people doubt that there's a God on earth that orders all the events of our lives? Why was I so driven to get an education? Why did I pick out this college of all colleges? Was it not because here was the man who had the knowledge that I had been seeking all my years?

That very afternoon, I moved in. On the way up the stairs, a suitcase in my hand, I bumped right into him. "Think only!" I cried with uncontrolled gladness, "I live now in the same house you live."

"Oh, is that so?" he said, in his quiet voice. And then I wondered if his voice was so extra quiet because my own voice was so loud with gladness.

The next morning I was wondering what hour he went to class. So as not to miss him, I was waiting for him on the doorstep from eight o'clock on. *Ach!* I thought. To walk and talk with him for the few minutes to college, what a feast of joy to begin the day!

At last he came out.

"Good morning," he said, and walked on.

"Oh, Mr. Edman, I'm going to college, too," I cried, catching up with him. I had a thousand questions that I had in my mind to ask him. But only after he bowed and I saw him walk up the steps to Philosophy Hall did I realize that I had forgotten everything that I had meant to talk to him about.

In the evening, as I passed his door, on the way up to my room, I heard him cough. I tried to go on with the lesson, but the repeated sound of his cough went through and through me so that I could not concentrate on my work. And before I knew what

I was doing, I was in the delicatessen store, buying a pint of milk. I hurried back to my room, heated the milk on my gas jet, and with the hot saucepan in my hand I knocked at his door.

"Hot milk is good for your cough," I stammered, as he opened the door.

He looked in surprise at me, and then slowly smiled. "Oh, you shouldn't have done this." He poured the milk into a glass. "Thank you," he said, handing me the saucepan and closing the door.

Because of the rain, I couldn't wait for him on the doorstep the next morning. I didn't hear him go out till the front door slammed. Through the window, I saw him walk quickly, with his head bent, through the rain. Quick as lightning I seized my umbrella and ran after him, crying, "Mr. Edman—Mr. Edman! You mustn't get wet. Remember, you have a cold. Here's my umbrella."

He stopped. He turned around. "Miss Smolinsky, you mustn't bother so about me. I don't like it."

His tone of annoyance hit me like a blow. I remained standing in the rain and let him go on. He hurried along the drenched pavement, and over him the quiet elms poured their cooling drops steadily.

As I watched him disappear down the street, I knew with sudden terrible clearness that he was going out of my life for ever.

Oh, Morris Lipkin! Was it all for nothing? God! Must I always remain such a fool! Such a fool!

Will even the hurts and the shames of my life teach me nothing? O God! Give me only the hard heart of reason!

A thousand years older I was by the time I dragged myself up the stairs to my room. I threw myself on the bed. My whole body ached with the bitterness of it all. Insane I've been—reaching for I know not what and only pushing it away in my clumsiness.

I want knowledge. How, like a starved thing in the dark, I'm driven to reach for it. A flash, and all lights up! Almost I seem to touch the fiery centre of life! And there! It was only a man. And I'm left in the dark again.

What was that flash of light that lured me into this blackness? Was it desire for the man, or desire for knowledge? Why does one kill the other and make everything that was so real nothing but an empty mockery?

For hours I lay listening to the breathing of the elm leaves in the rain.

Slowly, the clouding numbness left me. Work to be done. Work to be done. That's why I came to college.

Stupid *yok!* Always wasting yourself with wild loves. I'll put a stop to it. I'll freeze myself like ice. I'll be colder than the coldest. I'm alone. I'm alone.

Little by little, I began to get hold of myself. If I lost out with those spick-and-span youngsters like

Mr. Edman, I won with the older and wiser professors. After a while, I understood why the young men
didn't like me. I knew more of life as a ten-year-old
girl, running the streets, than these psychology
instructors did with all their heads swelled from too
much knowing.

With the older men I could walk and talk as a person. To them, my Hester Street world was a new
world. I gave them mine, and they gave me theirs.
What could such raw youth as Mr. Edman know of that
ripened understanding that older men could give!

As time went on, I found myself smiling at the terrible pain and suffering that my crush for Mr. Edman
had cost me. That affair, like the one with Morris
Lipkin—all foolish madness which, though it nearly
killed me, made me grow faster in reason than if I had
no such madness in me.

Each time, after making a crazy fool of myself over
a man, I was plunged into thick darkness that seemed
the end of everything, but it really led me out into the
beginnings of wider places, newer light.

Gradually, I grew up even to be friends with the
dean. His house was always open to me. Once, while
we were chatting in his library, I asked him suddenly,
"Why is it that when a nobody wants to get to be somebody she's got to make herself terribly hard, when
people like you who are born high up can keep all
their kind feelings and get along so naturally well
with everybody?"

He looked at me with the steady gaze of his understanding eyes.

"All pioneers have to get hard to survive," he said. He pointed to a faded oil painting of his grandmother. "Look! My grandmother came to the wilderness in an ox cart and with a gun on her lap. She had to chop down trees to build a shelter for herself and her children. I'm more than a little ashamed to realize if I had to contend with the wilderness I'd perish with the unfit. But you, child—your place is with the pioneers. And you're going to survive."

After that I could not go back to my little room. For hours I walked. I needed the high stars and the deep stillness of the night to hold my exaltation.

* * *

The senior year came, and with it a great event. The biggest newspaper owner of the town, who was a rich alumnus of the college, offered a prize of a thousand dollars for the best essay on "What the College Has Done for Me." Everybody was talking about it, students, instructors, and professors.

What had the college done for me? I thought of the time when I first came here. How I was thrilled out of my senses by the mere sight of plain, clean people. The smashed hurdle in the gymnasium. The way I dashed into the bursar's office demanding money for my failed geometry. Yes. Perhaps more than all the others, I had something to write about. Maybe they wouldn't understand. But if truth was what they wanted—here they had it. I poured it out as it came from my heart, and sent it in. Then I had to put it out of my mind because I was so buried deep in my examinations. Everything was forgotten in this last fight to win my diploma.

It was Commencement Day at last. Glad but downhearted I was—glad because I'd won, but so sad I was to leave the battlefield! The thing I had dreamed about for so many years—and now it was over! Where I was going now, will I be able to find these real American people again—that draw me so?

With all the students and professors, I sat in the big assembly room and listened to the long speeches that seemed never to end.

At last a man came up to announce the winner of the contest. "The student," he said, "whose essay the judges found the best is a young lady. Her name is——" God in the world! Who? Who was it? They were clapping to beat the band. I only heard him say, "Will she please come forward to the platform?"

I heard clapping louder and louder. Then I saw they were all looking at me. "Sara Smolinsky, it's you. It's you! Don't you hear? They're calling for you."

How my paralyzed feet ever got me to the platform, I don't know. So exciting it was! It was I, myself, standing there before that sea of faces!

The man handed me an envelope and said things

that flew over my head. How could I have the sense to hear or think to say something?

Then all the students rose to their feet, cheering and waving and calling my name, like a triumph, "Sara Smolinsky—Sara Smolinsky!"

BOOK III

The New World

Chapter XVII

MY HONEYMOON
WITH MYSELF

Home! Back to New York! Sara Smolinsky, from Hester Street, changed into a person!

Kid gloves were on my hands. All my things were neatly packed in a brand-new leather satchel. Who would believe, as I took my seat with the quiet still-ness of a college lady, how I was burning up with excited pride in myself. I was like a person who had climbed to the top of a high mountain and was still breathless with his climb. If only I could have taken out my diploma and held it over my head for all to see! I was a college graduate! I was about to become a teacher of the schools!

For the first time in my life, I knew the luxury of travelling in a Pullman. I even had my dinner in the dining car. How grand it felt to lean back in my chair, a person among people, and order anything I wanted from the menu. No more herring and pickle over dry bread, I ordered chops and spinach and salad. As I spread out my white, ironed napkin on my lap, I thought of the time only four years before, when I pinched pieces out of the loaf, and wiped my mouth with a cor-ner of a newspaper and threw it under the seat.

What a wonderful experience, to go to bed in a sleeping car behind those damask curtains! As I stretched myself out comfortably, between those silken soft linen sheets, my flesh relaxed so deliciously, it was a sin to fall asleep. For a time, I lay there luxuriously listening to the rhythm of the revolving wheels of the train. When I finally drowsed away, it was to live over again in dreams that last triumphant day at college. When I awoke, my ears were still ringing with the cheering and applauding and the chorus of voices calling my name.

The next day, in New York, I walked, for the first time in my life, on Fifth Avenue, devouring with my eyes the wonderful shop windows.

My hand was in my coat pocket, clutching a check book of a thousand dollars to my account. . . . I could buy anything now. Anything. I could begin my career as a teacher as well dressed as any of them. The dark night of poverty was over. I had fought my way up into the sunshine of plenty.

Shop after shop I passed. But I didn't have to buy the first thing in sight. I could choose now what I wanted. Oh, that pink ball gown! Grand! But not for me. Furs? That's too rich yet. A pearl necklace? Maybe for born ladies. I must be plain as I am without ornaments. Here's the Sport Shop— that's where the college girls get their college clothes. How I had dreamed of them and despaired of ever having them. What fine suits in that window. There! There! That graceful quietness. That's what a teacher ought to wear.

How cool my voice, how quiet my manner, as I walked through the huge doors and went up the elevator, and then to the department where suits were sold.

"I want a suit like this," I indicated to the saleslady. "Show me the best."

For the first time in my life I asked for the best, not the cheapest.

A smiling saleswoman handed me a chair. "Will madam be seated?" Then she showed me several suits from the rack and called for a model. One after another, the model put on these quality clothes, walking up and down before me, to show them back and front. The head of the department herself, as well as the saleslady and the model, stood before me, awaiting my pleasure.

I considered a blue suit, a gray, a brown. Finally, I decided on a dark blue. Plain serge only! Yes. But more style in its plainness than the richest velvet. I tried it on in a beautiful fitting room lined with mirrors. From all angles I could see myself. It was all I could do to hold myself in and not shout out my joy before the saleslady. She saw, even before I did, that there was a slight wrinkle in the shoulder of the jacket, and called for the fitter to make it just right on me. There seemed no pains too great to please me.

"Thank you, madam," the saleslady took down my address. "It will be sent you by special delivery."

I went on to the millinery department and bought a hat to match my new suit. Then I rode up to another floor, and chose shoes, stockings, new underwear, gloves, and fine handkerchiefs.

When my things came, I tried them on again before the big mirror in my hotel room—hat, coat, shoes, the whole outfit, even the new handkerchief. For the first time in my life I was perfect from head to foot. Now I laughed aloud in my pleasure. There was no saleslady around before whom I had to act as though I were used to it always. No prima donna dressed up for the opera ever felt grander than I, ready to be a teacher in the schools.

Now for a place to live.

How different was my search for a room now than a few years ago. It was merely a matter of going to a real-estate office. A polite agent greeted me with business-like courtesy. I told him the kind of a room I wanted and the amount I could afford to pay. He handed me a list of addresses. And in about an hour I had selected a sunny, airy room, the kind of a room I had always wanted. Dealing with an agent was as different from the tyranny of landladies, with their personal questions, as bargaining for my things at a pushcart was different from choosing them at a department store.

I furnished my room very simply. A table, a bed, a bureau, a few comfortable chairs. No carpet on the floor. No pictures on the wall. Nothing but a clean, airy emptiness. But when I thought of the

money=power

crowded dirt from where I came, this simplicity was rich and fragrant with unutterable beauty.

I sat down in my easy chair and let the quiet and the sunshine flow over me. A triumphant sense of power filled me. Life was all before me because my work was before me. I, Sara Smolinsky, had done what I had set out to do. I was now a teacher in the public schools. And this was but the first step in the ladder of my new life. I was only at the beginning of things. The world outside was so big and vast. Now I'll have the leisure and the quiet to go on and on, higher and higher.

Once I had been elated at the thought that a man had wanted me. How much more thrilling to feel that I had made my work wanted! This was the honeymoon of my career!

I celebrated it alone with myself. I celebrated it in my room, my first clean, empty room. In the morning, in the evening, when I sat down to meals, I enjoyed myself as with grandest company. I loved the bright dishes from which I ate. I loved the shining pots and pans in which I cooked my food. I loved the broom with which I swept the floor, the scrubbing brush, the scrubbing rag, the dust cloth. The routine with which I kept clean my precious privacy, my beautiful aloneness, was all sacred to me. I had achieved that marvellous thing, "a place for everything and everything in its place," which the teacher preached to me so hopelessly while a child in Hester Street.

Chapter XVIII

DEATH IN HESTER STREET

As I got ready to make my first visit home, I began to wonder what had happened to Father, Mother, and sisters in those six years that I was away. Would I find them changed? Would they understand that my silent aloofness for so long had been a necessity and not selfish indifference?

Till now I had no time to be human or enjoy sociability with people. Now I felt like a prisoner just out from a long confinement in prison. Love ached in me more than if I had been with them all the time. It was like a secret wound that I had kept covered for six years. And now that I bared it, it hurt.

How I longed to share with them everything that was mine! I had no great riches to bring them. But this beautiful, clean emptiness I had created for myself, this I longed to share with them.

I looked on the address of the last letter and searched for the number of the house. They had moved back to Hester Street, though on a different block. Father could never be happy unless he prayed in the same old synagogue, and Mother could never feel at home outside the block where we had grown in so many years.

The door of the flat was ajar. Hearing Mother's and Father's voices, I was panic-stricken at the thought of facing them, and I hid behind the door.

"Stay with me, *Moisheh*," came pleadingly from Mother.

"Woman! You want me to be late to the synagogue?"

"But see how sick I am. How can you leave me?"

"I never yet missed my prayers in my life."

"I'm afraid to be alone," Mother moaned. "I'm so helpless."

"Well, what can I do? I'm no doctor. But if I run quicker to pray, God will at once hear me, and send you a cure."

"Woe is me! Can't you see my days are counted?"

"I'll call the widow Mrs. Feinstein, she'll stay with you——"

"Her! That barrel of fat! I can't stand her near me. She's only waiting for my death so you could be her boarder——"

"Woman! Why are you keeping me? I'll be late on account of you. I can help you more by running to the synagogue to pray than staying with you." And off he rushed.

As I saw Father stamping away, the old, dominating energy still pounding in each step, I crept out from behind the door. Through the cracked mirror opposite Mother's bed, I caught a glimpse of her gray, wasted face. What a change! Almost beyond recognition. Pain and suffering on all her features. Only the shadow, the semblance of herself was there. I wanted to cry out, but tears of horror froze me. I thought of the time when I told her I must leave home and she begged me not to leave her. I remembered that freezing winter night when she came to me all the way from Elizabeth with a feather bed. She begged me then to come and see her, and I had answered her, "I have no time. I can come to see you later, but I can't study later." And now that I took the time to come, to find her so sick, so helpless!

"Mother!" I cried, falling on her neck.

"Sara!" She sat up, lifted my face in her bony hands. "You? You here? I was just dreaming of you. Every day I saw you in my dreams I knew you were coming."

selfless mother

I could only pat her precious hand, trying to gulp back my tears.

"How beautiful you look!" She touched the sleeve of my coat. "New clothes. You shine like a princess. I feel like Father Jacob after seeing his son Joseph, who he thought was dead."

Tears fell from her faded eyes as she gazed hungrily at me. "Why did you stay away so long? Where was your heart? All those years!"

"Mother! Don't excite yourself. Now I'll come to you often."

"Now—now? Don't you see it's my end?"

Weakness dragged my knees to the ground. O God! What can I do to atone? my heart cried.

"Are you already a finished *teacherin?*"

I nodded.

"I'm so glad I lived to hear it. If I were only not so far gone, this would make me live longer. But now, my strength is going out. Nothing can make me well any more."

"You will get well. You must get well. I shall look after you from now on."

I unwrapped a new purse and took out five brand-new twenty-dollar gold pieces, and displayed them to Mother. "From now on, your fight with the pennies is over. I'm a teacher of the schools with an all-year salary from the Government."

She smiled, but her eyes were so sorrowful above her smile.

"I'll stay with you every day, when I'm through school. Tell me only anything I can do for you."

"Be good to Father," she begged. "I'm leaving him in his old age when he needs me most. Helpless as a child he is. No one understands his holiness as I. Only promise me that you'll take good care of him, and I can close my eyes in peace."

"You have yet many years to live. I'll get the best doctors."

She shook her head. Then, moaning, uncovered the bandage of her foot. "Oh, *weh!* The pain! I don't get better. It only gets worse."

My eyes shut with horror. My God! Her toes

eaten with decay and gangrene spreading. I couldn't speak. I could only feel the anguish of her flesh rending me more terribly than if I could actually take upon myself her pain.

"If you'll promise me to take good care of Father, I'll pray in the next world God should send you good luck. You'll yet get a better husband than all your sisters."

While she was yet talking Fania came in, as stylish as ever, a huge bunch of red roses in her hand. She threw down the roses on Mother's bed and rushed over to me, in excited surprise. "Well, well! Of all people! Why were you hiding yourself so long? Was that what they taught you in college, to turn your back on your own people?"

"Sh-sh-sh!" admonished Mother. "Thank God she came now. Don't spoil my little joy in my last hours." Her thin fingers twined into mine. "Praise be to God! I lived to see my daughter a *teacherin*." Fania picked up the roses and held them up to Mother. "Smell them only! Aren't they beautiful?"

"What do I need flowers yet!" she sighed, pushing them away. "There'll soon be flowers growing on my grave. When I was well, I liked flowers and I never got any. Now I'm so sick it hurts me to look on them."

I gathered the roses up in my arms, and as I turned to take them to the kitchen, Mashah and Bessie came in.

"From where did you drop down? From Heaven?" they cried, embracing me.

How changed they were. Six years of poverty had pinched Mashah the beautiful into a ragged *yenteh*. And Bessie was grayer and drabber than ever before.

We looked at one another, our hearts wrecked with helplessness. "Good God! What has happened to Mother!" we flashed to one another in dumb silence. I would have broken down the next minute, but Bessie winked at me not to let go. She hid her own tear-filled eyes, bending down to smooth Mother's bed.

"*Nu?* What do you think of our new-found stylish lady?" Bessie forced a gay tone into her voice as she turned to Mother.

"Some style!" laughed Fania. "Like a regular old maid. Any one can see a mile off Sara's a school teacher." *Uno.*

But Mother chanted gratefully: "God be praised I lived to see my daughter a *teacherin*."

We sat around talking of old times, laughing with a gaiety that we did not feel in an effort to cheer Mother. But over the chatter of our voices, I suddenly heard Father's heavy footsteps, ascending the stairs.

"You—you here?" Father grew red with anger at sight of me. "So many years you left your mother. Aren't you ashamed for your heartlessness?"

"Leave the girl alone," Mother defended. "A lot you care for me. You get your meals upstairs by that fat widow Feinstein." meals and other things too.

"I have to eat and she's kind enough to cook for me."

"She's kind, is she?" Mother jerked to one side in the bed in a flare of wrath. "Wait! You'll see after I'm gone what a false thing she is."

"Mother! Don't excite yourself," I begged. But she wouldn't listen. She sat up with an effort and poured out a fury of smouldering jealousy at Father.

"I see you're already trimming your beard for your new wife. You're only waiting for me to close my eyes. You're only waiting for my lodge money to give it to that heartless thing. A fine wife she'll make you! Wait! You'll see the difference. Go—go—go—to her."

She dropped back in the bed, exhausted.

Then Father came over to her, shaking his head tenderly, and laid his hand over her forehead and smoothed her hair. "Woman! Woman! What do you want from me?"

The touch of his hand was like magic. Her whole face softened. A beautiful look came into her eyes as she gazed at Father, undying worship in her face.

"*Moisheh!*" she whispered. "Our Sara is already a *teacherin* in the schools."

"A lot I have from it. She's only good to the world, not to her father. Will she hand me her wages from school as a dutiful daughter should?"

The doctor came in. He sat down at the bed and was putting the thermometer in Mother's mouth when Father shook his arm anxiously.

"*Nu*, Doctor? What do you think?"

A grave look was the doctor's only reply.

"Doctor! Save me my wife!" Father implored. "Since she's sick my house is in ruin. I have to go for a drop of soup to a neighbour. No one looks after me. It says in the Torah, a man who loses his wife is like a man who has lived through the destruction of the temple."

"You've got to get well." The doctor gently tapped Mother's shoulder. "You see how your husband needs you."

"Doctor! You've already met my older daughters." Father proudly pointed to my sisters. "This daughter's husband is in the fish business. This one married the biggest cloaks-and-suits manufacturer in America. This one, a dealer in diamonds. I married them all off myself. And this, my youngest, is a *teacherin*. She has a head on her. Takes after her father, even though she's only a girl."

The doctor glanced at Father, knowingly, and smiled at me, while Father went on innocently singing his own praises. "*Nu*, Doctor! Where do you find a poor father letting his daughter go to college? It cost me enough, her education, all those years of wages that I lost."

On his way out, the doctor called Fania and me aside, to tell us that there was danger of blood-poison setting in, and that Mother's foot must be amputated immediately. It grew black before my eyes. Fania and I stared at each other, unable to grasp the hopelessness of the situation. Only despair nerved me with the courage to speak.

"Mother!" I began. "The doctor said you're getting better. But to get real well, he advises an operation in the hospital."

She shot a look of terror at me. "Hospital! To be cut up? No. Never. If I got to die, I'll die at home."

She stopped and tightened her lips as the widow Mrs. Feinstein entered. "*Nu,* how are you feeling, Mrs. Smolinsky?" the widow asked, with an ingratiating smile.

"The doctor said I'm much better," said Mother, with spiteful hardness in her voice. "I'll soon be well and out of bed."

"I only hope the doctor tells you the truth. Anyhow, if you'll get better, I'll teach you how to make *lokshen kugel* for your husband the way I make it. You ought to see how he licked his fingers from every bite."

"My poor husband! He must have been starved if he could eat your *kugel.*"

We motioned to the widow to leave the room, as she was only exciting Mother.

That same afternoon we got a day- and a night-nurse. For a few days the constant care seemed to make her better. We began to think maybe the doctor was mistaken. Maybe an operation was not necessary.

One day I had left Mother in a fairly hopeful condition, but by the time I came back from school, a change had set in.

Propped on pillows, she sat in bed, my sisters around her, weeping. Was that gray, ghastly face Mother's? Only the eyes that gazed at me seemed alive. What sorrowful eyes! What unutterable sadness looked out from their silent depths! What worlds of pain lay dumb in that helpless gaze! Two tears rolled slowly down her cheeks as she looked at me. The eyes seemed agonized with longing to speak, but only tears came.

My God! She's dying. Mother is dying! I tried to think, to make myself realize that Mother, with all this dumb sorrow gazing at me, was passing, passing away, for ever. But above the dull pain that pressed on my heart, thinking was impossible. I felt I was in the clutch of some unreal dream from which I was trying to waken. Tiny fragments of memory rushed through my mind. I remembered with what wild abandon Mother had danced the *kozatzkeh* at a neighbour's wedding. With what passion she had bargained at the pushcart over a penny.... How her face lit up whenever company came! How her eyes sparkled with friendliness as she served the glasses of tea, spread everything we had on the table, to show her hospitality. A new pair of stockings, a clean apron, a mere car ride, was an event in her life that filled her with sunshine for the whole day.

... God! God! She's dying. No. No. Is there a God

over us and sees her suffer so?... She had seized me by the hand. She had begged me to come and see her. And I had answered her, "I can come to see you later, but I can't go to college later...."

"Mamma—mamma!" I sobbed.

Suddenly the sorrowful eyes became transfigured with light. Her lips moved. I could not get the words, but the love-light of Mother's eyes flowed into mine. I felt literally Mother's soul enter my soul like a miracle. Than all became dark. Blackness drowned me.

When I came back to my senses, the house was crowded. I found myself on the lounge, Bessie putting cold towels over my head. Mashah and Fania were tearing their hair and shrieking hysterically, "Mamma—Mamma!" For the first time in my life I saw Father weeping, like a lost child. Never before did I see him suffer. How strange he looked! His old veined hand holding a red kerchief, hiding his face, his gray beard trembling, his whole body bent and shaken with sobs. For the first time I realized that he was old and that he was without Mother. Rushing over to him I flung my arms around his neck, and wept with him. he's weak.

People coming and going. Wailing and screaming. Tumult and confusion. I saw Mother laid out in her coffin. The eyes that but a few hours before filled me with light, those eyes were tightly shut, sunken deep in their sockets. The nose drawn in, bluish pallor staining the nostrils. Lower jaw dropped, revealing stubs of decayed teeth. Ears yellow as wax. This was death. This was not Mother. I stared and stared, and I felt myself turning to ice, staring.

I touched the sunken lids where they eyes had shone on me with such ineffable love. My hand withdrew, shuddering. Cold, icy Death. Mother no more.

Where? Where has it gone, that light, that spark, that love that looked into mine? What has it to do with that cold clay? It's here, here, here in my heart. She's in me, around me. Not in that clay.

I felt a hand under my arm leading me away into the kitchen. In one heart-breaking monotone Father wailed:

"Woe! Woe! My house has fallen! My burden bearer gone! Who'll take care of me now? Who'll cook me my meals? Who'll wash me my clothes? Who'll light me my Sabbath candles? For forty years I protected you, watched over you, prayed for you. Now you're torn away from me. Be a good messenger to God for me. Beg him not to forsake me. Not leave me in loneliness. O God! God! Help me in my woe! Give me strength to stand my loss." So selfish!

As Father crumpled into a heap, spent with grief, the widow Mrs. Feinstein began to howl at the top of her voice, wringing her hands and rocking herself over the coffin. "My best friend! My neighbour! Forgive me if I talked evil of you. I take it all back.

Handwritten annotation: Why does all anyone care about whether or not they'll get into heaven when mother is the one who died?

I didn't mean nothing. Who would know that you
would die so soon? Forgive me. Be a good messenger
to God for me. Pray in Heaven for me. Beg God to be
merciful to me and spare me all ills."

Other neighbours came in screaming, tearing
their hair, and beating their breasts. Falling on the
coffin and begging the dead body to forgive their evil
talk during her lifetime. Begging the corpse to be a
messenger in Heaven for them, to beg God to spare
them all ills.

The room became crowded with all kinds of old
and middle-aged men and women. Some moaning
with grief, others with stony, serious faces. In the eyes
of the old, fear of their own end.

A chorus of wailing neighbours gathered about
the body, rocking and swaying and wringing their
hands in woe.

"Such a good mother, such a virtuous wife,"
wailed a shawled woman with a nursing baby in her
arms and two little tots hanging to her skirts. "Never
did she allow herself a bite to eat but left-overs, never
a dress but the rags her daughters had thrown away."

"Such a cook! Such a housewife!" groaned a white-
haired old woman wiping her eyes with a corner of
her shawl. "Only two days ago she told me how they
cook the fish in her village sweet and sour—and now,
she is dead."

At this, all the women began rocking and swaying
in a wailing chorus.

"Only a week ago she was telling me she was getting better," began the widow Mrs. Feinstein. "But I saw it was her end."

"Yesterday morning, she was telling me if she'll only get well, she'll stop worrying and take it easy. And now . . ."

Floods of tears were shed by these strangers, but my eyes were dry. My heart was numb. My mind became a petrified blank. Suddenly I heard the undertaker, cold and unconcerned, announce:

"Members of the family take your last look!"

We filed around the coffin, frozen with grief.

The lid shut down. A shriek from the whole crowded room burst through the air as the undertaker ground the screws into the coffin. "Never shall we see her face again. Never, never!" it echoed and re-echoed. "Never shall we see her face again. Never."

The undertaker, with a knife in his hand, cut into Father's coat and he rent his garments according to the Biblical law and ages of tradition. Then he slit my sisters' waists, and they, too, did as Father had done. Then the man turned to me with the knife in his hand. "No," I cried. "I feel terrible enough without tearing my clothes."

"It has to be done."

"I don't believe this. It's my only suit, and I need it for work. Tearing it wouldn't bring Mother back to life again."

A hundred eyes burned on me their condemnation.

"Look at her, the *Americanerin!*"

"Heart of stone."

"A lot she cares for her mother's death."

"Not a tear did she shed. Her face is washed. Her hair is combed. Did we care how we looked when our mothers died?"

Four shabby-looking, frail, ill-fed poor men lifted the coffin on their shoulders. People pushed back on both sides to make room for the men to pass. Louder shrieks burst through the air again as the coffin was borne out of the house, through the crowded hall, and down the crowded stoop. Passers-by joined in the hysterical shrieks. They didn't know who died, but were drawn in by the common grief of death.

The coffin was pushed into the hearse. The door shut with a bang.

We stood jammed in by neighbours, waiting for the carriage to take us to the cemetery. All I saw were mobs and mobs of strangers staring at us. And all I heard was the clanking of coins in tin boxes, and insistent begging voices, exhorting the people, "Charity saves you from death! Charity saves you from death!"

Chapter XIX

LODGE MONEY

I had failed to give Mother the understanding of her deeper self during her lifetime. Let me at least give it to Father while he was yet alive. And so, every day, after school, I went to see him.

He did not look so forlorn as I thought he would. He looked like one who had straightened out his back after the strain of a long, heavy burden. Perhaps he was glad that Mother's sufferings were over. Then I noticed he began wearing his Sabbath clothes for every day. He began to polish his shoes and comb his beard like for a holiday. Once I found him gazing at himself in the mirror and smiling with an innocent joyfulness that made me wonder how he could be so childishly happy when Mother was dead. He still ate his meals upstairs at Mrs. Feinstein's. But before, he used to eat there only his suppers. Now, he ate there three times a day.

Often I wanted to ask him if he was getting his food cooked just right, but I hated to speak of that widow. The mere thought of that woman filled me with a blind dislike that I couldn't reason about.

One day, I came and found her sewing a button on

Father's shirt. After a hasty greeting she walked out.
She must have known how I felt toward her.

As the door closed behind her, Father exclaimed,
"What a womanly woman! What a virtuous soul! All
she thinks of is how to cook for me things I like and
how to please me the most. The more I see her, the
more I feel what a diamond treasure she is. How she
could make a man happy!"

I stared at Father. What had happened to him!
Was he bereft of his senses? That such a spiritual man
could find anything in that bold-faced barrel of fat!

"In my misfortune, God yet sent me a great good
luck," Father went on. "She's so kind, so nice to me.
God punished with one hand and blessed me with the
other."

I looked at Father's guileless face and longed to
shake him out of his blind foolishness, tell him about
the world, about scheming women. But I was too angry
to speak. My lips tightened, struggling to control
myself.

"You ought to taste her *kugel*, her *gefülte* fish! Her
cooking puts a new taste in life. And she's so quick
and handy. Her table is set with a clean tablecloth for
every day. And the knives and forks and even a paper
napkin is all laid out, waiting for me, when I come.
Every time I see her, her face is washed, her hair is
combed and a clean apron. Always there's a smile on
her face. The sun shines from her. I can see she's a
woman who don't curse like other women."

I shuddered, as he went on, exulting in that woman's virtues. After Mother's devotion, how could he turn to such a creature? The thought of her sitting in Mother's chair, occupying Mother's bed, revolted me.

A few days after, when I called, I noticed Father avoided my eyes. He walked up and down, awkward and uncomfortable, as if he had something on his mind that bothered him. Suddenly, he stopped pacing the floor, brought his chair in front of me, and sat down.

"I have something to tell you," he began. "You understand a little more than your sisters, because you have a little bit of my head on you."

He paused and again avoided my eyes. I felt something terrible coming. I waited, my heart pounding in my throat.

"You know I can't remain alone. And I can't live with any of you children, because none of you are religious enough. I have to have my own house and someone to take care of me. It says in the Torah, a man must have a wife to keep himself pure, otherwise his eyes are tempted by evil. It says no man needs to wait more than thirty days after his wife's death to marry again. And I couldn't find a better woman than Mrs. Feinstein."

The room began to rock. Everything whirled before me in a blur.

Thirty days! Mother not yet cold in her grave. And he already planning for a new wife!

"Father! That woman! Her thick lips—her fat cheeks—and you!"

"Would you want me better to marry a consumptive?"

I felt as if my heart were torn in pieces. I wanted to scream, but my voice stopped inside of me.

Now I understood why Father began to wear his Sabbath clothes for every day. Why he polished his shoes, why he had smiled to himself so happily in the mirror.

I had thought that Mother was talking out of pain and fever when she called him "the young bridegroom," and accused him of trimming his beard for his new wife. She had seen it all before her death.

"Father!" I implored. "Save yourself from doing this terrible thing. You know nothing about women if you can be taken in by her. Can't you see she's only after your lodge money?"

"I've seen enough in my life to a judge of people," cried Father angrily. "I know what I'm doing."

I seized his hand in mine. "There's yet time," I entreated. "At least, won't you think it over?"

"I've done all my thinking already. I married her yesterday."

"Married! Father! You married!" The words clawed themselves out of my heart. This man who thirty days ago had torn his clothes over Mother's coffin, this man telling me he's married! It was too much to bear. I could not breathe in the room where he was. Blindly, I rushed out.

How I ever found my way to Bessie, I don't know. But when I reached her home, my sisters were all there.

"What is it? Your face is ashes!" Bessie cried.

"*Mazel-tof!* Rejoice!" I dropped into a chair, weeping wildly. "*Mazel-tof! Mazel-tof!*"

"In God's name! What is the matter with you? What do you mean?"

"Rejoice! Father is married!"

"Married!" they screamed. "*Mashugeneh!* Are you out of your head?"

"Yesterday—he led her to the canopy."

In horrified silence we stared at one another. Worse than the shock of Mother's death was the shock of this sacrilege.

Suddenly Bessie gave a loud cry, "*Mammeh! Mammeniu!*" And she tore her hair and beat her head against the wall.

The room grew full of wailing.

"*Mammeh!* You're better off in the grave!"

"Forty years Mother lived with him, cooked for him——"

"Never will I see his face again."

"A bad father he was to us——"

"Mother's memory he dishonours so soon."

"That woman will fatten now on Mother's death."

We went on beating the air, weeping with shame and anguish. What good were all our tears? The shameful marriage had already happened.

For several months none of us would go near

Father. Neighbours told us from time to time that he was shining like a tree in spring. He was getting younger and happier every day, like a bridegroom on a honeymoon.

One day, as I stepped out of the classroom, a dirty-faced boy in the passageway handed me a letter. It was written in that flourishing hand that I recognized as the public letter-writer's. It was from Father's wife, too ignorant to sign her name. It said:

> Daughter
>   There's trouble in your father's house. Drop everything and hurry up, come at once. Remember, right away we need you.
>   Mrs. Smolinsky.

I shuddered. "Daughter!" That creature daring to call me daughter, daring to fling at me the name that had been my mother's, "Mrs. Smolinsky!" And yet, if Father was in trouble, I had to go.

Shining in a new silk waist, she opened the door. Her fat bosom bulged like a pillow under her heavy double chins. She led me to the front room and pointed to a red velvet morris chair for me to sit down. The flat, with its new gaudy furniture, new red carpet, hit me like an insult. I thought of the broken rags of things with which Mother had to keep house. I thought of those freezing winter mornings when Mother had to get up before everybody, and shake out the ashes from a cold grate, and with freezing fingers start up the coal fire, if we were lucky enough to have coal. And this woman living in a steam-heated flat with all the comforts of the world—bought with Mother's death money.

Forcing down my indignation, I asked, "What's the trouble?"

"There's trouble enough," she burst out, indignantly. "Your father don't earn a cent. He gives me nothing to live on. There's not a penny in the house since yesterday. What will become of us? How is the old man going to get along if you children have deserted him?"

"Where's all Father's lodge money?"

"What about this furniture? I had to fix up a new house, and it all cost money." She began to weep hysterically. "You think your father married a poor servant girl? I was a princess by my first husband. I had servants nicer than some school teachers. And the fancy clothes my first husband used to buy me! When I walked out, I shined up the block with my style. Everybody turned their necks to give a look on me. What did your father buy me outside of a fur coat and this diamond cluster ring? He promised me earrings and everything, and give a look only on my empty ears."

Dumb with disgust, I glanced at her huge ears. An overdressed, overfed cow. And she Father's wife. As she sat down, the buttons burst open from the bulging bosom of her waist. Pink ribbons peeped out from a new corset cover. Silk stockings, new shoes. All Mother's death money on her back. And she demanding more, like a leech.

"Do you mean to say you've spent all the lodge money in this short time?"

"What?" she shrieked. "Accounts I should give you? What was your poor father, a millionaire? He had a few rotten dollars, and it's long spent already."

Oh, my poor mother! If but one day in her lifetime she would have had half the things this woman owned now, how happy she would have been!

"He told me that all his children would put enough money together to keep him in comfort," the woman went on. "And on that, I got married. I could have picked myself out a younger man, but your father promised me such riches——"

In a fury, I jumped to my feet. "Father had money from four lodges. Enough to keep him a lifetime. If he were in need and alone we would have supported him. But we can't keep two people."

I rushed for the door, but she clutched my arm and held me back. "You mean you'll not support your old father?" she screamed. "I married to better myself. I'm not his servant to wait on him for nothing. If you and your sisters won't support him, I'll tell the charities. I'll tell them by the board of education that you refuse to support your old father."

"Go ahead. Do your worst. We'd pay Father's board if he lived alone. But we'll not keep two people in luxury."

"The heartlessness of his children! Talking luxury, when he don't give me enough for bread——"

Father's entrance at that moment turned her rage from me toward him. "You want your dinner yet?" she shouted at him in her shrill voice. "This is your last meal unless you bring me money. Your children don't want to support you. So to the court I'll go and have you arrested for not bringing me in a living."

"*Zeresh!* Snake!" Father spat his contempt in her face. "I've just come from the lawyer. He told me no man over sixty can be arrested for not earning money for his wife. You're younger and healthier and they'll put you to work to support me. Thank God, some laws of America are yet made by men!"

At sight of me, Father's angry voice ceased. Like a child, he turned to me for sympathy. "Hear her only! The vulture! What does she want from me? I should go to work! I should bring her money!" HYPOCRIT .

The woman lifted a towel from the chair as if to throw it at Father, but her hand dropped and the towel fell to the floor. "Woe is me!" she sobbed into her apron. "All I ask of you is to be a man like other men. Pay the rent. Give me bread. Buy me a decent dress. I married to better myself."

Father turned his back on her and began to talk to me. "You see, Daughter, how I fell in with a dummox? Can I sit down to eat or look into a book? I've got to get rid of this curse on me."

"God is my witness, I don't want to fight with you," she wailed. "But it's coming a holiday all over the world. In a few more days will be New Year. I ask you only, as a man with God in his heart, with what can I show my face before the neighbours? When they'll see me, they'll only laugh: Huh! She married an old crazy—and such a beggar! She hasn't from him even a new dress for the holidays."

Sobs drowned her torrent of words. Bucketfuls of tears seemed to flow out of her eyes.

"What have I from my life since I married you? I'm ashamed to go among people. The first thing I go anywhere, they give a look on my empty ears. They got no respect for me because they see me with empty ears. The butcher's wife, even the rag-pickers, they all got diamond earrings."

"*Ishah Rah!* Should I steal or rob to bring you diamond earrings?"

"A good husband steals and robs even, only to give his wife what's coming to her. I'm a young woman yet. I want to live. I thought if I'd have a husband I'd have a man who'd be company and pleasure——"

"Servant! Cow!" he hissed, furiously. "I should be your company? Could you with your dumb head, your thick flesh, ever understand what's under the nail of my littlest finger?"

"Then why did you hurry so much to marry me?"

"I wanted someone to cook for me, to wash for me, to carry the burden of my house for me——"

"You wanted to warm up your old age with my youngness. And now I'm not worth to you the dirt under your feet——"

A loud knock interrupted the quarrel. A man came with a bill.

"There!" she cried, snatching the paper. "Already two weeks the groceries not paid——"

"Why not paid? You got enough yet in Lemanofsky's bank to start yourself a business."

"Do you make me for a liar and thief? I already have consumption. My heart is affected from your meanness——"

"I want my money," the man demanded. "What for are you wasting my time? You got so much for new furniture and carpet, why not first pay your grocery bill?"

She motioned to the man to follow her in the hall. Through the crack in the door I saw her fumble in her stocking, take out a bill from a thick wad, and hand it to the grocer.

But when she returned, she was weeping as loudly as ever. "You think I'll slave away my young years for you for nothing? You'll not drive me to an early grave as you did your first wife——"

"Thing of evil! Don't dare take that saint's name in your evil mouth. You're not worth to speak her name." He staggered to a chair and lifted his eyes in supplication. "God of the Universe! Have I not always done Your will? What sin have I committed here on earth? How could You have created such an *Ishah Rah* and send her on my head?"

What was there for me to do? Useless for me to interfere or try to make peace between them. Blind with tears I rushed from the room, down the stairs, straight to Bessie's house. When I told my sisters of the woman's demands that we support her they flared up in indignation.

"Support that woman?" cried Fania. "I'd sooner throw my money in the gutter."

"It would dishonour Mother's memory if we gave that leech a cent," declared Bessie.

"As you made your bed, so you got to sleep in it," quoted Mashah, with scorn. "That's what he used to tell us. Now let him have a taste of his own preaching."

But as I came back to my quiet, sunny room, my heart ached for Father. What was my duty? Was it to give my hard-earned school money to this woman healthy enough to go to work? If she married Father to have it easy was it not her own mistake?

I tried to still my conscience with reason. But my heart ached with the unceasing question, "What will become of Father if we abandon him to the mercy of that woman?"

Chapter XX

HUGO SEELIG

The windows of my classroom faced the same crowded street where seventeen years ago I started out my career selling herring. The same tenements with fire escapes full of pillows and feather beds. The same weazened, tawny-faced organ-grinder mechanically turning out songs that were all the music I knew of in my childhood. How intoxicating were those old tunes of the hurdy-gurdy! I'd leave my basket of herring in the middle of the sidewalk, forget all my cares, and leap into the dance with that wild abandon of the children of the poor.

But more even than the music of the hurdy-gurdy was the inspiring sight of the *teacherin* as she passed the street. How thrilled I felt if I could brush by Teacher's skirt and look up into her face as she passed me. If I was lucky enough to win a glance or a smile from that superior creature, how happy I felt for the rest of the day! I had it ingrained in me from my father, this exalted reverence for the teacher.

Now I was the teacher. Why didn't I feel as I had supposed this superior creature felt? Why had I not the wings to fly with? Where was the vision lost?

The goal was here. Why was I so silent, so empty?

All labour now—and so far from the light. I longed for the close, human touch of life again. My job was to teach—to feed hungry children. How could I give them milk when my own breasts were empty?

Maybe after all my puffing myself up that I was smarter, more self-sufficient than the rest of the world—wasn't Father right? He always preached, a woman alone couldn't enter Heaven. "It says in the Torah: *A woman without a man is less than nothing.* No life on earth, no hope of Heaven."

Not one of the teachers around me had kept the glamour. They were just peddling their little bit of education for a living, the same as any pushcart peddler.

But no. There was one in this school who was what I had dreamed a teacher to be—the principal, Mr. Hugo Seelig. He had kept that living thing, that flame, that I used to worship as a child. And yet he had none of the aloof dignity of a superior. He was just plain human. When he entered a classroom sunlight filled the place.

How had he created that big spirit around him? What a long way I had to go yet before I could become so wholly absorbed in my work as he. The youngest, dirtiest child in the lowest grade he treated with the same courtesy and serious attention as he gave to the head of the department.

One of Mr. Seelig's special hobbies was English pronunciation, and since I was new to the work, he would come in sometimes to see how I was getting on.

My children used to murder the language as I did when I was a child of Hester Street. And I wanted to give them that better speech that the teachers in college had tried to knock into me.

Sometimes my task seemed almost hopeless. There was Aby Zuker, the brightest eleven-year-old boy in my class of fifty. He had the neighbourhood habit of ending almost every sentence with "ain't it." For his special home work I had given him a sentence with the words "isn't it" to be written a hundred times.

The next morning he brought it back and with a shining face declared, "I got it all right now, Teacher! Ain't it?"

"Oh, Aby!" I cried. "And you want to be a lawyer! Don't you know the judges will laugh you out of court if you plead your case with 'ain't it'?"

Poor Aby! His little fingers scratched his mop of red curls in puzzlement. From his drooping figure I turned, laughing, to the class.

"Now, children, let's see how perfectly we can pronounce the words we went over yesterday."

On the board I wrote, S-I-N-G.

"Aby! Pronounce this word."

"Sing-gha," said Aby.

"Sing," I corrected.

"Sing-gha," came from Aby again.

"Rosy Stein! You can do better. Show our lawyer how to speak. Make a sentence with the word 'sing.'"

"The boids sing-gha."

"Rosy, say bird."

"Boid," repeated small Rosy with great distinctness. "Boid."

"Wrong still," I laughed. "Children, how do you pronounce this?" And I wrote hastily on the board, OIL.

"Earl," cried the class, triumphantly.

"You know how to make the right sounds for these words, but you put them in the opposite places." And I began to drill them in pronunciation. In the middle of the chorus, I heard a little chuckle. I turned to see Mr. Seelig himself, who had quietly entered the room and stood enjoying the performance. I returned his smile and went right on.

"You try it again, Rosy. The birds sing-gg."

"Sing," corrected Mr. Seelig, softly.

There it was. I was slipping back into the vernacular myself. In my embarrassment, I tried again and failed. He watched me as I blundered on. The next moment he was close beside me, the tips of his cool fingers on my throat. "Keep those muscles still until you have stopped. Now say it again," he commanded. And I turned pupil myself and pronounced the word correctly.

As he was leaving the room he turned to me with great gentleness and said, "When you dismiss the class, will you step into my office? I must see you."

The door closed. I tried to go on with the work, but my mind kept going round and round the one thought, "I'm going to see him at three. What has he to say to me? Was something wrong with my work? And yet he seemed pleased and so gentle."

His face. The features—all fineness and strength. The keen, kind gray eyes. A Jewish face, and yet none of the greedy eagerness of Hester Street any more. It was the face of a dreamer, set free in the new air of America. Not like Father with his eyes on the past, but a dreamer who had found his work among us of the East Side.

For the next hour I was more rattle-brained than my worst children. How could I come down to geography and spelling? I kept looking at the clock, counting the minutes to three.

The bell rang. Thank God! It was time to dismiss the class.

I took a quick look at myself in the mirror, powdered my face, straightened my hair, and hurried to Mr. Seelig's office.

The moment I stepped into the room I was brought to my senses by the cold, business-like atmosphere. Mr. Seelig rose from his chair. Gravely, without even a word of greeting, he handed me an opened letter. "Perhaps you had better read this." And this is what I read:

To the Mr. Principal, School for the Public.
I want you to know about Sara Smolinsky who let her own father starve and no rent. So he should be thrown in the street to shame and to laughter for the whole world. Is it not a disgrace for the schools from America that you have a *teacherin* learn-

ing the children who is such a mean stingy to her own blood? If you have the fear of God in your heart, you will yourself see that at least half her wages should go to her poor old father who is a smarter man as she is a *teacherin*—

Every drop of blood seemed to leave my heart. My first impulse was to cry out to him, "It's false! All false!" and pour out to him the whole story of my wretched life. But I simply stood there trembling like a guilty thing. How could I ever make clear to him my father?

The blackness upon me was like the last gasp of drowning. . . . It's the end. He despises me. He'll send me from his school.

Mr. Seelig must have seen how I stood crushed with shame. For when I looked up, his head was turned. He was busy reading papers on his desk, as if he had forgotten that I was there.

I fled the room. Did he call me? I thought he spoke my name. But I had no strength to turn and look at him.

My hate for Father, which Mother's death had softened, boiled up in me like poison. Never would I look at him or his wife again. A blackmailer—a blood-sucker—that's what she was! This disgrace which they had heaped on me was the bottom end. I wanted to tear the roots of my father out of my flesh and bones, force my heart and brain to blot him out of my soul. But through that night of suffering, even hate bled out of me. I was a ruined thing without purpose—without hope. I was no more.

The next day was lead. Mechanically, I dragged my feet to school. Mechanically, I went through the routine of the class work. But the children were so much dead wood in front of me. What I was saying to them, or what they were answering, made no difference. I was so tired, I saw nothing, heard nothing, and yet what was left of me was waiting for the worst to happen—condemned to lose my job—my life—condemned by him.

Three o'clock came. The blow had not yet fallen. To-day, at least, I could get back to my little place and hide myself from my shame. The children seemed to crawl out of the room instead of running as usual. Aby Zucker and Rosy Stein lingered with questions about their home work. It was as if they were trying to spite my misery.

At last they were all out. And yet I had no energy to move. I stood paralyzed, waiting. . . . Suddenly, my breath stopped! There! Mr. Seelig. I felt him come in and I couldn't look up. . . . Let him dismiss me. I was dead anyway. . . . After a moment, I dared lift my eyes. Why, he was smiling!

"I have a compliment for you. Mrs. Stein says that Rosy is a changed girl since she had been in your class."

I just couldn't speak. It was all I could do to meet his eyes. That dreadful letter! He seemed to have forgotten all about it. He was still my friend!

We walked out of the building together. At the

street corner he turned to me. "Do you take the L or car?" he asked.

"I usually walk home."

"So do I," he smiled. "I think we go in the same direction."

We fell into step and for many blocks not a word passed between us. I only felt an enveloping friendliness going out of his heart to mine. A sudden commotion! Wild shrieks jerked us out of ourselves to the street around us. A little boy who ran madly into the middle of the street for his rolling marble was caught in the crowding traffic. Mr. Seelig and I rushed over in one breath and dragged him almost from under the wheels of a racing truck.

Before we could get to the curb, a woman, weeping and laughing hysterically, snatched the child from us.

"Gazlin! Murderer! How you blacken me my days! she cried, shaking and cuffing him. *"Tatteniu!* Only to get rid of this devil once for all!" It was some moments before we could rescue the child from the animal fury of the mother.

And afterwards we became aware that we had gripped each other's hands fiercely. Something in what happened had drawn us suddenly together. We were too filled for small talk the rest of the way, and before we knew it we had reached Thirtieth Street and stood before my house.

"We've arrived. I think both of us deserve some tea after our exciting adventure."

I fairly ran in my joy and rushed to my room a

whole flight of stairs ahead of him to see that everything was in order. I snatched up the stockings and
wash I had drying on the radiator and threw them in
the basket.

All excitement, I opened the door and showed off
my room for the first time. My plain room that I loved,
how would it look to another? Anxiously, I watched
him as he looked slowly around. "How beautiful and
empty!" he cried.

I sighed with happiness. "Years ago, I vowed to
myself that if I could ever tear myself out of the dirt
I'd have only clean emptiness."

He nodded understandingly. How great it felt to
break my long loneliness and warm up my home with
another presence. I lit the lamp under the tea kettle
for the first time for two instead of one.

"I like your nice dishes," he said, as we sat down.

"Because I live alone, I must have my table beautiful. It's company."

We got to talking about ourselves, our families, the
Old World from which we came. To our surprise we
found that our beginnings were the same. We came from
the same government in Poland, from villages only a
few miles apart. Our families had uprooted themselves
from the same land and adventured to the New World.

For a moment we looked at each other, breathless
with the wonderful discovery. *"Landsleute*—country-
men!" we cried, in one voice, our hands reaching out
to each other.

"What do you remember of Poland?" he asked, in a low voice.

"Nothing—nothing at all. Back of me, it's like black night."

"I remember a little," he said. "The mud hut where we lived, the cows, the chickens, and all of us living in one room. I remember the dark, rainy morning we started on our journey, how the whole village, old and young, turned out to say good-bye. When we came to the seaport, I couldn't eat their bread, because it had no salt. We thought we should starve going to America. But as soon as we got on the ship, they gave us so much that first meal that we couldn't touch another bite for days."

After that, all differences dropped away. We talked one language. We had sprung from one soil.

"How strangely things work out," I said, with a new feeling of familiarity. "You got this blackmailing letter. And yet here we are born friends."

"Why shouldn't we be? You and I, we are of one blood."

We fell into silence. All the secret places of my heart opened at the moment. And then the whole story of my life poured itself out of me to him. Father, Mother, my sisters. And Father's wife, with her greed for diamond earrings. As I talked my whole dark past dropped away from me. Such a sense of release! Now I could go on and on—I could never again be lonely!

"I understood everything the moment I read that

letter," he said. "It's queer, how people get to know one another. That mean letter, instead of turning me against you, drew me to you. I knew you weren't that kind. As for your father, I know just the kind of an old Jew he is. After all, it's from him that you got the iron for the fight you had to make to be what you are now."

I looked at him in wide wonder. "What a mind-reader you are! You understand not only me but even my father whom you've never yet seen. He used to call me *'Blut-und-Eisen.'*"

And then I told him of the hard heart. How I had to cut out everything soft in my life only to survive.

He took hold of both my hands. "You hard! You've got the fibre of a strong, live spruce tree that grows in strength the more it's knocked about by the wind. When men go to sea they set the spruce for their mast."

We had lost all sense of time and it was dusk when he rose to go.

"Next time when we are together we must spend it outdoors," he said, "and try to remember more about Poland."

Next time! So there was going to be a next time, my heart rejoiced!

I stood looking at his chair feeling him still in the room for hours after, and my last feeling as I closed my eyes was: I'm no longer alone. I'm no longer alone!

In the early morning when I swept my broom halted at Hugo Seelig's muddy footprint. He leaped up at me out of that spot on the floor. I felt again his voice, I saw again his eyes as he looked at me. "You and I—we are of one blood."

Chapter XXI

MAN BORN OF WOMAN

One day, three months later, I walked out of school. It was a cold, drizzling rain, but my heart sang with the gladness of sunshine. That night Hugo was coming to have dinner with me.

Why were my years of lonely struggle unlit by the hope that I might some day be as happy as I was now? Why did I ever feel cheated and robbed of the life that more fortunate girls seemed to have? And here I had so much more than my heart could hold!

But as I walked along through Hester Street toward the Third Avenue L, my joy hurt like guilt. Lines upon lines of pushcart peddlers were crouching in the rain. Backs bent, hands in their sleeves, ears under their collars, grimy faces squeezed into frozen masks. They were like animals helpless against the cold, pitiless weather.

Wasn't there some way that I could divide my joy with these shivering pushcart peddlers, grubbing for pennies in the rain? I felt like Carnegie and Rockefeller trying to give away the millions they could not spend. Why was my happiness so hard to be enjoyed? I felt like one sitting down to a meal while all the people around him were howling hungry.

I felt as if all the beauty of the world that ever was ached in me to pour itself out on the people around. I felt like the sun so afire with life that it can't help but shine on the whole world—the just and the unjust alike.

A longing to see Father came over me. What had happened to him in all those months? I could stifle my conscience no longer. Wife or no wife, I had to see what I could do for him. Even his wife I could not hate any more. For after all, it was her blackmailing letter that had opened Hugo's eyes to me.

Poor woman! Poor people of Hester Street! With new pity I looked at them. I hurried on, but the verve of my winged walk was dulled by the thick, shuffling tread of those who walked beside me. My own shoulders, that I always held so straight, sagged because of the bowed backs that hemmed me in.

The sadness of it chilled the glow I usually felt when I got to my peaceful room. Hugo's red roses on my table—almost I could have wept for them. So full and rich with lovely colour, so heartlessly perfect, so shamelessly beautiful that it hurt to look at them. I didn't want them if they were only for me.

I leaned out of the open window and saw the city as it lay below me, sharp and black and grimy. The smoke of those houses kept rising sullenly, until I couldn't help but breathe the soot of that far-reaching tragedy below.

Ach! You—with your always guilty conscience! Why can't you be happy when you're lucky enough to have a little respite of happiness? Why do you have to make yourself so miserable because for the first time in your life you know a little bit of love? Fool! Get yourself dressed.

I threw off my dark school dress and put on my new challis. I turned to the mirror. How becoming was that soft green with that touch of rose embroidery. How well it suited my pale skin and dark hair that I learned to braid so becomingly around my head! I hope Hugo will like it.

The telephone rang. It was Hugo, telling me that he was held up by the Board of Education meeting and asking me to join him at Orloff's Café on East Broadway.

So happy I was in a moment. Forgotten were the sorrows of the world. How could I most quickly get to him? I ran to the car. But when I got off at Grand Street, I was blocked by the usual jam of evening traffic. I stood impatiently on the corner with a crowd of people, waiting for the policeman to stop the stream of trucks and taxis. As his whistle sounded and we rushed for the other side, I was shoved against an old man with a tray of chewing-gum. The sudden impact knocked his wares out of his hands. In spite of my excited haste to get to Hugo, I stopped to help the old man pick up the rolling packages. With my fresh handkerchief, I wiped the mud from each piece and dropped it back into his tray.

"Thank you, lady!"

At the sound of that voice, my heart leaped as though a red-hot knife had been thrust into it. The old man's face was half hidden in the collar of his shabby coat, his bony fingers trembled as he recovered his soiled stock. But I knew that face, those hands.

"Father! You—you—here?"

He fell back against the door and stared at me, the sorrows of the whole world in his tragic eyes.

"Well—well," he jerked out, his teeth clacking together with the cold. "Let the world see the shame—the shame that my daughters heaped on me. What's an old father to heartless American children? Have they any religion? Any fear of God? Do they know what it means, 'Honour thy father'? What else can I do to support myself and her? She drove me out to bring her in money."

"You let that woman boss you?" I burst out, furiously.

"Have I children like other people's children who carry their father like a crown on their heads? Have they provided for me as God-fearing children provide for an old father? With all I have done for my daughters—the morals I soaked into them, the religion I preached into them from the day they were born—yet they leave me in my old age, as they left King Lear—broken—forgotten ... God! What have I sinned, to come to this? I, Reb Smolinsky—down among the pushcarts. . . ."

How changed he was! How old and suffering! He, the master—with the stoop of poverty on his back! And I had been so happy!

He began to cough, shivering with the cold. "His days are counted," my heart cried. Who would nurse him and watch over him? That woman? Mother's dying eyes rose before me. Her last words, "Be good to Father. I leave him in his old age, when he needs me most. Helpless as a child he is." I looked at Father with Mother's eyes. I saw in him only the child who needed mothering—who must be protected from the hard cruelties of the world.

"Come," I said, fighting back the tears. "It's raining hard. Let's better go."

"Where? Where shall I go? In your house shall I go?"

"I'll take you home. I'll see that you get what you need."

I took his arm and led him away. He trembled against me as we trudged along. When I looked into his face, his eyes were half closed and his lips blue. He did not speak. He walked on, in silence, proud as ever.

At his door I stopped. All visions of doing things for him were checked by that door. That woman! How I dreaded facing her! But he needs me! To hell with my feelings. He needs me!

I opened the door with determination and walked in. Thank God! She was not around! I could help him. He sank back weakly in his chair, and he let me take off his wet shoes and the torn rags of stockings that clung to his old feet.

Supporting himself on me, he staggered to the bed. As I tucked the covers around him, I felt the shrunken bones where once the rounded flesh had been. How he had wasted since Mother had died! How neglected he looked! How helpless! He's like a poor orphan with a stepmother. I had hated him. But where was that hate now? Whom else had he in this world if not me? How could I leave him in his need?...

Tears strained in my throat as I bent over him, offering him some hot tea. But he pushed away the glass, muttering deliriously. In a panic, I left him and ran for the doctor.... How could I have hated him and tried to blot him out of my life? Can I hate my arm, my hand that is part of me? Can a tree hate the roots from which it sprang? Deeper than love, deeper than pity, is that oneness of the flesh that's in him and in me. Who gave me the fire, the passion, to push myself up from the dirt? If I grow, if I rise, if I ever amount to something, is it not his spirit burning in me?...

When I returned, the woman was there. She met me with hostile daggers in her eyes and a shower of reproaches.

"Now, when your father is already dying. Now you come to him," she shouted. "When weeks and months passed and we were starving, you did not come near. Now, when he has only a few hours to live, now you come, dear, kind, good-hearted, dutiful daughter."

I paid no attention to her but went Father's bedside. He was burning with fever, groaning and gasping for breath.

"And what'll become of me now that he's dying?" she began to howl at the top of her voice. Selfish.

The doctor came and examined him. As I saw him sitting by the bed, I realized that he was the same doctor who had attended to Mother. I recalled the day when he had advised her to have her foot amputated. Mother's dying eyes. The gray, cold face in the coffin. Through fogs of fear I struggled to think how best to take care of Father. Should I hire a nurse or get a leave of absence from school? But the woman's howling lamentations would not let me think.

"What has God against me?" she wailed. "What sin have I done? Haven't I always been a good woman, an honest woman, a virtuous woman? Haven't I nursed my first husband to his grave? Haven't I done all my duties to him, my second husband? God! My God! Why is it coming to me to be a widow the second time!"

The doctor stopped her impatiently. "This is no time for noise," he said. "If you want your husband to get well, give him quiet."

It was not necessary to get a nurse, he thought, or even for me to be absent from school. The woman could wait on him the first part of the day and I could take my turn in the afternoon and evening.

The minute school was over, next day, I rushed back.

"Your father is worse," his wife greeted me. "He refuses to take his medicine. Maybe he can't swallow any more. He's an old man. And it's his end."

In her eyes I seemed to see a look of secret triumph. "Soon," those eyes said, "he'll die and I'll have his lodge money to marry again." Shuddering, I turned from her and hurried over to Father.

Yes. He was worse. His eyes were closed. His cheeks burning.

"Father!" I stroked his hot hand, gently. "You must take this medicine. It will take away your fever and stop your cough."

His dull eyes opened and gazed up at me pitifully.

"I'll take it from you. Only stay with me," he begged. "I'm afraid to take the medicine from her. She might do something." His fingers closed on my arm to pull me nearer to him. But the strength had gone from that dominating hand. In weakness and helplessness the poor flesh clung desperately to me. "I'm all alone," he whispered. "She isn't like Mother. She's only waiting for my death."

A cough shook him. He groaned with pain.

At the sound of his voice she hurried out of the kitchen. "Where does it hurt you? Are you feeling worse?" she asked.

"No. No. I'm better."

In her presence he tried to control his groans and hide his pain. He even struggled to sit up. His hand clutched at the bosom of my dress. "Bring me my book," he whispered. I brought it to him. His feeble fingers caressed the worn, yellowed pages of his beloved book of Job. With his last strength, his faded eyes strained to drink in the words that were his life.

Anxiety and lack of sleep had exhausted me. And in spite of myself, I dozed off at the foot of his bed. Then through the haze of semi-consciousness, I heard the woman pleading, slyly, "Tell me only, where do you keep your lodge papers? Is there any one who owes you money? Maybe you got yet insurance on your life?"

"Leave me alone," his faint voice reached me. "I breathe yet."

"But you're in God's hands. You can't tell what may happen to you the next minute. Don't forget it, you're a very sick man, and very old. You haven't the strength to fight a sickness like a younger man."

In a flash I was awake and on my feet. Never again while Father was alive would I leave him alone with her.

Hugo quickly got me a leave of absence from school. Night and day, until he was well, I stayed in that house with my father.

Day by day, I won his confidence and a sort of dependent affection. His old talkativeness returned. He told me legends of the Bible and explained the wisdom of the Torah. In more intimate moments, he told me of his unhappiness with his wife.

"The sages of the Talmud said, a man has a right to divorce his wife if she don't salt him his soup to his taste. And mine is guilty of worse offences. She's selfish and wants to live for herself, instead of living only for her husband.... I thought if I'd marry a young one, she'd have strength to work for me," he went on. "But she only wants pleasure and luxuries of the flesh. So maybe it would be better for me to go to an Old Men's Home where I could spend my last days in peace instead of living with a false wife who reminds me always that I'm old."

To please him, I went next day to the Old Men's Home. It was a beautiful building, but the moment I entered, the loveless, inhuman, institutional atmosphere struck me like a blow. They showed me the place. Clean. Cold. Choking with orderliness. Beds all in a row, spotless, creaseless, like beds in an orphan asylum. I saw groups of old men sitting lifelessly on hard, wooden benches.

"How much better off they are here than living by themselves," said the official, rubbing his hands. "They eat only food that's best for them, and their meals and their sleep are at regular hours. It's like a sanitarium for their last days."

But the very things the man praised up to me made me shudder.

No. This institutional prison was not for my father. Never would I allow him to have his will broken in such a place. He who all his life had his own way must continue to have it to the end of his days.

If he wanted to leave his wife, let him go to board somewhere where he can have his own room, his books around him, free to come and go as he wishes. Here, in this prison, were rules and regulations that he could never endure. My father would never stoop to ask permission to go out and to report when he got back. He would never obey the iron rule not to upset his bed all day long. He would want to go to bed or get up at any time of day or night, as he pleased. He should have a place that suited him. And not with his wife.

I came back to Father's house. As I opened the door, I could not believe my eyes. There was his wife on her knees, putting on his shoes for him. She was lacing them patiently and making the double knots, just as he dictated. I watched her with wide eyes. This was something new. It took me a minute or two to take it all in. I suddenly realized that this woman I hated was necessary to him. He could not live alone in a boarding house any more than in the Old Men's Home. He needed a wife to wait on him. It came to me that if we tried not to hate her, to be a little kind to her, maybe she would be more faithful to Father.

I followed her into the kitchen and put ten dollars into her hand. "I'm going to give you this each week, and I'll see that my sisters should give you ten dollars more regularly. Only take good care of Father."

Her eyes glowed with gladness as she seized the bills. "Sure," she said. "If I only get enough money in my hands, I know how to live good. You think I want him to die? Is it nice for me to bury already my second husband? But how could we live, if you children had no hearts?"

She became a new person, as the money came to her regularly. In a very few months the coveted ear-rings appeared in her thick ears. She got what she wanted in this world. A gloating look of smiling satis-faction came to her face. As she waddled with her basket to the market, she tossed her head coquet-tishly from side to side, showing off the glittering ear-rings to the passers-by.

Soon we all began to visit Father's house, and met his wife without hostility. We tried to make up with presents for the lack of real, warm friendliness that we could not feel.

Once I brought her a box of fruit for the New Year holiday. And in return, she made me taste her apple *strudel*. At that moment most of the old hostil-ity vanished from my heart. Next time I came with Hugo.

"Father, this is Mr. Seelig," I said, watching to see how the two would take to each other.

Father shook his hands and scrutinized him inquisitively. "Mr. Seelig? From where do you come?"

"Father, this is Mr. Seelig..."

"Warsher Gubernie—a long time ago," Hugo added, with a smile.

"And your parents with you here? By what do you work?"

"Mr. Seelig is a principal of a school," I interposed.

"So—a principal?" Father shook hands again with new respect. "Do they pay you good?"

"Well," sighed Hugo, getting into Father's spirit, "I make a living. But I'm not smart enough yet. And I came to ask you, would you care to teach me Hebrew?"

"Hebrew? An American young man, a principal, and wants to learn Hebrew? And you want *me* to teach you?"

"If a learned man like you would care to take a beginner like me."

Father leaned back in his chair. The old dream look came back into his glowing eyes. "Listen to me, Mr. Seelig—young man! I want you to know I don't trust much American young men. They're all deniers of God. One day is the same to them as another. Ask them the difference between a plain Monday and the Sabbath and they'll gape at you."

His eyes grew soft and moist. He looked most gratefully from Hugo toward me. "I thought that in America we were all lost. Jewishness is no Jewishness. Children are no children. Respect for fathers does not exist. And yet my own daughter who is not a Jewess and not a gentile—brings me a

young man—and whom? An American. And for what?
To learn Hebrew. From whom? From *me*. Lord of the
Universe! You never forsake your faithful ones."

His old eyes widened with a glance of sudden
understanding and he looked from Hugo to me and
from me back to Hugo.

"Even my daughter with the hard heart has come
to learn that the words of our Holy Torah are the only
words of life. These words were true ages and ages
ago and will yet be true for ages and ages to come. Our
forefathers have said, 'A woman without a man is less
than nothing. A woman without a man can never enter
Heaven.'"

The old pride flamed up in his face.

"Woman!" he called, ecstatically, to his wife. "Show
only this American young man all my holy books in the
bedroom."

Hugo's eyes sought mine. With a look of awe, he
followed the woman to the other room.

Delighted with the outcome I turned to Father.
"Aren't you glad," I whispered, "that you didn't go to
a home, or a lonely room in a boarding house? Here
you have your books, and all the comforts of your own
house, and her, ready to wait on you."

He wagged his head for a silent moment; then an
unbeaten fierceness came into his eyes. "Yes," he
sighed, ruefully. "It's like living in a beautiful garden with a snake in it. Never will I finish out my
days with that woman! Can fire and water live

together? Neither can a man of God live with a cow, an *Ishah Rah.*"

With his every word my high spirits sank. My breathing spell of happiness was over. Just as I was beginning to feel safe and free to go on to a new life with Hugo, the old burden dragged me back by the hair. Was there no place in the whole world for Father? My home! Must I give it up to him? But with him there, it would not be home for me. I suddenly realized that I had come back to where I had started twenty years ago when I began my fight for freedom. But in my rebellious youth, I thought I could escape by running away. And now I realized that the shadow of the burden was always following me, and here I stood face to face with it again.

"Father!" I ventured, hesitatingly. "Would you care to live with me?"

He looked at me, and in that look I felt the full force of his unbending spirit. "Can a Jew and a Christian live under one roof? Have you forgotten your sacrilege, your contempt for God's law, even on the day of your mother's death? I must keep my Sabbath holy. I cannot have my eating contaminated with your carelessness." He paused. "But if you'll promise to keep sacred all that is sacred to me," he went on, in an attempt to be tolerant, "then, maybe, I'll see. I'll think it over."

I almost hated him again as I felt his tyranny—the tyranny with which he tried to crush me as a child. Then suddenly the pathos of this lonely old man pierced me. In a world where all is changed, he alone remained unchanged—as tragically isolate as the rocks. All that he had left of life was his fanatical adherence to his traditions. It was within my power to keep lighted the flickering candle of his life for him. Could I deny him this poor service? Unconsciously, my hand reached out for his.

The look of bitterness faded from his face and he opened the Bible, his eternal consolation. Instantly he was transported to his other world.

Hugo returned. And Father glanced up with stern absent-mindedness from his book to bid us good-bye.

I could hardly wait till we got out of the room to tell Hugo about Father.

"Of course, the old man must come with us," he exclaimed.

"Do you realize what you're saying? If he lives with us we'll lose our home."

"Not at all. Our home will the richer if your father comes with us."

I laughed at his easy enthusiasm. He talked like a Tolstoyan.

So there it was, the problem before us—the problem of Father—still unsolved.

In the hall, we paused, held by the sorrowful cadences of Father's voice.

"Man born of woman is of few days and full of trouble."

The voice lowered and grew fainter till we could

not hear the words any more. Still we lingered for the mere music of the fading chant. Then Hugo's grip tightened on my arm and we walked on. But I felt the shadow still there, over me. It wasn't just my father, but the generations who made my father whose weight was still upon me.

The End